A door across the room burst open. Panic seared through me as I saw the glowing amber eyes. The brown-suited cyborg leaped through and lifted his hand toward Jason. He was crouched with his back to the door, fending off the beams from the other room.

"Jason, watch out!" I scrambled out, grabbed a chair, and threw it across Jason at the cyborg.

"No! Ruth!"

Everything was a blur of blinding light and flame and agony as a thin blaze from the far room sizzled across my shoulder. I could smell my skin burning as I screamed.

The room was suddenly exploding with people in brown suits. A cyborg crumpled into my thrown chair with his back torn open. I was falling. The light from the far room lanced out again at me. I couldn't twist away. I screamed . . .

SARA STAMEY

WILD CARD RUN

BERKLEY BOOKS, NEW YORK

The lines from ''Those Winter Sundays'' are reprinted from *ANGLE OF ASCENT, New and Selected Poems* by Robert Hayden, by permission of Liveright Publishing Corporation. Copyright © 1975, 1972, 1970, 1966 by Robert Hayden.

WILD CARD RUN

A Berkley Book/published by arrangement with
the author

PRINTING HISTORY
Berkley edition/April 1987

ISBN: 0-425-09705-6

A BERKLEY BOOK® TM 757,375
The name ''BERKLEY'' and the stylized ''B'' with
design are trademarks belonging to
the Berkley Publishing Corporation.

PRINTED IN THE UNITED STATES OF AMERICA

FOR HELEN AND NEIL—

"What did I know, what did I know
Of love's austere and lonely offices?"

—Robert Hayden,
    "Those Winter Sundays"

With special thanks to R.D. and Meredith, and, always, Jim.

prologue

It's only in the scattered half-durs of pre-entry that the human passengers are allowed to see what lies beyond the clear blister of the observation dome.

Of course, the passage of the shift would present a picture meaningless to our eyes—"inducing acute perceptual and cognitive schism" is, I think, the official cybernese—so the alloy shield clamps down tight. Even the hardened traveller tends to spend the pauses between jumps harvesting a quick crop of stars.

And the stars that turn into suns.

It had been a while since I'd seen this particular sun as more than a distant flicker. Now it burned sullen orange beyond the edge of the stressplex dome. Its innermost world sat like a pale-green and turquoise cat's-eye on a black matte gaming table, a last glittering target for the crystal shooter marble cupped in the palm.

What odds for a backboard ricochet into the tripling ring? The click of credit-counters around the table as you cradle the clear shooter and cock your thumb for the last chance to send it spinning down that long black table, connect cracking with that winking target, go for the big one, Go Home . . .

1

one

I was flying. Dark space stretched endlessly, sparked with stars and the distant shapes of galaxies. A glittering explosion of light showered past as I plunged through a veil of asteroids.

I reached out and flew faster. I could feel the immense openness, feel the windless speed as my body sliced darkness and my arms embraced it.

A streak of pale silver shot past, then another. I grasped the next, tucked, and swung as the clear lumiflex bar absorbed the impact, flung me around it, and added its spring as I opened out again and flew backward and up for the bar above it. I caught it behind my head, swung back, changed my grip, swung forward, and kipped around and onto it. Another swing and I was poised, legs taut toward the ceiling as a spiral galaxy swirled across my vision on one of the surrounding vid screens. It shrank, then exploded into racing stars that transformed up to down and then to no direction at all as I swung again, gathering momentum and dropping fast to fling myself through the bars.

I was past the slow warm-up, past the stage where hands stung with the slap of the bars, muscles in arms strained for the pull, legs tensed and struck momentum from the limber lumiflex, lungs strained for air, mind scrambled in quick calculations of angles and grips.

Now I was only a feverish, exalted rhythm, another particle flung through space by random forces, but caught in the fierce joy of it. My body gripping and flexing the bars, springing off one to spin around another, was only the engine driving the surge of space around me. It twirled and spun and the stars swept through me with their silent music. I was the music, I was the center, and I was flying, another bright sun flaring among the brilliant bits of light in their fathomless depths. I was—

A shrill alarm ripped the silence. A harsh red light flashed on and off.

Off rhythm, I caught the next bar just a milla late and wrenched my shoulder swinging around it. "Damn!" I lowered myself in careful swings over the last two to drop onto the resilient floor.

I worked my shoulder to loosen it up and threw a robe over my sweat-soaked microslick. I tore off my palm-grips, hit the kill switch on the doorbell, and tapped the button beneath it. "Be right with you."

Slinging a towel around my neck, I passed through the opening hiss of the membrane into my office and secured the door with a code number. I reached across my desk console to hastily blank out the landscape I'd programmed on the window vid. Restless, wind-swirled wheat stalks and distant hills faded into standard light patterns.

"Come in." The front door locks deactivated just as I noticed the letter—actually written by hand, and on paper— still lying open on my desktop.

I quickly swept it into a drawer, despite myself glancing again at the graceful, looping script: ". . . such a terribly long time. I've arranged for an enclave visit and a host, if you would only please come . . ."

Damn. I slammed the drawer and looked up at my visitor.

He was unremarkable enough, pausing in the doorway to eyeball the office, though his dark blue unisuit was definitely on the conservative side for the casino managers who generally sought my services in designing new games or modifications.

I punched up my calendar and the console screen scrolled as his eyes tracked across the plain desk, the subdued resinlay floor, and the three loungers around the alterant dispenser. Standard stuff, except for the skin of the big, freckled cat stretched on one wall, which usually got some sort of revealing reaction. The man's squarish face didn't alter beneath his topknot of graying hair. He turned back to me, his eyes running coolly over my grubby robe.

I laughed. "You caught me out. I didn't check my console this morning and I guess I forgot your appointment, Fra—?"

He didn't help me out, so I glanced at the screen display. There was no appointment listed.

I looked back at him. He was still giving me the stone face. A little irritated, I gestured toward the loungers. "I take it you'd like to discuss some consulting work? How about a drink, or maybe a smoke?"

A thin smile appeared. "I'd prefer to sit here." He walked over to the desk and reached a hand palm up across it, extending the formal two fingers. "I rejoice in our meeting, Kurtis:P385XL47:Ruth."

I automatically crossed his fingers with two of mine. "I rejoice in our meeting, Fra—"

He still didn't supply his name. He sat across from my desk and managed to maintain an erect posture in a chair that was supposed to make you lean back and relax. "Shall we talk?"

I wiped my forehead with the towel and threw it down. I sat across from him. "Am I supposed to know you, or what?" Maybe this was a new con game.

The thin smile passed over his face again and brownish eyes studied me. "We could have contacted you through the console, of course, but we thought—"

Something clicked. I jerked angrily to my feet. "Why aren't you wearing a breast badge?"

He gave me an approving nod. "We expected you to be quick. Not many people notice."

"How many of you are there around?"

"That needn't concern you. I understand your surprise, of course, but there's no need to feel defensive."

I aired one of my most creative Sethar curses.

He gave me a regretful smile. "So often angry, Sra Kurtis. We had hoped to minimize such a reaction by making our approach as personal as possible." He gestured toward himself. "But if you'd prefer the console—"

I shook my head, blew out a long breath, and sat down. "You're here now."

I couldn't help giving him an admiring once-over. He cooperated by rising from the chair, walking over to the spotted ferial skin, examining it, and returning to sit. He was pretty smooth. He breathed evenly, his hand had been warm, his face more expressive than a lot of people I could name.

He was almost human. A far cry from the awkward mechmen who so helpfully maintained order inside the huge orbiting rock that was Casino.

"What do you want?" No use wasting politeness on—him.

He actually blushed. "Can't we make this pleasant?"

I let him answer that himself. He had my psych-profile.

He sighed. "Your ten-year limit has nearly expired. You have apparently rejected your renewal option, but we have decided that would be detrimental to your well-being. You should make the visit to your homeworld, before you lose your clearance."

"Home!" My voice made the word a mockery. I swivelled in my chair to face the vid, glad I'd blanked out that field. But he probably knew what I'd programmed, anyway. Even though I gritted my teeth, I couldn't kill the faint stirring under too many layers, the regret, the wondering . . .

I pounded my fist angrily on the armrest and jerked back to face him. "Turn it off, damn you!"

The music hadn't even been audible, more like a whisper somewhere between my ears. Everyone used it in the casinos, it was no big deal, but that was at audible levels and the gamblers seemed to expect it. But this was me, and this was personal, and I didn't like it.

He blushed again and the gentle tug inside me faded. He faced my glare. "I do apologize. We'd simply like to make this easier for you."

"Easier! Make what easier?"

"Your renewal visit to Poindros, of course. We've decided. You're going home."

I stared at the cyberserf.

I found my mouth hanging stupidly open and snapped it shut. "*You've* decided! I'm going home!" I gave a short laugh. "Look, take my word, you'll never make it as a comedian."

He frowned. "I did not intend to trigger a humor response."

"Come on. I know the limits of the cybernetic benevolence directives—I've had to know. You're here to serve us. So, okay, I appreciate your concern. But I'm not going to be persuaded." I stood up. "You know the way out."

"I'm afraid you don't yet understand. We've decided you must go. You're mature enough to accept a helpful nudge."

"Like hell I am! The answer is no."

He sighed elaborately and reached over my desk to pick up my sunburst-crystal dice. "I would regret having to employ other means of persuasion."

Shaking the dice absentmindedly—absentmindedly!—in one fist, he reached down the neck of his suit and pulled out what looked like a cyberserf breast badge with a skin-cling clip, inserting it into the slot used for IDiscs. He touched his fingers to the screen, then punched up a display of my business account on the monitor readout. He obviously didn't need the voice-linked code. As I watched, the cheery figures faded and reassembled into an aesthetically displeasing configuration.

I clenched my teeth.

"Or we could be more creative. Perhaps you'd enjoy that?" I hoped one of us was enjoying his performance as he perched on the side of my desk and rolled the dice onto the surface in front of me.

"Two sixes. A good roll. One that would win me credits in a casino. I'd like to see it again." And he did. Enough times without a break from double sixes that it got to be boring.

He cocked his head sideways. "Or perhaps snake-eyes? You've found them profitable." He rolled the dice once more, the fiery crystals flashed, and I stared down at the two dots staring back up at me.

My hand jerked out and swept them off the desk. I paced the room and back. There was a cold, empty feeling spreading out from my stomach. I stopped by the desk. He sat calmly, waiting.

"You can't be doing this. The benevolence directives. You're here to serve us." I glanced over at the dice where they sparkled on the floor. "Are you telling me you cybers fix the games? You control who wins?"

"At times, yes."

I blinked. "But why? What's the point?"

"You do realize this is a Taboo conversation, Sra Kurtis. However, at this point it would be meaningless to register more violations for you."

"Wait a centa!" The cold was rising in a swamping tide, but I could feel sweat breaking out again on my back and palms. No doubt he was reading that, along with my increased heartbeat. "I'm way below the limit right now. You know that. You can't take me in for the Steps of Healing."

"You're mistaken. We could if we determined that to be

the best solution for you.'' He tilted his head toward the
spotted skin on the wall. ''We're well aware of your trans-
gressions of the visitor Rules on Sethar, you know. That
alone could qualify you for the Steps.''

''But . . .'' There was no way the cybers should have
known. My hostess, for reasons best unexamined, had covered for me, and Setharians rarely used their consoles anyway. No one had reported me for ducking the required
relocation orientation.

''While a straight-line projection indicates low probability
that someone of your worldplan would experience the hunting
customs of the Setharians as gratifying, you were obviously
strongly bonded to the tribe and your friend Jaréd. Is that why
you've refused skin grafting to remove that scar?''

Jaréd. I raised a defensive hand to the thin scar down my
cheek, the initiation mark I usually concealed beneath the
colored face-slicking currently the vogue among sophisticated
transients and leasers in Casino. I glared at the cyberserf.
''Fill in the gaps in my profile yourself, damn you!''

''Well, well. But we needn't look that far back for violations, need we?'' He rose and strolled over to the door to my
workout area, the locked membrane spiralling open at his
touch. He raised an eyebrow, glancing in at the tall chimney
of bars I'd built by breaking through into the second, illegally
leased apartment above mine.

''You consistently choose the hard way, don't you, Sra
Kurtis? Casino's public exerstim facilities do maintain quite
painlessly the muscle and heart tone necessary for health, you
know.'' He returned to his chair.

I sat, staring blankly at him—at it.

I couldn't even hang on to my anger. The cold tide of fear
was drowning me. None of it made sense. Were they going to
send me for the Steps of Healing? The thought sent another
icy wave running through me. I didn't want to be happy that
way. Maybe that meant I was truly sick. Maybe that was why
everything was turning upside down and spinning, like the
galaxies on the vids when I spun on the bars.

The cybers were ordained by the sacred Founders to serve
us. *And lo, though I walk through the valley of the shadow of
war, the cybers are with me and I will fear no evil*. The Book
of Words couldn't be wrong about our guardians. It couldn't
be true that we were only the pawns in their game.

The cyberserf smiled gently. His voice modulated into a

soothing tone. "I didn't intend to upset you. Now, I have made the transport arrangements for you. I will leave it to you to inform your family that you are accepting their invitation for an enclave visit."

It didn't even surprise me that he knew the contents of the letter.

"We would like you to stay until harvest, and when you return, we'll want to have another talk."

I blinked. "*When* I return? What if this trip succeeds brilliantly, and I decide to resettle?"

"We've calculated that likelihood as minimal."

I blinked again. "Then what's the point? Why send me home?"

"It should prove educational. Perhaps you'll see your homeworld and yourself differently now. We'll discuss your observations when you return." He rose and paused just before the point where the front door would cycle open. "Good faring, Sra Kurtis."

I glared as he used the Poindran leavetaking. He smiled and turned to go.

Something clicked again. "Hey, wait a centa!" I was around the desk and between him and the door. "There's more, isn't there? What's in this for you?"

He put on a considering expression, then nodded. "We calculated approximately even odds that you would ask that question." The thin smile passed over his face once more, and he crossed back to the console, activating the plate on the side. "I am authorized to provide a simplified explanation."

Wavering light-beams emerged and coalesced into a tri-D holofac of space, our galactic system floating among more distant stars. Near the center of the elongated spiral, a blue star flared and expanded, and I could see the jagged craters of a dark, barren planetoid orbiting it. Crimson words appeared below it, floating along in space. CASINO. CENTRAL INTERLOCK HEADQUARTERS.

Now several of the scattered suns flared into brightness, and planets orbiting them sprang into detail and color. Past the high-tech hub worlds, near the low-tech rim of the system, I recognized the three irregular continents of the planet orbiting close to an orange sun. More letters glinted beneath it, blue this time. POINDROS LOCAL SERVICE NETWORK. More blue marked other inhabited planets: PROTOS LOCAL SERVICE NETWORK, ANDURAN LOCAL SERVICE NETWORK, and so forth.

I turned back to the cyberserf. "Very pretty. So what's the point?"

He nodded toward the holofac. "Few humans are allowed to know that our cyber network operates within separate divisions. The limited construct I inhabit at present," he indicated his body, "is an operative of Central Interlock, the coordinating network inside Casino. CI regulates interplanetary transport and enforces the limitations on mutual influence between worldplans." The crimson letters rolled into a circle enclosing Casino, then sent out sparks of red light to other planets. "Each worldplan is administered by its own Local Service network, as you can see." Blue circles enclosed the different planets and the red sparks formed wider circles around each blue one. The holofac gleamed and faded.

He paused to give my inferior brain time to absorb it all, and I found myself contemplating the Taboo question: What kind of creatures *were* the cybers, living in their energy networks?

The cyberserf continued, "One of CI's data recombination studies has underlined an intriguing anomaly in the long-term figures for Poindran immigration and resettlement. We require further data on Poindros."

"That's it?" I wasn't going to admit I was confused. "You want me to go gather information for you? Why don't you go yourself? You'd pass."

He gave me his patient, imitation sigh again. "My appearance would 'pass,' as you say, among humans. However, CI operatives such as myself are prohibited within the LS spheres of control. Just as you humans are protected by your Rules, we cybers have our own. Even were I capable of violating *my* rules, I could not pass Poindros clearance. We cybers are capable of recognizing, but not duplicating, the energy emanations of the human brain."

He tilted his head slightly, studying me, not bothering to blink now.

"But . . ." I was still confused. "Why don't you just ask Poindros LS for the information you want?"

"We have determined that the data we need would best be garnered by the experience of a native returning for the visit."

"But why me? Surely you could find a more willing—" It hit me. "I'm not the first one you've sent back. What did you learn from the others?"

He should've dropped his eyes, if he wanted to look human. "The others chose resettlement, and we cannot contact them within the Poindran sphere of control."

For no clear reason, the icy fingers had clenched around my stomach again. "Did you tell them the trip was for their own good, too?"

"They did not question the benevolence directives." The voice held a mild warning. "They *did* benefit, since they resolved their escape syndromes. We are only trying to help you, Sra Kurtis."

I must have looked as unconvinced as I felt.

"You know that we are—"

"Right. You're incapable of lying to me."

He nodded and smiled, stepping finally through the spiralling door. "Good faring."

I wanted to call him back and ask more, but I didn't know what. I knew they couldn't lie, but it was clear as moonwater they didn't have to tell us the whole truth.

Hot sun glared over a dry, bare expanse of soil. A hand groped out of the cracked surface, then an arm, brown, veined and knotted with age, straining upward out of the earth. Fingers spread and stretched outward as the soil sprang to life and a stirring sea of copper-colored wheat flowed over the endless plain. The fingers melted into the spinning spokes of a great wheel spanning the height of a hundred men. The arm became the base of a giant tower, its roots sunk into the tremor of the earth. The wheel high at the top spun in the dry wind, bearing the silver-and-pearl glory of its sails around and around until the dancing lights merged to a pure white glow that enveloped everything.

Harmony.

Then, in the center, as always, it took shape. An eye, steady and unwinking, the iris a sphere of writhing yellow and crimson flames and boiling demon shapes of smoke, watching me and waiting. Watching and waiting.

"No!" I jerked up, cold and sweating, staring through the dark. Past the lip of my bedroom, the upper bars emanated a ghostly gleam of lumiflex. I closed my eyes. "Damn!"

It was no good. I'd tried every creative combination of Casino's drugs and even the rusty discipline of a Setharian trance-state, but the dream kept coming every night. I knew that damned cyberserf was right. I didn't want to know if the cybers knew about the dream. But somehow I knew it wasn't going to stop until I got on a transport for home.

The sullen orange sun's innermost world sat like a pale-green and turquoise cat's-eye on a black matte gaming table, a last glittering target for the crystal shooter cupped in the palm.

What odds for—

"Arrival stations for Poindros in one quarter-dur."

The social directives of the ship's operating cybers had chosen a sensuous alto voice for its on-duty persona this time. The toy planet out there rolled abruptly down the slope of domed sky, nearly targeting my starry jackpot as the ship swerved into a wide orbital approach. Poindros was swelling fast into a world.

Suddenly too fast—the comfortable dark distance shrinking, shrinking me until I could no longer fit that smooth cat's-eye into my pocket, until I was small enough to stand on its crust of dirt.

"Arrival stations for Poindros in one-aught-one-one eura."

Binary for the benefit of the group of Andurans bound past Poindros. So thoughtful of the cybers.

I glanced around the dome and spotted the shadowy figures hovering fearfully as close as possible to the ornamental plants in pots near the exit doors. They all looked from a distance like undernourished and humpbacked, hairy little old ladies in dingy nighties. Though they seemed to accept me in their skitterish fashion, I still hadn't penetrated their Taboo against speaking to outsiders, and I had no idea why such a timid bunch would be travelling from one far rim of the system to another.

I was curious, as usual, about things that were none of my business. Like the way they'd suddenly melt from a room when a cyberserf mechman was just about to appear to helpfully guide them around the transport.

"Hey, watch it!"

"By the Founders!"

The exit spiralling open silhouetted a small, dark shape against the bright hall beyond. It loped with long arms and short legs, barrelling through a startled group of travellers heading for the door.

". . . ought to be reported!" A rotund woman in a spangled coiffure swung around in an indignant swirl of light-emitting filigree as the exit snicked shut again. The small figure scrambled in the dimness past me, across the star-dappled expanse of stressplex flooring.

I recognized him as the young Anduran boy who'd caused such a gratifying commotion in the dining area when it'd taken three cyberserfs to get him down from his perch on the overhead tri-D. He made a scrambling, terrified about-face and headed for the tallest plant near the end of the row of exits. He swarmed up it and the triangular leaves quivered in agitation.

"Arrival stations for Poindros in fifteen centadurs."

It looked like the kid wasn't coming down. The Andurans were pretty worried, hunching with their Plan-tailored, too-long arms beneath the tree and nervously squeezing and releasing the two halves of their flesh mittens as if to reassure themselves they were still there.

The kid probably had a lot of violations going. I walked over. "Maybe I can persuade him."

I reached into my belt pouch and pulled out two polished and cubed F'earni sunburst-crystals. They'd been a lucky pair. The fiery heart of the crystals flashed irresistibly as I tossed and caught the dice.

"You know"—I glanced up for a milla and saw eyes fixed on the bright dice—"once you leave Casino, you're supposed to find the right person to pass your dice on to, otherwise your luck runs out. But they've gotta roll a two. Now where am I gonna find somebody to try?"

I whistled again and ignored the stealthy rustling above me. The boy dropped from branch to branch and then made an easy swing to land at a wary distance.

I looked into his amber eyes and smiled. "You look like you might have the knack. Like this." I crouched and rolled the dice on the floor toward him. They sparkled temptingly.

He bit his lip, then reached out a thinly furred arm, touching one crystal and jerking back his hand as if afraid of the fire in it. Then he scooped them up with the two thick fingers and shook them as I'd done.

I concentrated on snake-eyes, hoping I was still on a roll.

I shook my head. Inside glittering Casino, it had somehow made perfect sense that a useless talent like getting the right number of carved dots on a cube to land right-side up could produce lovely stacks of credits. That is, when my lucky streaks didn't suddenly dissolve into spectacular losses.

The crystals clicked against the floor, tumbled toward me, and settled against my boots.

"Snake-eyes it is, kid! Go ahead, they're yours now."

His eyes gleamed above an abashed grin as he scooped them up and started to run awkwardly back to the group. Then he spun around, the long arms swinging for tree limbs that weren't there, and loped back over to me. He reached into his pouch and quickly thrust something into my hand.

"Hey, thanks, but you don't have to—" I started to give it back, but he stood his ground, fixing me with an oddly intent look that silenced my protest.

He ran over to the others and his mother hugged him close. I shrugged and slipped what looked in the dimness like a flat chip of plasmeld into my belt pouch. I was about to follow him over to see if they needed help finding their station, when the same door the kid had used spiralled open. A mechman rolled into the dome with its metal leg-units in locked-in mode, moving faster than usual. It zipped straight over to the kid, flashed its lights at the mother, and rounded up all the Andurans, herding them toward an exit. The little people looked even more agitated than usual. I hoped they weren't in trouble. But of course the mechman was only *helping* them.

"Arrival stations for Poindros in ten centadurs."

The predictable last-centa exodus from the dome began. I eased through the crowd toward my exit, passing the Andurans as they fearfully followed the mechman. I opened my mouth to call out "Good faring," but the mother, clutching the boy's hand, suddenly turned to give me a look and quickly shook her head.

She gave me a fleeting smile and suddenly she didn't look so strange after all. Her eyes held mine. They were really very lovely, a deep, rich amber, thanking me as clearly as if she'd used words. Those eyes spoke too clearly. Suddenly I was the strange, furtive one, hunched inside my own silence.

The hearth and the calm, forgiving pools of her eyes . . .

I detached myself abruptly, striding away. "Okay, okay, so what's the big deal?" I hurried on to my station.

Before I got in my pod, I located the flat panel at the back. I cut my finger prying at the recessed catches, swore, then pulled out the chip the Anduran kid had given me. It was just a useless piece of plasmeld, the silvery-blue color of an IDisc, but thinner and uninscribed, with a shimmer that must

have appealed to the kid. I shrugged. Whatever it was, it fit
in the slot on the catches and the panel came loose.

I pulled the set of plugs for the headpiece speakers and
gave the valve on a small gas canister attached to the air feed
a twist to close it. I could do without their pleasant dreams
this trip.

I had some things to think about. I knew it was silly, but I
wanted to feel the descent to that world, feel the windy air
reaching up for me, curled in the spongy extruded-foam dark
as I was. That wind sighed in my ears as the headpiece closed
around me and the hatch locked me into my plasmeld womb.

Soft black, the foam softly embracing me, and the faint
hiss of the air feed and pneumatic seals.

I was alone, always excepting those guardian presences
inhabiting their energy networks and monitoring devices. So,
okay. One more descent. Only this time it's—

Thump-thud.

What's that? *Whose distant footsteps echo through the
corridors?*

No one, only your heartbeat, you idiot.

Fireblood, it's loud! No wonder they pipe in the mood
music. Can't have that disturbing throb of mortality upsetting
the cargo—I mean passengers—

". . . customary to defer to the authority of the Village
Elders for arbitration of minor disputes."

Thump-thud thump-thud.

The voice seemed to be inside me. Maybe the dream-gas
and music usually masked it.

". . . must remember the highest Poindran Taboos against
sexual impropriety. Casual touching and kissing are permitted
only to family members and older-generation friends. Under
no circumstances will the possibility of incestuous relations
be entertained or mentioned. It is especially important to
remember that the immediate family unit is defined by . . ."

What in blazes? The pedantic voice droned on, reinforcing
the purified word usage of the changeless galactic Plan and
drumming in the Rules for a visit to Poindros. But I remembered too well the Rules I had run from when I was sixteen,
dreaming of a worldplan that would free me.

Freedom. Right. I tried to shake my head, but the pod's
foam prevented me. I tried to feel myself hurtling in the
shuttle through the burning streams of air, back into the

windy arms of Poindros, but it wasn't real. I was floating, and I couldn't shake my head.

To hell with it. I sent the footsteps back down those inner corridors and managed a crooked smile, despite the foam. I was coming home. Everybody was happy.

Sure.

A faint jar and a hiss and the pod was sliding open, foam crumbling to dust and sucked away in sparkling motes. It looked, after all, like this ride down had been no different from any other. The yellow tiled walls of a processing center were pretty much the same everywhere.

I blinked and crawled out of the pod. I stretched, made a face at the cheerfully bright walls, and joined the file of travellers on the slowbelt. I was the only one wearing a frown.

I was tired and more than a bit punchy by the time I'd run the gamut of sonic soundings, immunization verifications, and an excruciatingly long interview with a lucite cube. But then that was my fault for getting creative with my answers. I took another slowbelt to clearance, swallowing down a cold ripple of unease as I remembered my weird conversation with the Casino cyberserf. I was about to pass from Central Interlock jurisdiction into Poindran Local Service control.

I was disgorged among a milling crowd of tourists waiting to pass the clearance gates. I reached into my waist pouch for my IDisc to reattach it to the necklace I wore because I didn't like the feel of the disc's skin-cling. My hand froze and the unease tightened into an icy fist clenching my stomach.

There was something wrong. The gates through the translucite wall were shut and amber lights were winking. On the other side, a group of brown-suited officials hurried our way.

"There will be a slight delay." A voice projecting calm authority filled the hall. "Cybernetic inventory indicates a missing transport item. Poindran officials will conduct a preliminary scan before you may enter the gates. Please form into the following groups . . ."

The voice droned off names and gate numbers and the tourists began lining up as the officials emerged on our side with handheld scanners. My name wasn't called.

There was no reason for my fear, for the nerve-tingling, charged awareness of threat running through me like the nearly-forgotten *timbra* state of the Sethar hunters. But my fingers clutched reflexively on my IDisc as a red-haired, freckled official headed my way.

"Kurtis:P385XL47:Ruth?"

I felt it now. An added thickness. I glanced down to see that the blank chip the Anduran kid had given me was stuck to my IDisc by the skin-cling.

I froze. Had the kid snatched it from the mechmen on board? It didn't look like anything much, but suddenly images flashed through my mind. The Anduran boy's terrified scramble into the dome. His intent look as he thrust the chip into my hand. The mechman hurrying after him. A console-count of my violation points ticking upward to the Healing limit.

I found my hand shooting out to thrust the doubled discs into the gate slot behind me. "It's about time! Can I go through now?" Relief flooded me as the gate accepted them and my name appeared on the lighted console.

"Pushy, aren't you? Your psych-profile was right." The man passed his instrument down me and it lighted up green. "Okay, you're clean. Get in the gate, quick." He cast a glance backward, shoved his own disc into the slot, and followed me in.

"Hey, what's—"

"Just shut up and listen." The gate opaqued around us. "We've only got a couple of centas, and I don't want us being connected. I work for CI and we just got some new information you ought to know before you head home. The resettlers—"

"You work for CI? But the cyberserf said they couldn't penetrate the Poindran system!" I stared down at the short, pudgy man.

"Hey, just listen, all right? It's not for us to figure why they do what they do, right? If they'd asked me, I'd've said from your profile you weren't up to this, but . . ." He shrugged. "Anyway, we just got some new data. The option visitors returning to Poindros have been getting cleared for unrestricted re-entry instead of being routed to the visitor enclave. That's why the Healing rate has been so high, I guess, since they haven't been properly reoriented. Your unrestricted clearance just came in."

"Hey, wait a minute!" The cold fist had tightened inside me again. "The cyberserf never said anything about—"

"Take it easy, okay? You were due for Healing, anyway,

and CI's just letting you slide, so what difference would it make? Anyway, they want you to avoid getting reported for Healing, so you'll remember everything. Just hop on the monorail like the others and go on home, keep your eyes open for what goes on.''

"That's it?" I took a deep breath. "Look, I don't like this. What's going on here, anyway?"

"You're asking me?" He rolled his eyes as the gate began to fade back into clear. "Just watch your points. CI wants you to stay until harvest. You can't contact me directly, but send CI a signal every decacycle or so by asking your console for a credit-account check. If everything's fine, transfer fifty credits from business to personal. If your point count's getting too high, transfer fifty from personal to business, and I'll send somebody out there to bring you back. Got it?" He prodded me forward out of the gate.

I blew out another breath. As the console on this side ejected my doubled discs, I reached out hastily for them. "Stick to the Rules, right?"

"Do that. Somebody on your family's console has been asking about your violation point status."

I froze again at the touch of that icy hand.

The official didn't seem to notice my numb state as he hustled me over to claim my baggage and lead me through a door labelled *Natives*. It did not cycle open automatically and give me a welcome speech. I had to push through it. In the stuffy, dingy corridor beyond, more officials dawdled along in their baggy brown suits. There were no mechmen in the Poindros worldplan.

Two women walked past, trying not to stare at me. I watched them sway with subdued grace down the hall. Even with the long, drab-colored dresses swishing around their ankles, they somehow exuded that elusively intense femininity I remembered so well. And the shrouding skirts were something I hadn't forgotten either.

"Hey, Leon!"

"Yes, Officer Hodge?" A young man in uniform coveralls stopped, stared at me, and hastily lowered his eyes.

"Take these bags over to monorail check-in, will you?"

Hodge turned back to me. "All right, you're cleared. Good faring back home."

"Right." I started to follow the boy.

"Hey, hold on a centa!"

I turned back warily, restraining myself from raising a hand to the extra disc on my chain.

"You're gonna trot on home looking like something out of their worst nightmares? Changing rooms're that way," he tilted his head. "Trade in that ridiculous outfit for something decent."

I was dressed in a conservative manner. My only real concession to the current vogue in Casino's caverns was my own—even unpowdered and unsilvered—hair, pulled back and wrapped around my neck, secured with a jewelled luck-charm. My friends there would have laughed at the severity of my green, opaque skinslicks, relieved only by pink and yellow bands around the waist and ankles.

I sighed. "The same old backworld Way."

The freckles stretched into a grin. "You wouldn't want to break any Rules, now would you? And for Founder's sake clean those green stripes off your cheeks."

I shot him a venomous look and started for the changing rooms.

He called after me. "Cheer up! You'll look almost pretty in a skirt."

Violation points be damned. I took the last opportunity to air an oath a lady would not use on Poindros.

two

I rode home in front of thirteen railcarloads of firewood. Some omen. And I'd given my Casino luck-charm to a departing Poindran.

There wasn't much to do on the long, boring ride except make those "observations" prescribed by the insufferable CI cyberserf, though I didn't see much point to it. My homeworld was exactly the same as it had always been. But of course he couldn't have meant *that* kind of difference. The Plan of the sacred Founders assured unaltering perfection, their cybers guarding us within each world's eternal Way.

Poindros still rolled in its calm cycles of repeating seasons. Railcars still rolled across its flat continents, delivering wood from cultivated timber stands throughout the settlements. Poindrans still actually burned it, though not for cooking and warmth like the Setharian nomads. The Poindros worldplan prescribed the milder discomforts of partial electrification.

The hearths provided something else. Splitting wood and tending a fire would've been a ridiculous waste of time inside Casino, but somehow on Poindros it wasn't. High-tech simi-flames just couldn't hold a candle to the real thing.

I groaned. Here I was, touting that damnable, laborious Poindran Way already. But the traditional nightly gathering around the hearth was one reason I'd delayed catching a railcar. I figured as long as I was wallowing in nostalgia, I might as well come home in the dark to the warming glow of that firelit circle. It might soften some sharp edges.

Another reason was that I was scared stiff.

I hadn't, after all, let them know I was coming. I'd figured I would just knock around as a tourist in the enclave for a while, getting my ground legs and taking in the spectacular scenery of the Penitent's Crack. The Cracks were the only reason tourists from the high-tech hub worlds would bother with a rim dirt ball like Poindros.

I remembered from a childhood excursion the steep, multi-colored canyon walls, the weird, twisted shapes of stone scoured by sand and ceaseless wind, the steaming rock pools of mud and mineral water that seeped from a pressure cooker far below the surface to soak away what ailed you. The Cracks made for interesting places to visit, but without the cybers keeping tabs on the seismic quirks of Poindros, the whole surface would've been as unstable as its jagged seams. The cybernetic tower-rods that evened out Poindros's constant tremor to a smooth hum also kept the earthquakes from raising much of a ruckus.

Anyway, Officer Hodge had nipped my little detour in the bud. No more procrastination. No, just plain old cowardice.

I hadn't kept in touch during those ten years, beyond a cyberfax now and then to let them know I was alive. Occasionally a forwarded and battered letter from Mother had found me. So I knew she'd recently married again, and my twin brother Joshua had also married and moved to a farm farther inland.

I leaned back against the faded, scratchy upholstery with its smell of dust. The cars clanked and creaked along the single rail at a crawl compared to what a flitter could do. But there were no sleek flitters for Poindros. Not even a bird was allowed to break free of the dirt. Only when you climbed one of the soaring windtowers, claimed the immense sweep of its wings for your own, could you almost touch that deep bowl of hot blue sky and taste the freedom of the wind . . .

But that was Taboo. I turned to look through the streaked glass, but I couldn't see the grain fields stretching without break through the night. Only my face hung white and tense against the dimly reflected seat.

It was the face of a stranger, oddly demure in the Poindran fashion. My hair, somehow tamed by the changeroom attendant and pulled back into a plain knot, blended into the darkness beyond the window. My face floated in the night like a pale ghost mocking, the long scar burning a darker trail down one cheek. Without cosmetics, it looked ridiculously young. And almost as defiant as that sixteen-year-old face must have looked, facing away from home.

It wouldn't do. I tried to superimpose the bored mask of the Cypher Fives player on those features, but it kept slipping.

Damn! My gaze dropped to the high neckline of the dress, which managed to discreetly advertise the gentle swell of my breasts and make my waist look even narrower above the full folds of the long skirt. At least the gangling height of that skinny young girl had filled out to a closer miss of the full-figured Poindran ideal.

I turned from the window, arranging my skirts in the old reflex gestures. I fingered the heavy, glossy fabric, a dark green that in daylight would almost match my eyes. It was really too fine for the farm, but I was sure Helen would have an old dress or two I could borrow.

Helen. Dressed like this, I almost began to look like her daughter, except that, instead of my dark auburn, her hair was a more fiery red. Like everything about her, it was richer, more vibrant, eclipsing without effort or design whoever dared stand in the shadow of her beauty . . .

But she would have changed, too. Maybe that was what the cyberserf had meant. I shrugged impatiently and pressed my face against the window, just as the signal light for our village swept by outside.

The cars clanked to a patient stop when I pulled the stiff cord. The only other passenger, a balding man in faded blue, glanced up as I inserted my IDisc into the exit gate. I returned his sleepy nod, relieved that I didn't look as foreign as I felt.

The cars creaked away and I followed the rail through the hiss of dark grain until I could see the low light of the house beyond its ring of trees rustling in the wind. My heart was beating fast. I took a deep breath and climbed to the front porch, left my shoes with my bags, and tiptoed to the winking eye of the uncurtained window.

Firelight from the hearth, the family circle, and the Way—I was grateful for even the fragile shield of the glass. The window winked again and I peered through at the figures gathered in the rising and falling tide of light from the hearth. Flickering firelight gleamed from the focus of that circle, where my eyes were drawn to the reflection of flames sliding up the polished wood of the lyre she held.

Her hands were still lovely, long-fingered and trembling over the strings, the chords rippling at her touch, and I could hear it softly, there on the dark porch. Her voice stirred through the harp-song, quiet beyond the glass, but clear, and warm as ripened grain weaving in the wind of the swelling chords.

It was one of her own. A new one. The song ended, and I released the skirt clutched tightly between my fingers. I looked up from her hands.

She could still make me catch a quick breath. And it had nothing to do with the kindness of firelight. A touch of gray in the bright hair would be more apparent in daylight, as would the new hints of lines about the eyes and mouth, and she was slightly heavier. But as she sat back in the huge chair, cradling the lyre, her face a deep pool with the light playing over it, the changes seemed irrelevant. Her beauty was only richer, that aura of femininity more pervasive than ever.

So bowed am I before thy mystery . . . Helen.

Beside Mother and to her right, Sam sprawled in a smaller armchair, feet up on a stool and pipe in hand. Beneath the cap of gray hair, his weather-beaten face looked the same and wore the same mellow smile. His eyes were closed and his chin rested on his chest, above the comfortable mound of his belly.

On Mother's left, with his back to me in the shadows, a young man sat on the braided rug, his arm and bent head resting on the padded armrest of her chair. That would be Joshua home for a visit.

Across from him, apart and back from the light, a tall man sat straight in a wooden chair, knees apart, feet planted squarely. His arms and shoulders, bare in the sleeveless underwear beneath his overalls, were sun-brown and muscled, the strong hands gripping rather than resting on the knees. Black, curling hair on his head and chest showed just a sprinkling of gray. Even his stillness was tense as a coiled spring, betrayed only by the dark eyes devouring Mother's face. Aaron.

I stepped back from the window and turned the knob of the door. The hall was dimly lit by the opening into the front parlor. I remembered that no one used front doors except for bindings or a gathering to scatter ashes. To hell with it. Celebrate the prodigal's return.

Mother's voice. "Who is it?" The scrape of chairs. Sam, blinking and rubbing his chin, met me at the firelight's edge.

He let out a comically surprised little snort. "What? Well, by the Founder, it's Ruth! Honey, you . . . I . . ." Turning to the others, "I knew she'd come!" He engulfed me in a warm squeeze, bristly cheek against mine, then held me back so I could see the faded blue eyes, lower now than mine.

"Ah, girl, it's good to see you home! How'd you get out of the enclave so fast? We didn't even know you were on your way." Another hug. "Helen, look! I knew she'd grow up beautiful! And tall, by the stars!"

Mother's voice behind him, catching, rushing on over an eager, throaty laugh. "I *will* look, Sam, if you'll only let me!" She took both my hands and turned my reluctant face toward the fire. I wasn't sure I could meet her eyes.

I could hear her take in a quick breath as she lifted a white hand to touch my scarred cheek. Then she said, softly, so that only we could hear, "Oh, Ruth, I've missed you so. Why did you stay away so long?" I looked into green eyes as bright as mine with unshed tears, and then we were clasping each other tightly.

The crash of the overturned chair startled us.

I jerked back defensively to see Aaron standing stiff, face gone blank and pale beneath the deep tan. The dark eyes pinned me and the almost-forgotten shock of his angers ran through me. "The mark of Cain. Changer . . ."

Probably no one but me heard his faint whisper. The fixed glare I remembered too well pinned me in my old fear of his sudden launches into righteousness. It condemned me of all the sins I had and hadn't committed against the Rules. I was once again that naked young girl—caught in the innocent abandonment of a spring dawn, when I had thrown off my clothes and decked my hair with wildflowers to dance and twirl in the warm wind, opening my startled eyes to see Aaron planted before me in the field, his eyes darting the flames of Hell as his voice shook and thundered, "Jezrial! Spawn of the sin of Eve! Whore!"

I bit my lip and met his eyes, realizing all at once that they weren't even seeing me. And I wasn't that young girl.

I was surprised by the easy smile that came to my lips. "Hello, Aaron."

He blinked and the color flooded back into his face. He slowly picked up and righted the chair. "How did you get here? You should be in the enclave." He gave me an oddly wary look.

"Hardly killing the fatted calf, Aaron! Aren't you going to welcome me home?"

Helen hurried forward, her confused look quickly erased by a calm smile. She touched Aaron's arm. "Aaron, dear, aren't you happy to see Ruth home at last?" She turned back to me, her smile becoming indulgent. "You couldn't resist surprising us, could you, sweetheart? I'm so happy you've decided to resettle. This is where you belong."

I swallowed. I couldn't explain my unrestricted clearance to them. They thought I was back to stay.

And Aaron was clearly less than thrilled about it. Of course, he was the one who'd inquired into my violation point status.

His eyes flickered from me to Helen, hesitancy sitting strangely on his features. They smoothed then into a mocking smile. "So you've found the way again, little Ruth? 'And there will be more joy in Heaven over one sinner that repenteth, than over a hundred upright men.' We welcome a repentant heart."

On impulse, I stuck out my hand to him. "Thank you, Aaron."

He stood looking at my hand for a centa while I held it out stubbornly and stiffly, the gesture twisted into a challenge. The edge of his mouth twitched downward and he reached for my hand. Instead of shaking it, he turned it palm down and kissed the top with a show of formal courtesy.

I managed not to snatch my hand back. Helen slipped her arm around my waist and guided me to the figure who had risen quietly in the shadow cast by firelight. I was surprised to see how lanky Joshua's boyish stockiness had grown. She pulled him gently into the light and he raised his head in a quick, shy motion.

It wasn't Joshua. For a startled moment, our eyes met. It could only have been a milla, but it was frozen somehow, and I almost thought I saw recognition in his eyes. He looked quickly away to Helen.

If he was comparing me to her, he was probably as shocked as I was. But there was no reason for *my* surprise. I should have realized she'd choose a younger husband.

Mother took my hand. "Ruth, this is Jason. Jason, Ruth."

He was about my age. But it was normal for a matron to take a young husband. It had simply caught me off balance. In the confusion with the cybers and the self-absorption that was no doubt part of their psych-profile on me, I hadn't stopped to wonder about her new marriage.

Helen offered my hand to him. "In a way it was you who brought us together, Ruth. Jason was working as an enclave host when I first went to inquire about a visit for you." She smiled. "I'm sure you two will become as dear to each other as you are to me."

His hand was large and callused in my grip. As we murmured rote phrases, he raised his eyes only as far as my nose, so I couldn't be sure of the color of the eyes I'd met in that oddly intent first glimpse.

Mother urged me to sit on the cushioned stool in front of her armchair, seating herself in a graceful flutter of skirts, and I cast another look at the quiet Jason. He was somehow monotone, the sort of young man you would pass on the street and not notice. Maybe that was a good quality for a mediating host.

He had resettled on the rug, but his lanky height had an awkward look even in sitting, and the big hands, despite their work-toughened strength, contributed to the gangly image. He kept his face turned down in apparent contemplation of the rug. His hair—thick, straight, and shaggy—was a neutral brown, sun-streaked lighter to blend into the sun-dark skin. The brief glimpse of his face had left me only an impression of broad cheekbones and the indefinably colored eyes that somehow matched his overall tawniness. I wondered what had attracted Helen to him. She could have her pick of men.

She and Sam reclaimed my attention. Their questions were too eager, Sam's laughter too hearty, but I pretended not to see the puzzled tilt of Sam's head, the banked coals of Aaron's glare, and the warm vivacity that masked the concern in Helen's eyes. They told me more than I wanted to know.

I listened to my brittle voice produce a coolly amusing story of the travels that had taken me a roundabout course from the humid tedium of a year on an orbiting hydroponics station to the perpetual glittering night inside Casino. I didn't tell them I designed gambling games. I didn't need to get Aaron started on "the wages of sin."

I knew I couldn't answer the questions they really wanted to ask. "I'd love to hear you sing, Mother. It's been a long time."

"Your lyre is still upstairs, waiting for you. I suppose it's silly, but I felt sorry for it when you left." Her eyes managed to convey at once gentle reproach, quick forgiveness, and the shared feminine secret of our music. I felt myself stiffening against the response she could trigger as easily as plucking the strings of her instrument.

She turned to reach for the lyre Sam was holding out, her hands pale against the dark wood. *The lotus-leaves which heal the wounds of Death lie in thy hand.* . . . No, Mother.

She began softly, an old ballad, one she knew I loved. Her voice was the balm she meant it to be. Still stiffened in resistance, I closed my eyes, but suddenly weariness flowed over me with the gentle notes and I stopped fighting. Her voice melted the song into warm waves. They rose and fell against me, then crested to carry me into the final passage of the ballad. I opened my eyes and she was no longer Helen, no longer Mother, but purely the lovely instrument of the song.

My voice was lower than hers, and huskier, without her rich resonance. But it formed a pleasant enough alto harmony in the falling chorus.

I didn't care if my face mirrored her serene smile, that she was charming me as she did the men. She leaned forward in a smooth movement to place her lyre in my hands. It was pleasant to hold, the balance fitting naturally into my shoulder. The wood was warm where she'd touched it, but cool beneath, and solid. Light gleamed from the strings as my fingers sought a chord, drew it forth from the sinking flames. It moved out into the room, reverberating . . .

My palms closed abruptly on the strings, killing the sound.

I handed her the instrument, keeping my voice light. "It's been too long. I'm afraid I've lost it."

She accepted it, content for the night. "What nonsense! You'll never lose that gifted touch, Ruth." Her fingers barely brushed my shoulder as I turned away to watch the fire.

Sam heaved himself out of his chair with a grunt and placed a stick on the fire. He returned to pat my head. "You'll play another night, hon. We're wearing you out on your first night back."

I grinned up at him. "I'll never get tired of gazing at those handsome features, Sam."

He made a horrible face and puffed out his chest, holding up his belly with both hands. "I can well believe it, Mistress." We laughed, almost without effort.

"Sam, you old fool." Mother only called him that when she was especially happy. She went on about some dresses that "would just fit you now." Sam was fiddling with something on the hearth and whistling nervously.

Mother laughed softly. "I think Sam's trying to ask if he can make a picture."

"What?" I drew a blank. "You mean a sense-cube?"

Jason raised his head to give me an odd look just as Helen said, "A sense-cube? What—?" She colored and dropped her eyes.

Aaron leaned forward in his straight chair. "You see? She hasn't learned." He turned to me. "It's best said now. We abide by the Rules here, Ruth. Don't try to bring your offworld sins to us."

"Aaron, please."

He turned back to her. "There'll be no changers in this household! Maybe Ruth's repented her waywardness, and if the guardians give her leave it's not for me to question. But the Book tells it plain, Helen. 'The righteous shall be like the eyes of the Founder.' I won't let any changers defile the Plan, spread their sickness like Ruth touched our family before. And now Sam with that sinful contraption of his, and even young David courting sin with his talk of spacers—"

"Aaron!" Helen's voice was still low, but with something beneath the velvet that stopped him. "This changer talk is only lack of charity and foolishness. The guardians protect the Plan for us, and all they ask is that we help each other along the way. Now, don't ruin Sam's pleasure in his toy. And I won't have you saying such things about David. He's a sweet, loving boy."

Jason's quiet voice defused the tension. "You'll like David, Ruth. He's very bright."

"David?" I was still puzzled by Aaron's reference to "changers."

Jason's eyes remained lowered in reserve. "Joshua's son, now he's married to Marda. Helen brought him for a treat—he was so excited to see the Crack—when she came to the enclave."

"Aaron?" Helen waited calmly. She didn't need to remind him that she was Hearth-Matron here.

He spoke grudgingly. "No offense meant, Ruth."

Right. "None taken, Aaron. I'm sorry, Mother."

She smiled, smoothly covering my lapse in mentioning the contraplan sense-cube. "Let Sam show you his toy, Ruth. He just had to have one when we saw them at the regional fair.

Then we'll all get some sleep. You look tired, dear, and—''
She bit her lip and turned quickly. ''Go ahead, Sam.''

He was eager. ''It'll only take a centa, Ruth.'' He held out
a flat object, handling it carefully with his battered, gnarled
fingers. ''Here, look.''

It was a thick paper, stiffened by a thicker edge. On it was
an odd, 2-D representation of Helen, like looking at her
reflection in a mirror, but static and drained of color, with
only tones of dark and light left. It was strange, but somehow
appealing.

Sam was fiddling with knobs on a bulky, boxlike contraption that rested on the mantel. ''Of course it's not
real woman-art, but I get a kick out of it. The camera
does most of the work, after I set it up with this film
stuff.''

I stared at the mechanical box, vaguely uneasy. I'd never
heard of such a thing, and I wouldn't have hesitated to say,
like Aaron, that it was contraplan. But if it was being sold
openly, it couldn't be. I looked back at the 2-D, the ''picture'' that was so different from the cybernetically reproduced
movement of a sense-cube. It was disturbing. It was like
Mother and yet unlike her—capturing and emphasizing one
moment, one mood. Her face was serious and she looked
stiff, and yet when I thought about it, I could see the fluid
gestures into and out of that frozen moment. I was stupidly
afraid of what moment of myself might be trapped on that
paper.

Sam puttered about the room, finally persuading Aaron to
join the rest of us, grouped around Mother's chair. There was
a buzz, a long, stiff wait, and it was done. Sam withdrew the
flat result from the box and rested it against the wall on the
mantel.

''When it dries, it'll be finished.'' He sounded pleased.

''I believe it's time to retire.'' Mother's voice was the cue
for one more ritual.

Sam, the eldest. He gave Mother a hearty smack on the
cheek and wrapped me again into his rough-shirted warmth.
''Welcome home, daughter, back where you belong.''

I squeezed him. ''Dear Pateros.'' My father's eyes shone
as he left the room.

Aaron took Mother's shoulder and turned her slightly
toward him before bending down to kiss her lips. He took my

hand and stiffly spoke the prescribed words. "Welcome home, daughter."

"Thank you, Aaron." Mother stirred, but I would not call him father.

As he left, Jason took Mother's hand and gave her a brief kiss. Again he avoided my eyes. "Welcome home, daughter."

I took his hand and gave it a matter-of-fact squeeze. "Thank you, Jason."

Mother gave me a quick, surprisingly amused smile, then her face became serious. She folded her arms around my shoulders and gave me a firm hug. She drew back and touched my hair. "It's true, you know. You have grown beautiful."

I jerked my head impatiently. "You don't have to say that, Mother."

She sighed. "Why don't you get your things, Ruth, and I'll go on up and prepare your bed." She turned in the doorway, smiling. "Welcome home, daughter."

Tears threatened to spill, but she was gone. It was hopeless. I'd almost forgotten that devastating smile of hers. And it was so terribly genuine.

My hands remembered the trick of lighting the oil lamp, and I fit the glass cover over it, turning to go fetch my bag. I paused, then walked back to the hearth. The picture was nearly dry.

The firelit family circle. Helen was the still center, her hands gentle on the lyre, her eyes gazing into a point below and beyond me as I held the picture. Her halo of braided hair gathered a rich light, and her lips were barely parted in the start of a smile.

Aaron stood with his shoulders back, his head turned obliquely, looking down and to his left, at Mother—or at me? One eyebrow was raised slightly, the edge of his mouth twisting, though that was probably my imagination.

Sam's face, lower than Aaron's behind Mother's chair, happy, eyes narrowed with laughter beneath shaggy eyebrows.

Jason knelt in a stillness that seemed to be his habit. His hand rested on the arm of the chair, his head turned toward Mother and me, his eyes lowered. His broad cheekbone had caught an interesting angle of shadow, but his face was calmly expressionless.

Finally myself, sitting among the soft folds of my skirt,

leaning dutifully against my mother's knee, my head sleek and neat with the hair drawn back. And my face, pale and tense, staring straight into the camera, the eyes shouting defiance.

I set the thing down and went to get my bags.

three

The world was poised on a shadowy line between night and day. The back porch planking was rough and dusty beneath my bare feet, the breeze almost cool through Helen's thin housedress as I bent over to slip the supple leather moccasins on my feet.

A sleeping hush whispered with the wind over the dirt yard. I passed the ring of rustling shade trees and Helen's kitchen garden and wandered past the barn with its half-finished coat of new brown paint, the tool shed, and the five tall grain silos. I didn't look into the lightening sky until I stood at the edge of the first field, pulling up my long skirt and cinching the fabric above my knees with the sash.

Then I raised my eyes to deep blue and the bright blaze of orange sun peering over low, distant hills. Sunlight flowed onto the fields and a sea of molten copper and silver lapped at my feet, hissing in the dawn. The wind tugged at my hair and eddied over the restless stalks, painting fast swirls of blue-green in shifting patterns before the froth of the ripening grain closed behind its path. A rich smell of dust and grasses rose into my nostrils and my eyes stung and watered. From the wind.

Past the first field the closest of the high towers rose from the stirring wheat. Sunlight gleamed down its alloy spire. Its mylar sails swept past the dim footing of three straddled legs and up again into the light—vast, fluttering wings of silver blue dipping and soaring around the tower, above the fluid earth. Down the valley to the base of the far hills the towers

31

strode among the fields, the last looking in the distance like a child's spinning pinwheel. The wind murmured over it all.

Home.

I took a deep breath and closed my eyes and it was summer, I was twelve, and we had just been released from a long spring term of village school. My rebellious legs free beneath my bound-up skirt, I opened the close kernel of my heart to the morning, all elbows, knees, and pigtails, spinning, laughing, twirling into the head-high, ripening wheat.

I was running into the windy surge of it, the stalks furrowing and closing about me, tripping and laughing. I ran with the firm kernels of grain striking my face, the tough stems whipping my legs, the smell of the grasses rich around me. A crazy exultation rose and spilled over me as I plunged on through the windy field, running to the sails of the closest tower.

Finally, gasping for breath, I fell against one leg of the tower and leaned into the cool kiss of metal on my back.

I closed my eyes and dug my toes into the dirt to search out the tremor radiating from the deep-sunk core of the tower. The vibration rose through the soles of my feet and hummed through me, the voice of Poindros itself, and that long-forgotten flush of well-being flowed up through my legs to each fingertip. Something held tight inside me eased and opened to the banished memory of the old harmony, the earth-tremor and the wind in the wheeling sails and eddying wheat.

"Breathe deep and slow, Ruth." I could almost see the sharp blue eyes, the craggy, wind-seamed face. "There—feel it? The tower in tune with the wind and the earth-tremor. . . ."

"Yes, Isaac, I feel it. Can we climb now?"

The slow, dry chuckle. "Simmer down now, young pup! We'll get to your 'air-dancing' soon enough."

I shook my head and broke away from the touch of the humming metal, squinting up at the glaring signals flashed by the sail tips as they rose and swept through sunlight. My toes found, through the thin leather, the knobbed projections of the tower's leg. I scrambled up and sat where the broad slope of the leg flattened for the nearly horizontal sweep toward the central shaft. The thick ribbon of steel alloy curved to its intersection with the other two legs, where they joined and rose to enclose the generator-spinner. And the tremor-rod inside it, the rod that helped even out the seismic quiver to a frequency that nurtured the hybrid wheat, Poindros's only export. My eyes followed the gleaming spire up to the ring that held the wind-spun wheel of the sails.

Sunlight slid over my face as I lay back on the still-cool slope of the leg and listened to the brisk snap of the sails. Their thin, tough mylar sheeting was clear if you held a piece and looked through it, but when it was stretched into the frame of the immense sail arms it came alive and flashed pearl and sapphire-silver in the sun. I lay and watched as the wheel spun its lights.

The wind shifted and with a rush the sails were carried by the extension bar and the central gimballed mount to a position directly over my head. They swept by so close their breath tugged against my grip on the tower's leg.

I closed my eyes and breathed with the rhythm of their cycle. The rushing arms counted off the days curving into another cycle before me, spinning out with a comforting sameness, drawing me back to the earth. The sails and the tremor whispered a song I had only to learn their harmony to share, drawing me close to the warm heart of Poindros, spilling generously like sun-ripe kernels of grain from Helen's overflowing, cupped hands.

The wheel shifted again with a sharp crack. I sat up, shaking my head as a jitter of misaligned tremor shook through me. The harmony of Poindros wasn't meant for me. The fields and towers were Taboo for women.

I climbed down from the tower leg and edged through the wheat to the beaten-earth track that widened to a clearing beneath the tower, where the central shaft disappeared into the roof of the controlroom. I could really feel the tremor now through my feet, shivering up from the restless layers of rock beneath our fields.

There was a dusty, battered rollcart parked near the controlroom door, crouched at unloading level on its long, jointed resfoam-wheeled legs. Its rear bed was half filled with tools and the odd bits of cord and sacking and crumpled gloves that always seemed to accumulate of their own will.

Damn. I hadn't heard it drive up with its quiet electric motor. It was really too early for the men to be in the fields.

I was beating a hasty retreat back into the stalks when the figure crouched by the recharging receptacle straightened and turned toward me. The camouflage of his dusty beige coveralls and his own tawny colors had blended him into the background. It was the Monotone Man, Jason.

I hadn't even been back a dwodur yet, and already I was racking up violations. Jason stood rigid, his eyes travelling from my wild, wind-snarled hair to my bared legs, then hastily back to my eyes. His face slowly suffused with red, destroying his neutral palette. I sighed, dropped my hem modestly to my ankles, and walked over, yanking my hair back with a ribbon.

He lowered his face and turned quickly to the rollcart to reach into its bed for a tool box. He kept his back to me as he crouched to inspect its contents.

I leaned against the rollcart, feeling the vibration buzzing through it, speaking above the roar of the tower and the wind. "Hey, Jason, I'm sorry. I suppose Aaron's told you all about my demonic nature, and what a Rule-breaker I've always been. I didn't mean any harm, but don't worry. I mean, I won't hold it against you for reporting a violation."

He only shook his head and didn't look up.

He couldn't really be afraid to look at me, like the Poindrans who thought all spacers were possessed of demons. He'd worked in the enclave. I looked over his shoulder. "Pretty interesting tool box you've got there."

I was relieved to see a smile twitch at the corner of his mouth, but he got it under control. He carefully closed the box and stood, still blushing faintly but wearing a properly paternal expression of reproof. He didn't meet my eyes. "Yes, Aaron told me about you. Why do you do it, Ruth? The Rules are for our good, you know."

I shrugged. "Yeah, sure. Go ask Aaron, he'll be glad to fill you in. He's got it all nailed down." I turned to go.

"Wait, Ruth. I'd rather hear it from you."

I turned back warily. His face was neutral, judging. "Look, if you think this is your paternal duty or something, it's all right. You don't have to bother." I started to turn away.

"Wait, Ruth, I'd really like to know." He took a quick stride to grasp my hand, stopping me. I jerked around as a crackle of static prickled up my arm in the dry air and I met his eyes. He didn't lower them this time.

Amber eyes.

Bright, oddly arresting. Amber. Like the timid Andurans? No, light brown, actually, with gold flecks, really quite striking, not at all monotone. Like Sethar's ferial, with his tawny colors. Or the gentle gizu-doe it preyed on? A confusion of carefully buried memory broke loose and whirled inexplicably

through me. Another pair of eyes, deep brown and warm in a
dark face, his slow smile splitting all at once to a gleam of
teeth. Jaréd's deft fingers clasping mine . . . No. Amber eyes
holding mine, seeing too much.

I jerked my hand free and looked down, clearing my
throat. "I . . . it's getting warm already, isn't it? I forgot
how hot the summers are. Have you got a water bottle?"

Jason had lowered his eyes and the blush was glowing hot
again beneath his tan. He glanced quickly at me, then turned
to reach into the rollcart for a plasmeld flask. I had already
unstoppered it and was tilting the water down my throat when
he reached again to politely hand me a cup. Swallowing, I
shook my head.

He stood, holding the cup, blushing deeper. He looked
down at it, then suddenly tossed it into the rollcart, spun on
his heel, and strode toward the controlroom.

I stood with the flask in my hand, staring after him.

So maybe he really was worried about spacer germs. I
shrugged and returned the flask to the rollcart.

He'd left the door to the controlroom open, so I figured I
might as well make some of those observations, since I was
already pegged for violations. The metal frame vibrated beneath my hand as I peered down the stairs into the dimness. A
light went on then, and I moved down the steps into the
tangible shock of the tremor and the loud humming roar.

Jason looked up, startled, from some gauges across the
room, moving almost protectively in front of them. He shouted
above the roar. "This is Taboo for you, Ruth. You know
that."

"I know." I raised my voice. "Look, Jason, I've already
committed my violation, and I just want to see it again. Don't
worry." I probably knew our towers better than he did,
anyway.

His lips tightened and he turned back to the generator
controls. It looked like they'd done some modifications since
my last childhood visit here. There was a new synchrometer
unit, and one of the panel readouts had been replaced with a
different configuration. I gave Jason a wide berth, letting him
ignore me, and wandered around the circular room, running a
hand along the smooth lucite water pipes and the routing
valves. A lighted board indicated the positions of the main
valves beneath the fields. Field Three was on trickle right
now. I walked on past the seismic scales, the readouts on

wind flux to the tremor-rod and counterbalance thrust. I quickly pressed a test button on one of the seismic scales, and the needle jumped and wavered in the satisfactory range.

I glanced over at Jason's back and whistled casually, wandering over to the thick rod running down from the ceiling through the center of the chamber. Fingers hooked into the protective mesh enclosure, I watched light from the ceiling bulbs flicker across the shiny steel alloy.

The tremor-hum pulsed through my hands and the soles of my feet, overwhelming now. Here at the heart, I could feel its power surge from my toes to my fingertips, stronger than my breathing, stronger than my heartbeat, coursing through me, filling me. I could feel each eddy of the narrow, solid tremor-enhancement and dispersal rod that ran deep into the buried rock through and beyond the hollow generator-spinner whose metal surface flickered its fast lights.

I pressed closer against the screen, drawn into the spinning pattern of light.

It was the tower wing slashing across hot blue sky in a dazzle of sun down snapping mylar, as the ground and the tawny gleam of wheat spun around and past, the wind catching us up for the lift. Isaac's voice, a calm center in the whirling maelstrom of earth and sky: "Go with it, Ruth. Let it take you, feel the tremor in the sail arm—that's your base. Let the sun twirl around you. You're the center when you're riding the spinner bar. Now, feel how it all moves together."

And for a centa that could have been eternity I was part of it again, part of the cycles within cycles, the smooth roll of the world and the spin of the sails, the twirling rod and the smoothed-out tremor singing beneath the soil and nurturing the rich fruit of the wheat, the energy humming through the wires and dials of the tower, responding to the touch of fingers.

But there was something else. Something wrong.

The imbalance I'd sensed when I lay on the tower leg. It was there, a physical jolt, a quiver not aligned with the power flux and the tremor-rod. I could feel the jarring eddy out of synch with the wheel and the rod, like a wheel spinning the wrong direction against the cycle. There was something wrong with the field flow. It was—

"Ruth!" A strong grip closed over my wrist and wrenched my fingers from the screen. Jason dragged me back from the screen, his face angry and worried and paternal.

"Wait, Jason—"

"Are you out of your mind?" His hand tightened painfully around my wrist and he dragged me toward the stairs. I caught a last confused glimpse of the dials, then I tripped in the long skirts as he yanked me up the stairs and my shoulder twisted in his grasp.

I was blinking in the hot, bright sun as he stood blocking the door. I jerked my arm free from his hand, my shoulder shooting out a little stab of pain. "What in hell was that for? I was only looking!"

He flinched as I swore, glaring at a point somewhere near my shoulder, not meeting my eyes. "Look, I don't know what you're trying to prove, but you've seen enough. That machinery can be dangerous. You're a woman, you belong back at the house."

I rubbed my shoulder. "Okay, I'll go. But there's something out of synch with the power flow. Check it out."

He looked even angrier. "That's crazy! Aaron was just out here yesterday, calibrating the synchrometers. Maybe he's right, maybe you think you know better than the Way, but you don't. Go back to the house and leave our work to us." The door slammed behind him.

Wonderful. I'd managed to antagonize my gentle new father into an un-Poindran display of anger in record time, even for me.

"You watching out there, cybers? Is this what you wanted? Damn you!" The wind swallowed my words and whirled past me.

I slowly retraced the path of my wild plunge through the bruised stems of wheat. Maybe I should've just gone for the Steps of Healing. It would've been a lot simpler. But something in me panicked at the thought. I was unreasonably afraid of more than the social stigma. I recalled the mellow smile and the odd memory blanks of an acquaintance in Casino who'd returned from the Healing. But he *had* seemed happier.

I sighed and sank down in the stems, lay back and crossed my fingers behind my head, looking up at the criss-cross pattern of shifting wheat against blue sky. I closed my eyes and CI's cyberserf smiled patiently in the dark. "Maybe you'll see your homeworld and yourself differently now."

Right. Lying against the pungent soil, I could feel the

world rolling, bearing me home on the returning cycle of the changeless wheel, and I was right back where I'd started ten years ago. I could almost hear Aaron's voice, "Go ahead, daughter, trample the wheat the way you do the Rules. Maybe you've forgotten what it's like to work for an honest living."

I could see Helen's eyes trying to hide her concern as I flared back, "Yes, you're so *honest*, Aaron," like the tower controls lighting up indicators in programmed anger whenever the same sequence of buttons triggered its relays. It was all so pointless.

So arbitrary, like the Poindros worldplan. Like the fall of a spinning credit-chip deciding if a boy- or girl-child would be born. Of all the gifts Helen tried to give me, I wanted only one thing, and that was something she couldn't give me.

If only I'd been born male like Joshua, it all would've made sense. It would've been right that I'd inherited that gift from our truefather, Isaac, his feel for the nuances of earth-tremor, the subtle shifts in wind, the humming song of the towers and the instinctive balance of them all that made riding the spinning sails so much more than the mundane job it was for my twin brother. But I was a woman now. Banned from the high freedom of the air, I was bound to the hearth, as blind to the joys Helen described as Joshua was to the magic of sunlight on tower wings.

I sat up and shook my head. Of course Jason would ignore my presumptuous advice, but that flux imbalance at the tower had been real. I sighed. It probably didn't matter, anyway. A minor skip wouldn't hurt things. But it'd had a funny feel to it, something I'd never felt before.

I absently fingered the IDisc that had slid on the chain from beneath my bodice. The red-gold scales of my lucky necklace glimmered and the tiny emerald eyes of the snake-head clasp winked slyly.

I deactivated the skin-cling and the chip attached to it came free. I turned it over in my hands, but it was only a feature-less, thin piece of silver-blue plasmeld. I wondered why the cybers had made such a fuss about it. I wondered why they'd let me slip by the Steps of Healing and sent me here to observe, since I was obviously such a misfit. I shrugged again and reattached the chip to my IDisc. Maybe I was just another minor imbalance, and I didn't really matter.

I shook my head and rolled quickly back and forth in the

sweet, scratchy wheat stems, like a pet pardil cleaning itself. I jumped up and ran back to the house.

"Ruth! What are you doing out here?"

I whirled around and backed a step toward the side of the barn. Bloody hell! I'd been longer than I thought, and they were already up.

Aaron stepped closer, scowling openly without Helen's eyes on him. "You've been out to the fields, haven't you? Haven't you?" He stood over me, fists clenched. "Listen, slut, I'm watching! You're not going to get away with it this time. If I catch you out by that tower—"

"Oh, there you are, Ruth." It was Jason, stepping through the side door of the barn with a bucket of foaming milk. "What did you think of our new livestock? I think old Bathsheba still remembered you." He met my eyes briefly, a slow smile splitting all at once to a quick gleam of teeth, tugging at memory and vanishing.

I stared. No. It was only my eyes playing cruel tricks of familiarity on me.

Jason shifted the bucket, his expression once again bland. "Morning's getting on, though. We'd best get back to the house or Sam'll have all our breakfast gobbled up."

Aaron looked from Jason to me, his eyes narrowing with suspicion. "I'm watching you, Ruth. You hear me? You go out to that tower, you'll be sorry!"

"Come on, Aaron, let's go in. Ruth knows the Rules."

Jason urged us on as I shot a quick look at his usual neutral expression, still astounded that he'd lie for me. He avoided my eyes, looking out to the fields. "Wheat's getting high already, Aaron. We'll have to string line soon." His eyes flickered unreadably across mine. "Founder with us and barring a bad wind, we'll have us a good harvest."

four
_____

"Oh, Matron Henrietta, I couldn't possibly. This is much too extravagant! Well, really, if you insist . . . oh, it's just too lovely, my dear! And you made this yourself? Well, of course Ezekiel helped, but still. . . ."

Henrietta shifted her heavy posterior, shook her double chins, and clucked in gratification.

I simpered. "Well, thank you, Matron. I'll treasure it."

She edged over obligingly as I rummaged beneath her ample thighs. I held up the last fist-sized egg, set it carefully in the overloaded wickerwork basket, and stroked the trotter hen's soft, tufted back. She hopped off the perch, stretching out the feathered stumps of vestigial wings, and landed with a thud beside me. She uttered a low cooing noise and rubbed her plumed head against my leg.

"Keep up the good work, gals. It's back to the house for me!" I'd about exhausted the allowable outside chores in the past few days, and there wasn't a weed left in Helen's garden.

"I thought I'd find you out here." Helen opened the gate to the pen for me, the filtered morning light through cracks in the barn boards glinting like spun copper in her hair. Her eyes gleamed bright green. She was completely unaware of the dazzling halo illuminating the contours of her face. Her smile transformed the marble-pale brow, the high cheekbones, the delicate, straight nose and slender, winglike brows from an almost too-perfect coolness into a warm promise of ripening

summer. It seemed impossible that she carried the weight of
nearly twice my years.

I touched her hand impulsively. "Mother, it was worth the
trip home just to see you look like that."

A faint rose touched her cheeks. "Why, thank you, dear."
She squeezed my hand, then released it. "My, the hens are
really laying, aren't they?" She reached over the pen to rub
the ear tufts of the trotter cock. Ezekiel closed his eyes and
crowed sleepily.

I chuckled, hefting the basket and pausing to pat the smooth
flank of the old milker who shuffled over to hang her head
out of the stall. I rubbed the knobby lump of bone on her
forehead. "See you later, Bathsheba."

I paused in the doorway. "Poor old Ezekiel looks a little
frazzled, trying to keep it up for all those females. Maybe he
needs a younger frateros to take the load off a little." I
chuckled again. "Unless he'd be as jealous as—" I bit my lip
at Helen's reproachful look.

She followed me across the dirt yard, turning to glance
back at the coat of brown paint I'd completed the day before,
using scaffolding I'd improvised on the back of a rollcart.
"Ruth, Aaron meant well yesterday. You really oughtn't to
do such reckless things. And I don't know what they wear on
those other worlds, but you're a woman now and you must
dress respectably."

"I didn't really think Joshua's old coveralls were 'showing
the shape of my legs like a harlot.' "

She colored faintly, hesitated, then reached up to place my
dangling shade-hat on my head. "We wouldn't want that
pretty skin all sunburned for the gathering."

I walked on to the house and dumped the heavy basket onto
the porch, lunging to catch an egg that tumbled off the pile. I
stood rolling it from hand to hand for a centa, then looked up.
"Helen, I hope you're not getting all built up for a letdown."

"What do you mean, dear?" Her eyes flickered, then
steadied on mine.

I sighed, dropping the egg from palm to palm. "Just don't
expect too much at the gathering, okay? I mean, people are
going to remember about me. I'm not sure they'll want a
spacer sitting among them."

"Nonsense, Ruth! You're resettled now. It will be good for
you to meet the young people again."

"Especially the bachelors?" I caught the egg and held it. "That would solve a lot of problems, wouldn't it?"

Helen sighed. "Ruth, please be patient with Aaron. If only you could see his loving side, as I do. I'm sure he would respond if you could only be more gentle with—"

"Gentle!" I laughed harshly. "Listen, Mother, if *you* only— damn!" The thin eggshell cracked in my hand and a yellow mess oozed through my fingers. "Fireblood and—"

I threw the dripping egg onto the ground, muttering in exasperation as I wiped my hand down my skirt.

"Ruth, here now! We can't leave it like that." She pulled the fabric straight and dabbed at the mess with her kerchief.

"Damn it, Mother, stop fluttering over me!"

"Ruth!" She looked shocked, her face flushing beneath the bonnet. Her eyes were hurt and disappointed.

"Oh, to hell with it all!" I stomped up the steps and slammed through the screen door.

Burnished copper beneath a hot sky. The wind sighed, softly now, and swelled, sweeping through the heart of the land . . .

> In the fields of Illyrion,
> Over the shining sea,
>   Who guards?
> Over the shining sea,
> Between bright Heaven and Earth,
>   Who guards?
>
> Deep-rooted strong, I stand,
> High-reaching, far-seeing, wind-full.
> Between bright Heaven and Earth
> I lift my arms; Behold!
>   I guard.
> In the fields of Illyrion,
> Wind-rushed wings of light.

. . . and the wheat surged, copper-pink and gleaming beneath the silvery dazzle of the sails. The great tower thrust upward to the sky, wings dipping and rising into the joy of wind and sun.

The last rising chord rang out and lingered between the stifling walls of my room. I let it fade slowly into quiet. My hands soothed the strings as I held the lyre against me, savoring the feel of the smooth, cream-colored wood threaded with darker veins. Of course I regretted my childish outburst in the yard. Maybe when I'd practiced more, I'd surprise her and play my new song for the evening gathering.

"Ruth?" A soft tap on the door.

I stood hastily and set the lyre back on the chest of drawers. As I turned to call "Come in," my hand brushed the strings and a faint discord rose into the air to greet Helen.

Her eyes went first to the lyre and her grave face lightened, but she said nothing as I stepped in front of it.

We stood regarding each other in silence. I recalled the mirrors in a certain casino I knew, where the patrons laughed at their grotesque, warped reflections. I was one of them, taking in Helen's beauty and giving back only ugliness.

"I shouldn't have come back."

She didn't reply, only walked slowly past me to look out the window, over the fields. Her hand reached up to absently stroke the smooth curve of the lyre as if the act were a habit. The hand trembled and she drew it back quickly.

A dismaying pity moved me to throw my arms around her. "Mother, I'm sorry. I don't mean to hurt you."

She held me tightly. "Ruth, Ruth." Her voice was muffled against my shoulder. "Don't run away again. Give yourself a chance to learn the Way once more. Don't you remember how you used to laugh and sing when you were a girl? You had such a happy smile."

I held her against me as she cried, disoriented by this reversal, at a loss in the role of comforter. I guided her to sit on the bed and found a grubby handkerchief in my pocket, gave it to her. I sat, arm around her, rocking slightly.

"Don't be upset, Mother. I won't leave." The lie popped out without thought.

She dried her eyes and raised them, still bright green with tears, to mine. "You *can* be gentle! I'm so glad."

She spoke to my downturned face. "Ruth, please let me love you. I've tried not to push. But it's been hard, not knowing, fearing I had failed you, that you wouldn't have gone away if I'd shown you better the joy and fulfilment of becoming a Hearth-Matron and mother. I see now it's there in you, though you fight it—the need to nurture. You've been hurt. But I'm sure now you will find peace."

I drew back and sighed. "Mother, you're wrong to feel

you could fail me. You can't be responsible for another person's life.''

Her hand touched mine again. "I'll always be your mother, Ruth. Whether you feel you need me or not. That responsibility is a joy to me, not a burden. But you know the meaning of love—things will come right for you.''

She kissed the top of my head and was gone with a sighing of cloth and the soft click of the door.

I sat on the bed, my hands clenched in the blanket. She was just as stubborn as I was.

I paced over to the window and looked out, over to the door, back to the window. I seized the lyre and sank to the floor with it, wrenched a chord from the protesting strings, and stared at my fingers until their focus dissolved in a long, fluid glissando.

five

Helen sat in her armchair, hands gentle on the lyre, calm face gazing past me. Sam grinned and Aaron raised his mocking eyebrow. Jason knelt in his quiet reserve, those remarkable eyes lowered. I clenched my teeth and my strained face stared back at me from the picture on the hearth.

I swore under my breath and threw the feather-duster onto a chair, yanked up my clinging skirts, and stalked back and forth across the empty parlor. The picture brought me up short again. I took it reluctantly in my hands, fingering the odd, stiffened paper of the 2-D.

The family circle. Emblem of the peace and stability of the Poindros Way. The picture should have been a perfect part of the Plan, preserving its moment of the eternal family unit. But something about it made me uneasy. Maybe because it pinned down that one moment so exactly, to stay that way until the paper frayed and tattered. It wasn't like the sense-cubes of high-tech planets, imparting their brief experiences in a single glimpse and then self-erasing for reuse. This picture couldn't change. It wouldn't show the time to come, my absence when I left Poindros again. It didn't show the before-time with Joshua, gone now to another family, or Isaac, taken by death. Or even farther back, Isaac and Sam's first wife, Hearth-Matron here before Helen, whose name I didn't even know. The family remained through the endless cycles of matrons and patera and sons and daughters, always the same.

But in a few years, that picture would show us just how

surely we *had* changed. Maybe other things changed, too. But that was a Taboo notion. Could the picture really be contraplan? I gripped it tighter, staring into the flat surface as if those frozen faces would give me an answer. We weren't supposed to think about the questions they stirred.

I sighed and set the thing back on the hearth. If I wasn't careful with *my* questions, I'd rack up more of the violation points Aaron was itching to pin on me. My eyes slid from his dark gaze to Helen's patient smile to my own defiant stare. She didn't deserve that look from me. Maybe I could make something for her, something to place there on the hearth to soften what that picture said.

Yes. I'd have to order supplies. I turned eagerly, striding from the room. I groped for the oil lamp at the top of the cellar stairs, fumbling in my pocket for matches. Shadows fluttered up from the flame and I hurried down. The consoles weren't used all that often on Poindros, so most of them were out of the way, like ours, in the cellar.

I descended into dim coolness and the light picked out a detail here and there among a jumble of castoff or forgotten possessions—a chair with one leg missing, a frayed songbook on its seat; a straw-stuffed puppet from the harvest festival; a dusty, cracked vase; a coil of climbing line that still looked good, except for one frayed spot that needed splicing; and the draping of an old rug making a vague animal bulk out of a pile of boxes far back in the dark.

Down the hall, I set the lamp on the floor and groped for the button to the cyber cubicle. The door slid open with a whoosh and electric light flared inside. It was the only room that had it, of course.

I stepped into the sleek, res-walled chamber, feeling the change in the filtered air, and it was like walking into another world. For the first time, it seemed odd to step from the rough-plastered cellar into the cyber cubicle, and I wondered why more Poindrans didn't wonder why the cubicles and tower controlrooms used electric light while their homes had only oil lamps, why they had electric stoves but had to heat bath water in pots, why . . . I shook my head.

I pulled over the battered metal stool that had somewhere along the line replaced the sleek plasmeld chair that belonged in the cubicle. I sat down before the bulky cabinet with its lighted indicators and pressed the activator button. As long as I was down here, I might as well send CI and Officer Hodge an OK signal, since Aaron hadn't yet caught me out in anything serious. I started to reach for my IDisc, then remembered that the persona would still be cued to my voiceprint.

A green light flared. "Good morning! How nice to have company! And what can I do for you today?" The speaker exuded her irritating presence, an overweight village matron bending close to breathe her mothery tones over me.

"First, I'd like to—"

"Why, it's Ruth! I'm so happy to hear your voice again, my dear!" The voice interrupted with nicely calculated, mild excitement. " 'Let the fields clap their hands! May the hills be joyful together!' May I add my welcome to that of the family?"

I took a deep breath, remembering the heavy psych-slanting of the Poindran personae. "Oh. Sure. Thanks, Matron."

"I have a message for you, my dear, from your brother."

"That's all right, Helen already passed it along." Joshua couldn't get free to visit, which was understandable since the season was well under way and they were underhanded at his farm, but I'd see him at the binding ceremony for his wife's upcoming third marriage.

"I do hope you're settling in happily, Ruth. You know, you really ought to put on a little weight, but I'm sure Helen is taking good care of you. She's such a wonderful Hearth-Matron! If you have any little troubles readjusting, now you be sure to talk to her all about them, won't you?"

"Oh, sure. Everything's fine." I rolled my eyes before I remembered that she'd be scanning me. "I've got a job for you."

"Oh, good! How may I help you?"

"I want you to contact my credit accounts on Casino—YBA-42E8—and transfer fifty credits from business to personal. Account key: Saint-seducing Gold. Got it?"

"This is a little complicated, dear, since I have to contact central records . . . there we go." She sighed. "You know, Ruth, you really ought to have your credits transferred to a Poindran registration, now that you're back home."

I swallowed, then answered hastily, "Oh, oh, sure. It's just that I . . . I'm waiting for some credits I'm owed there to clear, then I'll have everything transferred back."

She sounded doubtful. "Well, this is a little unusual, my dear, but it's not strictly a violation. . . ."

"Good. I want you to do something else for me. Contact a

licensed courier on Sethar—EKL-3A79—and transfer contingent credits from my personal account to his or hers. Let's see, a hundred-fifty should do it, and there'll be a bonus if the courier can light a fire under Anáh . . .''

I smiled, remembering the cranky old woman, her skinny legs bare as she crouched in the dirt, her brown, toothless face crinkling in disdain of my first blundering attacks on the practice-wood. ''You, Young-soft-pale-offworld-one, must use only the Tohr-wood''—the wood without soul—''until you learn to give it life. Then, perhaps, your fingers will not kill the many creatures of the Lianarr.''

Of the Lianarr—the woods of the Sethar sculptors, those imbued with life that skilled hands could awaken—I had longed to work with a piece of the mirō. Finally, even Anáh had allowed that I'd mastered the trance-states, and she'd given the first small piece into my hands, where I'd felt it stir and pulse, like blood shot through with dazzling sun. The fire-lizard, Ni-Pohn, awoke through that feverish night in my hands, darting his quick tongue. Beside the ashes stirring in the next morning's breeze off the river, Anáh had laughed, like dry twigs snapping, and said it was a good totem for me.

''A fire?'' The Matron's querulous voice cut across my thoughts. ''Beneath a human? Is that part of the instructions to be relayed? I'll have to check Sethar's customs, my dear, but are you sure that wouldn't be a violation?''

''Okay, Matron. No fires, just a bonus for quick work.''

''Now remember, dear, these impure word usages really aren't proper. Perhaps we'd better have a standard-speech refresher one of these days.''

I sighed. ''Tell the courier to contact Elder Anáh of the Tribe of Dehbarroth. . . .'' My hand raised involuntarily to the raised ridge of my scar and I jerked it back into my lap. I closed my eyes. Maybe this was a mistake.

I could feel the finished carving in my hands again, the ebbing of the trance-state as I'd opened my eyes, blinked, and found a set of dark eyes in a face as dark fixed on mine. It was Jaréd I'd first seen as I awoke. When the face with its jagged scar across the forehead had warmed in a slow smile and he'd put aside his spear to reach down a hand to me, I'd known that I would be accepted in the tribe, after all. It was Jaréd who had been my first real friend, my teacher in the hunt, had been—

"Ruth, is something wrong? I read indications of distress. If you're ill, you should ask Helen for an elixir, my dear."

I shook my head. "No, no, I'm fine, really." I blew out a long breath. "Let's see. I want the courier to deliver a message. Why don't you give me the vid screen? How about half-centimeter characters on a twelve-wide scrolling field, white letters on green?" I wiped a beading of sweat from my forehead.

"I could help you compose an appropriate message, with my culture-tapes, Ruth. It would be much easier."

"No, that's all right. How about that screen?"

"Very well." She sounded definitely put out, but the screen slid up from the console top.

"Okay, first line: 'The voice of the fire-lizard has'—wait, erase 'has'—'speaks in the heart of. . . .' "

By the time I'd completed the long, roundabout appeal to Anáh, the console-Matron was responding in an offended tone that warned me I wasn't behaving like a proper Poindran. "Very well, Ruth, I will convey your instructions, but I really can't approve of your sending for this offworld wood."

"Look, it's not contraplan. If you've checked your Rules, you know Sethar's even lower-tech than Poindros."

"Very well." Her voice was curt, disapproving, exactly like Elder Katherine berating me for rough-housing during a play-break at the village school. "Will that be all?"

"I guess so . . . no, wait, Matron." The green energized light blinked into a pulsing holding pattern. "No, I didn't mean go on hold. I just wanted to ask you something else. What do you know about these cameras? Why haven't I seen one before?" Sam's gadget still didn't seem right to me, not on Poindros. Maybe not anywhere.

"Camera? I don't understand, Ruth. I have no such word in my data-loops. I'm afraid I must register a violation for you if you are introducing contraplan concepts."

"No, no, wait! Maybe I got the word wrong. It's nothing wild, really, just a box that paints a sort of picture for you if you stand in front of it."

"Checking." Her voice was curt. "Verified. No such construct exists within the Poindran worldplan." She sounded upset now. "Ruth, I must inform you that possession of a contraplan mechanism constitutes a serious violation."

"No, Matron, you don't understand!" I took a deep breath. "I don't have one, I just heard about it, and I thought it was allowed here. I—I guess I'm still a little confused, resettling and all, you know.'' I held my breath. I didn't want to get Sam in trouble, though how the contraption had gotten circulated openly beyond the Spaceport black-marketeers I had no idea.

"Ruth, I am sorry, but I'm afraid I must register a three-point conversational violation. Your confusion indicates a readjustment problem. I'd suggest you have a talk with Helen about it. She'll help you.''

I let out my breath. "Yes, that's a good idea, Matron. I'll do that.''

"Good, Ruth.'' She was playing soothing mood music now, just barely audible. "You go on now, talk to Helen, and you'll feel much better.''

"Thank you, Matron. Oh, before I go, could you tell me my status now on violation points? I'm really trying to improve myself, and I'd like to say my penitence at the next gathering.'' I bit my lip and started to roll my eyes again, then stopped in time.

"Very well, dear. Your current status is seventeen points. That's not too bad, Ruth, though it could certainly be better.''

"Yes, I know. The family's trying to help, too. They checked on my status for me before I came home, didn't they?''

Her voice sounded puzzled. "I have no record of such a request, my dear. Are you sure you're not mistaken?''

"But they said they did. You're sure no one asked you?''

She sounded amused now, the music swelling a little louder. "Now don't tease me, dear. You know I have a little trouble understanding humor. You know I can't be mistaken. You go on, now, talk to Helen. She'll advise you about achieving the proper attitudes of a Hearth-Mistress. It might help to remember these words:

> Fevered is the daughter who cannot look
> Upon her mortal days with temperate blood,
> Who vexes all the leaves of her life's Book,
> And robs her fair name of its maidenhood.

I am glad you're trying, my dear. Good faring.''

"Good faring, Matron.'' I reached out slowly to deactivate the console, and the green light faded into the blinking ambers and blues of the automatic monitoring functions linked to the tower controls. I stared until the colors blurred and ran together.

It didn't make sense.

The cyber consoles never made mistakes. End of discussion. But Hodge had told me one of the family had inquired into my violation status. Aaron, obviously, since he was so eager to catch me out in more of them. He had a definite interest in this camera business, too. Something funny was going on. All at once I felt like a camera in the hands of CI, sent home to passively snap pictures that wouldn't make sense to me until CI brought me back and interpreted what was captured on my film of memory. I didn't like it.

Could there actually be something wrong with the console interface? I hesitated, glancing nervously behind my back, then took a firm grip on the cabinet and pulled. It stuck, then slid with difficulty away from the wall. Dust sparkled in the light as I looked down at the thick cable running from the box into the cubicle wall.

I crouched down and read the notice on the back: CYBER-NETIC ACCESS ONLY. DANGER.

I took a deep breath and pried at the recessed catches with my thumbnail, swore, sucked the cut, and tried the Anduran kid's handy plasmeld chip again. The catches loosened and the heavy plate fell free into my hands. I leaned it against the wall and took a look.

A mass of gray insulated wires converged into the outlet cable. I peered into the tidily bundled and branching maze of leads. I didn't see the terminal numbers or color code the cybers used in the simpler circuitry of the tower cabinets they let us repair and maintain. I picked out the small, boxlike units of relay switches and bell-shaped backs of speakers that created the persona voice. A seamless black bulk took up most of the interior.

That had to be where the real business went on, where the cybers lived. I stared at the opaque, impervious shape, wondering what mysterious Ways the cybers followed in there. The black surface stared smugly back at me.

Some of the wire leads had to carry alarm signals of an unlikely interface defect or short-circuit to the automatic surveillance and repair dispatchers. I poked an edgy finger among them, half expecting the Matron's voice to snap a reprimand at me. But all the connections looked good.

I blotted another uneasy beading of sweat from my forehead. It looked like I could rule out tampering of some sort. It would have to have been done by humans, anyway, since of course the cybers couldn't break the Rules. And no human could have the Taboo knowledge to do that. I took another long look in the cabinet, reclosed it, and shoved it hastily back against the wall.

Either Hodge had been lying, or the cyber console had just made a mistake. I wasn't thrilled with either possibility. I turned to leave.

"Something wrong?"

"Blazes!" I jerked backward in alarm.

It was Aaron leaning in the cubicle doorway, the coil of frayed line slung over his shoulder, one eyebrow raised, the slight twist to his lips just revealing his strong teeth. "I see you found it."

"Found what?" Had he seen me closing up the cabinet?

"The console. What else? You maybe looking for something else down here?" The words held an insinuating emphasis and his smile widened into an unpleasant grin as he glanced from me to the winking monitor lights and back.

"Look, Aaron, I'm not in the mood to play games." I started to step past him, but he shifted just enough in the doorway to block my way.

"Games? I thought that was your specialty, little Ruth. I know what you've been doing, out there," he jerked his head vaguely upward, "with your gambling and whoring and—"

"Is that why you're so interested in my violation point status, Aaron? Must have been a disappointment to find how low I am."

His nostrils flared angrily. "I don't count up points on you—that's for the cybers—but the sooner they decide you need Healing, the better. You and the rest of the Rule breakers, trying to bring the Plan down. I'm watching, I see the demon at work in you. I warn you, I'll stop you."

"You're telling me you didn't ask the console for my point status?"

"Now why would I do a thing like that?" The nasty smile was back on his face. "Running scared, aren't you? Go ahead, ask the Matron." He tilted his head toward the console. "Go ahead."

I shrugged. "It doesn't matter, anyway." He knew damn well what the Matron would say. But what was he up to?

I straightened my shoulders and met the hostile brown

eyes. "Look, Aaron, what's the point of all this? It's been ten years. Whatever arguments we had with each other are wind over the wheat now. For Helen's sake, why don't we start over? I'm willing to forgive and forget—isn't that what the Book says?" To my reckoning, I had more to forgive than he did.

He shook his head. "You can't fool me with your wiles." His eyes narrowed. "You've learned how to use them, haven't you? You've grown up. You're even pretty now, aren't you— almost like a *real* woman? Sort of a pale imitation of Helen."

I could feel the angry flush rising through me, my nerves jumping for a fight, but I refused to be baited in the same old way. "All right, Aaron, have it your way. I've got better things to do."

I started again for the door, but he shot out a hand and grasped my arm. He leaned closer. "I know why you came back, bitch! And you think Helen's going to shield you again? Maybe you're not so grown up after all."

I tried to pull my arm away, but he only tightened the grip painfully. "I'm about the same age as Mother's new husband, I expect. Is that what's got you, Aaron? Can't stand sharing her?"

His eyes glittered furiously as he drew in a harsh breath, and he yanked me angrily forward. "You demon, you—"

I stamped on his instep as I snapped my free forearm quickly beneath his grip, twisting and moving back to break his hold. I stood, crouched slightly forward, taking a deep breath. "Don't touch me again, Aaron."

He looked briefly disconcerted, then laughed and moved back from the doorway with a mocking bow. "Don't let me stand in your way, Ruth. Do you really think you could tempt me? You? When I have a wife like Helen?"

He was laughing as I hurried past him to the stairs.

six

Bright blue arched over me. Hot wind tugged at my hair and tangled the long skirts about my legs. The wheat surged and rippled around me, hissing rage, shame, and discomfiting pity. But Aaron had been right about one thing. That young girl wasn't as far behind me as I'd thought. I still fled to the fields.

I yanked up my dress and ran, fighting the tangible resistance of tangling wheat stems, clinging skirts, hot wind, trying to outrace the nerve-twisting tension. But when I stopped, panting, it still hummed down my spine, insistent, warning, and I found myself crouching, turning to rake the long grasses with my eyes.

I shook my head. Aaron was a different kind of danger.

I walked on slowly, wondering what he knew about the console and my violation points. Did he really believe I was a threat to the Plan, or was that only an excuse to take out his resentments on me? Was he connected with the imbalance CI wanted me to observe? Could there actually be something *wrong* here on Poindros, some flaw in the perfect Plan? The cybers hadn't told me enough.

And I suddenly realized how little I really knew of Aaron. Helen had brought him home for the courting visit when Joshua and I were thirteen and I was still allowed in the fields with Isaac and the others. Though Isaac was strong, it was clear that his time on the towers was going to end as surely as mine. The men needed a younger frateros. But the centa I saw Aaron, tall and too handsome, his arm possessively encircling Helen's waist as his eyes passed over our faces with the same look he cast on the sagging boards of the house and the leaking barn roof, I knew he was wrong for us.

Oh, he was upright in the Way, as he read aloud the Book of Words in the evenings and his voice drove sharp nails into our farm's sins of ease and comfortable dilapidation; as he tried to drive the sins from me when I wouldn't follow his paternal dictates with Joshua's eagerness to please. But I saw now what the rebellious girl of sixteen who'd finally run away couldn't have seen, that Aaron was almost as much a misfit in the Poindran worldplan as I was.

Even Helen couldn't smooth away the sharp edges of Aaron's righteous angers. And the un-Poindran possessiveness that must be burning him now like the fabled flames of war, now that he had to share Helen with Jason and me, as well as easygoing old Sam. Who knew what that rage might drive him to?

The same cold slivers of fear I'd felt during the Spaceport clearance prickled inside me. I could feel the charged tension race down my nerves in answer, and suddenly the full state of *timbra* blossomed through me—the heightened awareness of the hunt, muscles taut, nerves focussed to a fine balance of calm held over readiness for instant reaction. Ready for the fight.

As if on cue, a stealthy rustling rose over the sound of the wind in the wheat stalks.

I swung around to locate the source of the noise, swallowed now by the hiss of the wind-stirred wheat. My senses sharpened, expanded to take in the sound, smell, feel of whatever waited before me, or perhaps to the side, or behind, ready to pounce from a hidden vantage, make me the prey . . . There, to the right.

"Don't be too confident, Ruth. You may not get a second chance." Jaréd's voice—calm, steadying. "Make your mind like the smooth sand by the river. Your body is the water, not moving, yet moving. Let the ferial show you his dance. Then you will flow with and around him."

A flash of tawny fur among the wheat. Or only the wind ghosting like memory through the tall grass? Like speckled shadow among the shifting shapes overhead in the vine-draped dhama boughs of Sethar's green jungle, as my grip tightened on the long spear. I crouched, knees flexed, weight forward on the balls of my feet, ready to turn, or launch forward, as my hand reached down to my hip for—

The wheat stems tore apart, erupting with noise and threat.

A streak of tawny yellow shot through them and landed scant meters before me, tensed to spring again. Color flowed and solidified into a clear, frozen crystal of time, etched with the shape of a sleek, lionlike creature, crouched low on four muscled legs. The frozen *milla* shattered as the huge cat quivered with readiness, its tufted tail twitching as its amber eyes burned into the quarry.

My heart slammed in deep, hard thrusts against my ribs, pumping charged readiness to meet the tensing leap of the clawed legs. I stared back with a strange sense of dislocation into those pitiless amber eyes. My hand jerked at my hip and grasped air where my knife should be. The tawny legs shifted forward, gathered to spring—

A high, terrified squeal sounded beneath my feet and a small, scaled burrower darted behind my skirts, its long tail disappearing into a hole in the dirt.

I threw back my head and laughed.

The strung tension of threat lapsed into the laughter I couldn't stop. The *timbra* state dissolved with the jungle of Sethar into farce. There was no reason to carry a weapon on Poindros.

The amber eyes registered bewilderment and the tufted ears of the pardil twitched forward inquiringly.

"Hey, Ela! Hey, boy," I crooned softly. "I must've given you more of a shock than you gave me." His tail twitched broadly back and forth. "Hey, boy, doesn't anybody play with you?" I feinted from side to side.

He gave a mock growl and moved his left paw toward me, the big, tufted pads blunt with the claws retracted. I laughed and darted forward, then back into the stalks as he reached out again with a lazy swipe.

"Ha! Bet you can't catch me!" I danced past his face again and ran through the wheat as he galumphed slowly after me. I pivoted and ducked past his butting head to grab the end of his tufted tail. He growled and twisted and I jumped onto his back, grabbing a handful of thick mane. He shook, ran forward, then rolled over. I found myself sprawled on his warm, dusty belly in the thick fur, trapped by his legs.

"Okay, big guy, you win!" I laughed and stopped struggling against the strong paws that held me so gently. I scratched him under the chin and a low rumble of pleasure revved up into loud purring.

Ela followed me through the stalks to the track, and I turned to head back. I paused, looking up to the sails of Tower One. Two small figures moved slowly up the curve of one leg, climbing on spider filaments of mylar line. Aaron and Jason. I squinted and made out the small rip in a sail. They must be climbing to replace it.

I could almost feel the rush of wind up there, the transformed perspective as the wheel stopped spinning around you and you were the center as the complex motions of sky and earth whirled around your high vantage. I could feel the song of the tremor humming up through my legs, and the way it would harmonize with the rush of the high wind. I envied them up there, riding the cycles within cycles while I was anchored by the Rules to the ground.

It didn't hit me until I was nearly back to the house. What had Aaron been doing in the cellar at that time of day? He must have gone back for that frayed climbing line.

A dark, sickening suspicion swelled in me. It couldn't be. But all I could see was that frayed climbing line. And Aaron following Jason with his smoldering eyes as the younger frateros reached with that slow, gentle smile to help Helen lift a heavy pot from the stove this morning, Helen's hand lingering a milla on his. And years ago, Aaron glaring in just the same way at Isaac when the older frateros had silenced one of his righteous tirades with a few wry words. The morning before Isaac had mysteriously fallen . . .

I was racing down the track, Ela leaping beside me, alarm screaming through me as I gasped in burning air and my legs flailed at the skirts.

But I was too late. By the time I reached the clearing beneath the tower, they were only two tiny shapes climbing the gleaming lines to the hub of the wheel. I shouted, "Jason!" and waved my arms, but there was no way he would hear me over the roar of the wind in the sails.

I tried to quiet my pounding heart. I squinted past the curve of the nearest leg, up the tapering spire, and I could see that Aaron was ahead, almost to the platform beneath the extension that held the wheel hub. Jason climbed behind him, the extra weight of the new sail in a bulky webbed carrier on his back, his feet braced against the spire as he pulled himself up the thin line winding back onto the takeup reel on his harness.

I took a deep breath. Maybe I'd panicked for no reason. He was almost to the top, and his line had held. I held my breath until Jason reached the platform and I could see the small figures disengage their lines from the reel mounted there.

But I couldn't shake the uneasiness shivering through me. I squinted against the bright, silver-blue gleam of sunlight on the sails as Aaron led the way across the massive extensor-shaft that held the wheel away from the spire. Mounted on a ring that allowed the entire wheel to shift around the tower with the wind, it transferred the wheel's spin to a system of gimballed synthadamantine gears. They spun the hollow generator-rod and powered the frequency modulators for the tremor-rod inside it.

I could see the doll figure that was Aaron reach out an arm to help Jason with the awkward carrier onto the hub. Now they climbed up, outward, down, clinging to the raised grips as the wheel turned them, slowly there at the center, but faster as they climbed outward onto the thick base arm bearing the damaged sail.

There was a wind change coming. I could feel it eddy, then swirl, then shift. The great wheel rolled above me, roaring in the hot wind, shifting around the tower on the extension's ring as the sails fluttered in a dazzling shimmer of light. The spinner arms on each of the eight wings rotated around the stable base arms as the wheel turned, settling the sails into a new position.

I could feel the eddy in the tremor beneath my feet, smoothing out into ripples as the sails realigned on the slip-ring mountings of the spinner arms.

But something was wrong. There was again the odd flux imbalance I'd felt the morning I'd visited the tower. The sails weren't readjusting properly. The balance was off.

I squinted upward again and found the two men. There, edging outward on the grips running down—up—the sail arm, stretching the new sail over the damaged one, working outward to the racing rim of the wheel. After that, they would loosen the grommets of the old sail and roll it toward the hub. Jason was inching his way out the narrow spinner arm, ducking beneath the offset sail carriage.

The spinner arm was less stable during a wind shift than the thicker base arm. With the flux out of balance this way—

I cast a last look upward, then ran to the controlroom, slapping the light panel and hurrying down the stairs. I caught a quick glimpse of blinking indicators and tools scattered from a box as I hurried to check the seismic readouts. They were within stable range. The imbalance wasn't emanating from below. Anyway, the cybernetic alarms would've indicated a potential earthquake.

I moved around to the controls for the sail arms. The tension on the slip rings was cybernetically monitored here and kept within limits. The slip rings held the sails at different angles to compensate for changes in wind velocity, so the wheel would turn at the required rate to produce the proper stress needed on the tremor-rod to regulate seismic tremor. It was too complicated for me to explain in the cybers' terms, but when you were riding the sails, you could feel when it was all balanced. That was why Isaac and I used to manually fine-tune the slip rings up there, for a smoother ride.

But of course Aaron had always mocked us for that, insisting you only needed the control panel dials. I checked them now, but the test button for each arm moved the gauge into satisfactory range for the cybernetically calculated wind factors.

I shook my head. I could really feel the flux imbalance now, pulsing through me in the roar of the generator-rod, a jagged extra thrust instead of a smooth hum.

I ran over to check the generator voltages. It took me a centa to orient myself to a new readout system Aaron must have installed. I didn't understand the purpose of some of the indicators. But the important ones were clear enough.

The small feed to the house was steady. So was utility voltage. The fraction siphoned from this tower for the village line was in the right range. But the voltage to the tremor-modulator units connected to the rod was way low.

It didn't make sense. The total power output indicated a normal figure. But the drains didn't add up to the total. Something was siphoning power.

A lot of power.

It was throwing off the tremor. And that would throw off the action of the sails, which were adjusted to compensate for tremor and wind. It could be dangerous to Jason and Aaron up there. I wondered why they hadn't felt it. Maybe it had started after they'd gotten up there.

I stood staring at the indicators, wanting to do something but not knowing what. I couldn't figure why the cybernetic monitors hadn't triggered an alarm. I didn't know the function of a couple of the new controls. But it didn't feel right. I hurried over to take another look at the sail controls and seismic indicators, but they still wavered in the satisfactory range.

"Fireblood and thorns!" I shook my head.

The jarring tremor drummed and shook through me now. The whirring rod roared deafeningly. It was making me jumpy. My nerves were screaming, "Do something!" I shot a last look at the controls and ran back outside.

Were the sails shivering more than usual, the mylar not quite filling? The tremor still jarred me. I craned my neck back and saw that they'd nearly finished. The new sail stretched between base and spin arms, and they were unfastening the last grommets on the old sail. Jason reached up—down, now—for a new grip as he climbed from spin arm to base arm across the bulk of the rolled-up sail. He slipped, lost his balance.

"Jason!" The wing swept down to the bottom of the cycle, hiding him.

"Founder and guardians protect—" I broke off in relief. The wing rose again and I could see him, grasping a rung. I watched as they grappled the bulky sail, pulling it toward the hub where they could drop it through free space to the ground. They were moving awkwardly, using the handles more than usual. The imbalance must have been bothering them.

On the hub now, Aaron reached for a better grip on the slippery mylar to toss it down. I could see him wave an arm and shout something to Jason. Jason shifted back to another handhold on the hub. Aaron leaned forward.

It all happened too fast. Aaron shoved the rolled sail toward Jason, leaning down over the hub, and must have seen me on the ground. He jerked back and thrust an accusing arm in my direction, twisting to shout something at Jason. He tore angrily at the roll of mylar and Jason was pulled off balance. He fell, flailing across the slippery mylar, reaching for hand-holds that weren't there.

I was too shocked to even cry out. I could only stare helplessly as he slipped faster.

The bulky sail glared blinding sunlight and fell toward the edge of the hub. Jason scrambled across it toward Aaron, who was clinging at the edge. Jason was moving fast, he could make it. He surged toward Aaron as the sail flashed silver-blue and tumbled free. He twisted to reach an arm toward Aaron. All Aaron had to do was reach out his hand.

The heavy mass of mylar fell toward me, blocking my sight. I jumped out of the way as it crashed to the ground in an explosion of dust. I squinted through it.

Jason was falling, past the hub, his hand still stretched up to where Aaron clung to his circling grip.

"Jason! Founder, no! No!"

I stared, horrified, as he fell. He struck one of the dropping sails and slithered helplessly, rolling, across the slick mylar. He hit the base arm with what must have been a stunning blow, but I could see his hands scrabbling frantically to grab one of the climbing rungs. He almost caught hold. His hands slipped across the metal as he was thrown down the arm. The momentum of his fall was broken, but he couldn't grasp on. He tumbled partway along the arm. Then the sail dropped toward the bottom of the cycle and he was thrown the rest of the way to the ground.

"Oh, no, oh no!" I ran past the crumpled sail to where he lay, twisted on his back, staring glassily up at the spinning wheel and empty, glaring sky. He was dead.

I closed my eyes as a sickening wave of horror and sorrow and fury swept over me. It wasn't Jason's empty eyes I was seeing, but Isaac's, seeing his broken body after he'd fallen from the tower he'd always ridden so surely. "By the Founders, Aaron, you'll pay, I swear it . . ."

I looked down again. Had something flickered in the flat brown of Jason's eyes? I knelt to listen for breathing. There was nothing. No heartbeat. His eyes were lifeless, one pupil shrunken and the other dilated. But I could have sworn I'd seen them move.

He hadn't fallen straight the whole way. Maybe he was only stunned. I refused to think about a broken neck or back. I tried to remember Helen's lessons on treating accidents. I eased the harness straps loose from his shoulders and listened to his chest again, but there was nothing. I was afraid to move his neck, but if he didn't get some air soon, it wouldn't make any difference, anyway. I felt carefully around his head and tilted it enough to clear his windpipe. My hand came away with blood.

Another cold wave of horror passed over me. "No! You can't die. You can't do this, Jaréd! Please the Founders . . ." Someone was whispering gibberish.

I shook my head. No. *Jason*. Think.

I ripped off part of my skirt and padded it beneath his head. Swallowing again, I pinched his nostrils, sealing his mouth with my own and forcing my breath into him. I could see his chest rise and fall. Good.

But still no heartbeat. I straightened his twisted position and leaned over his chest, pressing down in the way one of the elders had said could bring back a soul that was hovering and wasn't ready for Heaven. More breaths. More pumping on his chest. No reponse. More breaths, more pumping.

I paused to listen again, cursing the loud rumble of the tower. Then his body abruptly jerked in a spasm and his chest heaved. I tore away his coveralls to listen. There was a jerking, uneven beat. It stopped, then started up again, fast but regular.

Relief made me light-headed. He was breathing again, though his face was still too pale, a dull lead color beneath the warm tan. His eyelids had closed.

"Jason?" I whispered into his ear, but there was no response. I lifted his eyelids, but the pupils were still uneven, the eyes staring blankly.

"See what you've done now! You've killed him!"

I jerked around to see Aaron standing, purple-faced and furious, shaking as he tried to catch his breath, pointing in accusation.

I jumped to my feet and faced him, suddenly filled with the same rage. "No! It was you! I saw it this time, Aaron! You could have grabbed his arm, but you didn't. Is that what you did to Isaac? Is that what happened when he had his *accident* on the tower? They were both in your way, weren't they? So you decided to kill them. Jason's line held, so you had to push him!"

His face paled and he looked shocked. He looked guilty, as guilty as he'd looked that day he'd brought Isaac's broken body back in the rollcart and I'd run from the porch, screaming my accusation at him.

He stepped back a pace, then shook himself. "You're crazy! You're sick with sin. What were you doing out here? You were inside the tower, weren't you? Weren't you?"

I suddenly came to my senses. "Aaron, there's no time for this! He's alive, but he's badly hurt. Bring the rollcart over, we've got to get him to the house."

He didn't even hear me. "You were in there, weren't you? What were you doing?" He leaned down to grab my wrist.

I jerked free and slapped his face. He slowly raised a hand to his cheek, blinking, stunned.

"Did you hear what I said, Aaron?" I made my voice even and low, like Helen's when she meant business. "Bring the rollcart over here, and I mean now!"

He blinked and turned stiffly to get the rollcart. I knelt beside Jason again, hearing the faint heartbeat.

"You're going to be okay, you hear me, Jason?" He lay unmoving. I raised my eyes past the towers to the hot glare of the sun. "You hear me, Founder, you and your damn cybers? He's *going* to be okay!"

seven

"You really think he'll be okay, Mother?"

She turned to me, pale but smiling. "Yes, I think so, dear, if a brain fever doesn't come on. He was lucky you were there. You did exactly the right things." She put her hand over mine and squeezed it.

I paced across Jason's small, neat bedroom, wiping my damp brow with my sleeve while Sam fussed with the covers, tucking them carefully around Jason's splinted arm. I took a deep breath. "Mother, I really didn't touch anything in the tower."

She put away the needle and thread she'd used to suture Jason's gashed head. "I know you didn't, Ruth. Aaron was upset. He knows it wasn't your fault. It was only an accident." She rose to touch my shoulder. "Like Isaac's." She searched my eyes.

I dropped my gaze from the deep green of those compassionate eyes. They had the same look they'd turned on Jason's injuries. Only she couldn't stitch and splint me. "Yes, Mother, like Isaac's accident."

She looked relieved. "Ruth, I'm sorry I had to report you, but Aaron *was* right about that. Even though you saved Jason, you know you shouldn't have been out there."

Below me in the dark, Bathsheba moved with a dull thud of hooves. The trotters rustled on their perches and subsided. I set the lantern away from the hay and stepped out of my dress, pulling on the coveralls I'd hidden in the loft. I slipped on the climbing gloves, tightening their cling tabs.

Shadows shifted, fluttering grotesquely in the cobwebbed rafters as I crouched and sprang for the lowest bar. I kicked and swung around and onto it, then kipped for the next one, moving upward through the four scaffolding bars I'd mounted in a corner of the high loft.

They were rough and not limber enough to take the shock out of a passing grab, but once I got into the rhythm of it I was almost flying, spinning around the bars, catching, arching to the next, somersaulting and flipping, then swinging back and up again. My mind could focus to a narrow beam of concentration on reaching arms, tensing legs, and deep, laboring breaths.

But somewhere beyond my sweating exertions, uneasiness still stirred. It rustled like the plumes of the trotters, fluttering suddenly below me as Bathsheba clomped in her stall and resettled into sleep. Questions stirred as they had through a restless night and during the day when I'd taken over Helen's watch in the sickroom. She'd assured me that Jason had awakened last night, though he was confused and rambling. He'd been quiet again all day, under the influence of Helen's healing elixir.

But I couldn't erase the picture of him tumbling from the hub of the tower, slithering across the sails, crashing to the ground. The quick, bright eyes I'd known so briefly gone blank. I couldn't quite believe he had survived. And I kept feeling that unbalanced jar in the tremor, seeing the power readouts that didn't add up, hearing Aaron's furious voice—

"What are you doing here?"

I gasped and jerked a startled face around, almost missed the second bar, and wrenched to a stop, hanging from it.

Aaron climbed up through the hatchway, holding another lantern that sent distorted shadows over his scowling face. "You should be helping Helen. What are you doing, dressed like that? Are you lost to every proper feeling?"

I took a deep breath and swung slowly, kicking over and onto the lowest bar. "What proper feelings, Aaron? Yours, when you didn't catch him?"

He glared up at me. "*You* dare accuse *me*? You'll never change. Casting off your maiden's skirts! Any decent woman would be burning with shame."

I rolled my eyes. "Come off it, Aaron! I'm just getting

some exercise. Aren't you satisfied with getting Helen to report my violations?''

His eyes glittered in the shifting light as he stepped forward with the lantern. "I warn you, Ruth. Don't mock the Way. Don't mock me.''

"Why not? Somebody should. Why don't you climb down from your high tower? Even Helen thinks you take yourself too seriously.'' Maybe one of his demons did have hold of me this evening. I couldn't help taunting him, sitting on my high bar above him, swinging my legs, free from the detested skirts for once. "Don't think you fool me, Aaron. I've been watching you, too.''

"Bitch! Get down from there!'' He lunged forward and grabbed my ankle.

"Hey!'' I lost my balance and started to fall. I kicked and twisted back to grab the bar, but he was pulling me down and my hand slipped. The side of my face cracked hard against the bar as I dropped.

I fell heavily onto the loose hay, stars swirling before my eyes. I sat up, blinking, raising a hand to my face. "Fireblood and thorns, Aaron! Do you have to be so blazing—''

I broke off when I saw his face. He'd gone pale beneath the tan, backing away from me, staring down at his hand and looking almost comically horrified.

He cleared his throat and said in a gruff voice, "Helen said I ought to apologize. That's why I came out here.'' He raised his eyes to mine and the lantern sent flickers of light and shadow across his troubled face. He started to say more, then hurriedly climbed back down the ladder.

"Hey, Aaron . . .'' But he was gone. I rose slowly and let out a long breath. Finally I shrugged. Beneath the floor-boards, I could hear the trotters cackling in agitation, then settling back in a rustling of plumes on their perches.

The gaudy bruise down my face made a dandy excuse to duck the village gathering the next morning. I told Helen I'd tripped feeding the trotters, and for some reason Aaron didn't mention my brazen sinning up in the hayloft. I didn't know if it was guilt or shame he was hiding, or something else.

I convinced Helen I could take care of Jason, who was still under her sleep cure. I knew she didn't want to miss this gathering, since she was godmother to young Elizabeth, a village girl who was being presented as Hearth-Mistress.

I wasn't eager to join the women's circle, to witness the lighting of the ceremonial candle and donning of the girl's first long skirts, the expectant hush and her voice rising in the song of dedication to the Hearth. To see the rapt young face kissed by candlelight, flushed with the culmination of the month-long sequestering in the Sororal House, glowing with eagerness to fulfill those newly-learned womanly mysteries. I didn't want to remember my own shaking hand as I finally lit that candle, the joyful song that fell like a dirge from my lips as the ceremony sealed the death of the air-dance in me. I was a woman, and I was banned from the open fields and the high wind.

" 'O that Thou shouldst give dust a voice to cry to Thee, and then not hear it crying . . .' " I shook my head as I realized I'd whispered it aloud. I wrung out another cool cloth and placed it over Jason's hot forehead.

He moaned and twisted away from me. He was hot, sweating. I tried to soothe him, but he was shaking his head now, back and forth, muttering. He fussed and threw the sheet away from him.

"Jason, hush. Lie back, everything's all right. You have to rest." I blotted the sweat springing up on his hot skin, gleaming across the smooth chest with its triangle of darker skin at the throat. I paused, surprised by the beauty of his lean, strong young body. I hastily pulled the sheet back up.

He shuddered again, moving restlessly. "No, wait . . ." He muttered something I couldn't hear. "What is it . . ? Aaron, wait . . ."

I froze, then leaned closer. "Jason, what did Aaron do?"

He was thrashing now. I tried to hold him still, afraid he'd hurt himself. He pushed me away. "Aaron, no . . . why would she—Aaron, no!" He sat sharply upright.

"Ruth!" His eyes snapped open as his uninjured arm shot out to seize my wrist in a painful grip. He stared, gold flecks in his eyes melting over the brown into burning amber, transforming his face. Again that shock, almost recognition, that I'd felt in the field when my quiet new pateros had suddenly met my eyes with a bright gleam of fire. That jolt of Taboo attraction, stronger now, almost crackling between us. It was crazy, disturbing, like a memory buried but pushing free, some answer or truth his eyes demanded. Their bright amber held me, blazed through me as if they could read from a dream every sorrow and sin and joy etched in my soul.

"Ruth." His hand tightened on my wrist.

"Jason, no!" I flinched and tried to free my hand.

He blinked and looked around the room, confused. He refocussed on me. He flushed deeply and let go of my wrist, falling back onto the pillows and closing his eyes.

I could feel my own face burning with the thoughts that had flashed through me. "Jason, are you all right?"

He opened his eyes and stared in confusion at the splint. "Was I dreaming? Were you there, Ruth? I thought I heard you, calling me back. I was afraid, I was in a dark place, but burning, and I didn't know which way to go. Then I felt you there. It was strange, like the way the wind feels and sounds way up on the sails, like it was blowing through me."

He swallowed. "But you said . . . Ruth, who is Jaréd?"

Despite myself, I started, drawing back and raising a hand to my scarred cheek.

"I didn't dream it?"

"No." I cleared my throat and fiddled again with the cloth, rinsing it out. "Jason, you ought to drink more of this elixir." I put the glass into his hand.

"Who is he? I've never heard Helen mention the name."

I looked down. "I . . . knew him on Sethar. He's dead." I touched the glass. "Now drink."

He hesitated, then emptied the glass and handed it back. "I'm sorry, Ruth."

"So am I." I turned away, then shrugged. I could hear him settling back among the pillows as I meticulously rinsed out the glass, recapped Helen's bottle, straightened the cloths.

Jason's voice was drowsy now. "Sethar. Was it there, Ruth? That scar?" His voice was slower, slurred, but he was fighting the drug, fighting sleep. "What's it like there? Never been off-planet."

"Jason, you know I'm not supposed to talk about it."

He sighed, nodded, and closed his eyes.

"That's right. Sleep."

He moved restlessly. "No. Nightmares—"

"Hush, Jason, sleep." I hesitated, then took his hand and squeezed it. "Don't fight the dreams, Jason. On Sethar they seek themselves in the dream world. That's what the scar is about. It means you've met the shape of fear in dreams and learned its dance."

He shook his head, eyes closed. "No! I'll fall! Don't want to die!" His hand clutched mine.

I bit my lip. I leaned closer, whispering, and my voice seemed to calm him, "Jason, listen. Feel my hand. I'm here, I'll guide you through the dreams."

I closed my eyes, felt the Setharian drug take me and the firelight pull me into lapping, flickering dream, felt Jaréd's hand and heard his voice through the nightmare images as he guided me to the place where dreams and waking fused. "Jason, I'm there with you on the tower. Can you feel the wind, hear it singing in the sails?"

He sighed, squeezed my hand.

"Good. We're there, we're riding the sails, the tremor is smooth and humming beneath us. Can you feel it?" Again he squeezed my hand, and I felt that tumbling wheel of earth and sky whirl around us as we poised on the arm of the flashing sail. "We're together, Jason. Listen to the wind. We're going to jump now, into its arms."

His hand jerked convulsively.

"No. Listen, Jason." And I listened to an almost forgotten voice. "Fear is there in the wind, but joy, too. They dance together. We're going to jump into the wind, sing with it, let it take us to learn the dance of fear. Now. Jump with me."

"No! We're falling!"

"Yes, we're falling, Jason, but listen to the wind. The sky and the earth are a wheel spinning around us to its song. Dance to fear, Jason, feel how fast it's taking you. It can kill you. But you can't run. Listen to it. Learn its voice." His hand tightened in my grasp. "There, that's it. Dance around it."

I squeezed his hand as it gripped mine. "The ground's rushing at you, but look, there's the sail arm, it's cycling beneath you. You're dancing now, flying. You can catch the sail. There, you've got it. You can rest now, let it carry you."

His hand had gone limp in mine and he breathed deeply and evenly. I sighed and laid his arm straight on the bed, pulling the sheet over his shoulders.

I touched my cheek, feeling the raised ridge, feeling again what I hadn't shown Jason. The horror and fascination of the blade winking in firelight, the fear of death hovering at its sharp tip, whispering its ultimate promise. My hands grasping the knife, touching it to my smooth skin, pressing, tasting the fear and blood flow over me, drawing its mark to remind me I would always face it.

When was I going to stop running?

I sat for some time, watching my young pateros lie in healing sleep, his chest rising and falling smoothly, face calm and remote. I sat like a dutiful daughter, watching my mother's husband.

But I was seeing past the still room as I absently rubbed my bruised wrist. Jaréd, looking up as he knelt on our blanket sharpening a knife, his dark hands strong and deft. The white smile splitting his face as he reached out a sinewy arm to pull me down and we laughed and tumbled like pard pups in the hot sun. Jaréd's face, muddy-gray and distant as the blood pumped out of him and I knelt helpless, refusing to accept, cursing the cruelty of that world, cursing the Plan for not allowing med-techs that could have saved him, cursing myself because I was failing once more the lessons of the Way.

I sat watching my sleeping pateros, the bulky splint on the arm that the cybers would have quick-knit on a different world. I sat thinking thoughts that were against the Rules. I rose and leaned over to kiss Jason's forehead, then let myself quietly out of his room.

eight

The console winked its ambers and blues in the glossy, seamless cubicle, blinking its monitoring indicators. I pulled over the battered old stool and sat nervously fingering my IDisc. I could almost feel the cybers in there, waiting inside that opaque black shape, watching me.

But that was silly. I hadn't even engaged the interface.

I needed some answers. I really wanted to run out to the tower again to investigate that power imbalance while Aaron and the rest were still gone, but I couldn't leave Jason that long.

I reached out and pressed the activator button.

"Good morning! Lovely day, isn't it?" The console-Matron was as irritatingly cheerful as ever.

"Good morning, Matron."

"Why, it's Ruth!" Her voice modulated into concern. "My dear, why aren't you at the village gathering with Helen? You know, she and I decided it would be a good thing if you had a nice talk with Elder Rebecca." She sighed. "I was disappointed to hear that you'd violated the Rules again, Ruth. And after you'd told me you were going to try harder!"

I found myself about to respond to the chastising tone, to offer explanations, but stopped myself and took a deep breath. "Yes, I am sorry, Matron. But right now I need information. I'm concerned about a possible power imbalance. Please connect into the Tower One monitors and give me seismic readouts."

I took another slow breath, trying to exude normality,

wondering if my "Rogue" interrogation technique would work on the Matron. My console on Casino hadn't been so heavy-handed with its persona characteristics.

Back in Casino, I'd accidentally discovered a way to cut through some of the console psych-slanting cued to my profile. I'd been designing a specialized version of the popular Knights in Tarot card game, to attract the large contingent of leasers repatriated to Casino from Venebia. I'd been toying with the Rogue card—a wild card that changed function according to chance events in the game. I'd tried questioning the console and responding with the attitudes and mannerisms I'd observed in the Venebians, trying to get more information about their Way. The console had begun to adjust its psych-slanting accordingly.

Maybe if I treated the Matron the way my patera would, instead of like a guilty, Rule-breaking daughter, the persona would respond.

She cleared her throat. "Ruth, don't you think you should leave these technical affairs to your patera?"

I closed my eyes and took another deep breath. "Isaac trained me to understand the tower functions. If there's a malfunction, don't you think we ought to find it, Matron, so we can alert the men? We wouldn't want any more accidents."

"No, no, of course not. This is irregular, but. . . ." The Matron hesitated. "Yes, I will help you investigate."

"Good. First, give me a preliminary scan of the Tower One readouts."

"Very well." The Matron recited a long list of wind, seismic, temperature, and moisture factors, her voice dropping into a relative monotone. "All factors within normal range."

"Power outputs?"

"Well within the norm."

"Does total power production equal total of outputs to utility functions, household, village, and seismic modulator demands?"

"Within tolerable error margin. Deviation would trigger alarms. Backup systems check operative."

"Hmm." I tapped my fingers on the console. "Check records on those totals for the last three days. Any significant deviations?"

"No deviations."

Damn! "Any deviations in seismic flux over that time?"

"No deviations."

I took another breath. "What possible malfunctions could conceal such deviations from detection by you?"

"Please repeat the question." Her voice had picked up an edge of confusion.

Damn. I repeated it.

"Ruth, I'm afraid such a question indicates serious adjustment problems. Why haven't your patera approached me?"

"Uh, Sam and Aaron went to the gathering with Helen, so I stayed to watch Jason. He's still in bed." I bit my lip. "He was awake briefly, and he asked me to question you about the imbalance. He discovered it before he fell from the tower."

"Oh, I see." Her voice sounded relieved. "Perhaps Jason is still confused from his injury, Ruth. I have now completed a test of alarm backups, and all functions are intact."

"I see." I sighed. "Thank you, Matron. I'll let him know."

I reached out to disengage the persona. Fireblood and thorns! I *knew* what I'd seen on the power indicators, and what I'd felt out there. Again I had two possibilities—either the Matron was mistaken or she was lying to me. But she couldn't lie. Then how could the power drain be concealed from her monitors?

I found myself hunched on the stool, turning my IDisc over and over in my fingers. I slowly straightened, looking down at it, feeling the extra thickness of the mysterious chip attached to it. The plasmeld that looked like a blank IDisc. A wild card?

I bit my lip and decided to give it a try. I held my breath and reached out to engage the console, quickly slipping the featureless chip into the IDisc slot that visitors who weren't cued by voiceprint could use.

The green light flickered and then pulsed into a holding pattern. A female voice that was like the Matron-persona's in tone spoke, but it was without inflection. "Contact established. Field agent identification?"

I froze, afraid to breathe, afraid the console sensors would read my racing heart, the sweat breaking out on my palms.

"Field agent identification required." The voice was blank, holding no expectation or impatience.

Founders curse him! I should have known better than to believe his apology.

So he *was* in on it. I hadn't imagined the gloating amusement in his eyes that day. He'd known why the console-

Matron hadn't been aware of any questions about my violation points. Obviously Poindros LS had its own hidden agents, just as CI did—maybe that was the "imbalance." But why? Aaron was so insistent on protecting the Plan from . . . changers. Maybe that was it. Poindros LS was clearing visitors for resettlement without reorientation, so they were sure to be sent for Healing. A purification program gone a little too far? It would be just Aaron's cup of tea.

I shot out my hand to disengage the console, and the slot opened to eject the plasmeld chip into the tray. I slowly picked it up, staring down at it. It was blank. As blank as the voice that had and hadn't been the console-Matron's. The voice waiting for a response from the field agent.

nine

So we were playing a game, Aaron and I, card for card. I didn't know how high he was wagering, but I wanted to win. If he was the Ebony Knight, the power card, there was no defeating him with a straight play. Only the Empress of Flowers, with her pale, lovely face and heart-shaped scepter, could do that. I would have to be the Rogue, the wild card, and wait for his next move.

And, anyway, I really had no choice but to wait for the "field agent" to reveal his strategy. A couple nights after the gathering, when Jason had no longer needed watching, I'd slipped out of the sleeping house and through the moon-stirred wheat to the first tower to investigate that worrisome flux imbalance. But the Matron had been right. There'd been no odd jarring to the tremor, no inexplicable power drain. All the instruments had read normal.

I pursed my lips, wondering for a milla if I'd only imagined the disturbance in my fearful haste the day Jason had fallen. I shook my head. No.

"Ruth?"

I blinked and looked up to see Jason's calm face bent to mine as he reached with his unsplinted arm to help me with the heavy hot-water kettle on the stove. "Oh. Thanks, Jason, but I can manage." His hand remained a centa on the handle as I lifted it, touching mine. His face colored faintly and he turned hastily to the table where Helen sliced berries.

"Now Jason, dear, you're supposed to be resting." She

gave him a warm smile and I turned quickly back to the dishes.

"Helen, I'm right as shine now. Aaron and Sam need help with the line stringing before heat-storm time. Come a bad wind, we could lose the wheat, it's that tall now. It's no good, me dilly-dallying about the house."

I glanced over to see Jason's eyes on me. He looked quickly away to watch Helen's hands deftly slice the red fruit. Aside from fading bruises he did seem surprisingly none the worse for the fall and fever.

"Wheat's growing fast now, Helen. We'll have trouble, we don't get those lines in their proper places." Jason shot me another look. "Ruth knows. It's true, isn't it, Ruth?"

Maybe I was imagining an emphasis in his quiet voice. Maybe he'd forgotten his fever dreams. Maybe *I'd* dreamed those brown-gold eyes blazing their quick fire through me. I answered levelly, "Yes, Pateros." I looked at Helen. "They do need his help, Mother."

She sighed. "We could hire one of the village boys . . ."

"No need. I can at least stretch line. Don't fret, Helen." He touched her face gently with his big, callused hand and I turned back to the dishes. "I promise, I'll be—"

The screen door crashed against the wall. "Demon whore! Destroyer!" Aaron stalked past Helen's startled face and planted himself before me. "You'll pay this time!"

I froze a milla in confusion, then finished drying the plate in my hand and turned to place it in the cupboard. "And a fine morning to you, too, Aaron."

"Don't mock me! 'And the words of her mouth were deceit and blasphemy.' Don't think you can hide your guilty face from me, with its mark of sin!" He grabbed my wrist and the plate flew from my fingers to shatter over the tiles.

"Aaron, whatever are you saying?" Helen's face had gone even paler than usual.

"Calm down, Frateros. What's wrong?" Jason started toward us, his voice low and reasonable.

"Wrong!" Aaron glared at Jason, a trickle of sweat running down his flushed face. "It's plain to see how she's brought her offworld sin to curse us, just as the Book says! 'And lo, the sinner Jezrial did mock the Way, and the land was stricken for her blasphemies. A blight fell upon it, and it brought forth no more of fruitfulness, but foulness only.' "

"For Founder's sake, Aaron! What's all this gibberish about?"

He swung back on me, furious. "You'll stop your mocking, you—you—" Literally choking with rage, he raised his arm.

Helen cried out and stood, but before I could even think about jumping out of the way, Jason had somehow darted in and grabbed Aaron's arm in his one good hand. "Aaron, that's not the way." His voice was still quiet, reasonable.

Aaron whirled around on him, his face nearly purple now with fury. Could he be acting? The muscles in his arm knotted as he broke free from Jason's grip. "Don't cross me, boy! Has she used her wiles on you now?"

Jason's face flushed a deeper pink and Helen stepped closer in a quiet rustle of cloth to take Aaron's arm. "Hush, my dear! You're upset, but you mustn't speak so. Tell us what's happened."

"Why don't you ask your daughter who she serves, what she's done to bring this curse upon us?" He glared at Jason and me. "I tell you, wife, you won't stop me this time. I'm going to talk to the console-Matron. Time the cybers dealt with her." He shook off Helen's hand and strode through the swing door to the hall.

"Aaron! It's not your place to be reporting." Helen's face was pale but set as she followed him.

The screen door to the porch clattered open again and Ela lolloped through, a silly feline grin on his face as his tufted tail wagged in excitement. Behind him, Sam rushed in, red-faced and panting. "Ruth, are you okay?"

"Take it easy, P'eros!" I urged him into a chair. "What's wrong with you two?"

"Phew! No, no, I'm fine." He mopped his sweaty face with a large red kerchief. "But Aaron, he was acting so crazy, I didn't know what he'd do! The way he was talking, Ruth, I thought he might. . . ." He looked up at me and shook his head. "He was spinning like a tower in a heat wind, I'll tell you! Gave me a turn, too, it did. Never seen nothing like it. It's danged bad."

"Sam." I knelt and took one of his gnarled old hands. "What happened out there? Aaron didn't make much sense."

He swallowed. "It's the fields, Ruthie. What he was saying about the sinner Jezrial. Never seen nothing like it. Some kinda blight in the fields, horrible-looking it is, and spreading so fast it ain't natural. I'd swear you can see it swellin' before your eyes.'' He swallowed again, the sun-faded eyes beneath shaggy gray brows troubled and strangely frightened. ''It's real bad.''

The cybers weren't doing anything about it.

Even I was shaken, but the family was numb with shock during those tense days of the blight. The guardian cybers were supposed to take care of such disasters. Helen had consulted the console-Matron, who had cheerfully assured her that the blight was ''under control.'' The men were to plow swathes around the affected areas, and the cybers would take care of the rest. But they hadn't done anything. Each night the men returned exhausted from their efforts, only to report that it was still spreading. We'd already lost an entire field.

And the day cycles spun us closer and closer to the season of the wind storms. The supporting lines weren't yet strung. Once the word had gotten around the village, there'd suddenly been no one free to hire out to help us. They were afraid of contamination. I knew Aaron wouldn't be the only one whispering the words about Jezrial and the retribution for her sins.

I sat on the battered metal stool, staring at the blinking monitor lights on the console and fingering the plasmeld chip I'd detached from my IDisc. I was risking the game, but I had to try my wild card.

I reached out to engage the interface and quickly slipped the disc into the waiting slot. Again the green signal flared and winked into the holding pattern. Her voice, flat and devoid of emotion, repeated the words I'd heard before. ''Contact established. Field agent identification?''

I took a deep breath and stared down at the IDisc clutched in my sweating hand. Aaron's IDisc.

''Field agent identification required.'' The voice waited.

It was now or never. I'd found Aaron's IDisc with the soiled work clothes he'd dumped outside the tub room, and I'd have to put it back before he missed it. I rubbed the disc on my skirt and slipped it into the slot.

A blue light pulsed and blinked on the console. The voice was apparently waiting for me. I took another deep breath. ''I need more information about the field blight. How did—''

Her voice interrupted in even, colorless tones. ''Identification inconsistent. Error.''

A ragged breath caught in me as a wave of cold fear lapped through me. I sat frozen, waiting.

The slot ejected both discs and the console-Matron's green light pulsed into a steady glow. Her voice was cheerful and eager to please. "Good evening. May I help—"

I jabbed a finger to silence her. I let out my pent-up breath. "Bloody, blazing . . !" My hand clenched around Aaron's IDisc into a fist.

I was caught in a losing skirmish, but the game wasn't over. Aaron couldn't know that I had a card in reserve—red-haired, freckled Officer Hodge, the "Jester." I didn't like the way he and CI had set me up, but at least they'd throw me a catch line if my points climbed too high. I decided I would ride this sail as long as I could, maybe even until harvest, after all.

Maybe the cyberserf had been right. Maybe I was learning some things from my visit. But I wasn't ready to scrutinize my reasons for wanting to stay. I jumped off the stool and hurried from the cubicle.

"Ruth, it's not your place to go out there!"

I looked down from the rollcart, at the new lines of worry etching deeper into her brow in the morning sun. "Mother, I've got to help if I can, with what I learned in the hydroponics satellite. The cybers aren't doing anything."

She shrank back. "Ruth, it's not for us to question their ways. You know that."

"Mother, I only want to save the wheat. How can that be wrong?"

"I know where your heart is, Ruth, but sometimes you choose the wrong path. This will only hurt you. Please stay here." The hot wind eddied swirls of dust around her skirts and tugged loose a strand of flame-bright hair. Her eyes pleaded and I was tempted to give in.

I sighed and activated the motor. "I won't be long, Mother."

She didn't answer, only held me with her eyes, deep green seas holding all of human grief and pity. I forced myself to feel only anger at the cybers for making me what I was, for making Helen pay the price in feelings they would never know except as data bits in the webs they wove with human souls.

I wrenched at the steering rod and turned onto the track leading to the back fields.

The dry song of the wind tugged and pulled me through the glistening waves of wheat. The fringed tops swayed just below my feet as I rode, gliding over the surface of a shimmering copper sea. The sun blazed its way up a hot blue, cloudless sky. I passed the circling arms of Tower Four, cresting a low ridge. I stopped, staring.

The whole of Field Five was a blackened expanse of ruin. The blight was spreading now into Field Six. A rollcart pulled its plow through the field, cleaving the bright wheat and crushing it beneath alloy blades, making the first pass of a new swathe around the diseased area. This circle would have to be big. The rollcart passed closer below me and I saw Jason at the steering rod, but he didn't look up. Farther over, in the plowed stretch, a smudge of gray smoke was scattered by the wind. Aaron and Sam were burning off the remaining stubble.

Alarm flickered through me and I drove on over the ridge. If it was what it looked like, they mustn't try to burn it. I pulled onto the perimeter of Field Five and reached out numbly to shut off the motor. An acid taste of nausea rose in my throat.

Sam's description may have lacked poetry, but it had been accurate. It was real bad.

Somehow it was worse for finding its dark roost here in the middle of the sun-shimmered fields. It didn't belong here, where the summer wheat etched its fine copper lines against clean blue and the sweet, dry wind sang over the open stretches.

Something in it whispered of violation, of hidden secrets, breathing out the fetid, moist air of swamps and the shadowed places under rotting wood. The blight was a huge, monstrous creature of gray, puffy flesh, reaching out its grotesque buds and swellings and split, oozing excrescences like the stubs of gangrenous limbs. They reached out to engulf the slim stalks as they dragged forward the innumerable gaping, swollen-lipped, sucking, voracious mouths of the thing. The gray, slippery flesh of the fungus oozed outward in an irregular ring to pull more of the field into its alien embrace, leaving a central hollow of blackened stubble and wasted land.

Foulness only . . .

I blinked and saw Aaron standing rigid with his torch, glaring at me. His face was drawn and smudged with smoke, his lips pulled back over his teeth, his dark eyes boring through me as if I were as vile an outrage as the blight.

I shook my head. I jumped off the rollcart, striding toward the gray mass. Yes. Offworld all right. Fungal. Extremely fast-spreading. Thriving on the heat, no doubt. But how could it be sucking up enough moisture, here in this dry wind?

Sam doused his torch and hustled over to me, casting a look back at Aaron, who was stalking toward us. He took my arm, the faded blue eyes tired and exasperated. "Now, Ruthie, you've gone and done it! What possessed you to come out here? Aaron's like oil on a hot stove today, and you'll be tinder, we don't get you out of here. Go on, quick now!"

"Sam, wait. Just a quick look, then I'll go. And for Founder's sake, don't start burning it! You could have this whole valley infected."

Sam looked taken aback. "But, Ruth, you know it's not your place to—"

I blew out a long breath and clutched up my skirts to scramble over the plowed stretch and onto the trampled stalks around the blight. "Right. I ought to have that just about memorized by now, Sam." I passed a thin fringe of still-standing wheat, absently pulling down the tops to break off the heads and roll the hard, unripe kernels in my palm.

Sam hurried after me, still protesting. I dropped the kernels and pushed through the trampled stalks, my nostrils flaring as the wind carried the smell to me.

I stopped at the edge of it and prodded with my toe one of the smaller mounds of the wartlike, mottled gray and brown buds that were separately delineated yet joined to the common body of the thing by an elastic-looking, glistening membrane over the surface. It cracked where my moccasin touched it, oozing a fluid that sent thick waves of the smell over me. I forced back nausea.

Behind me, I could hear Sam laboring over the tangled stems.

"Looks like an advanced stage, Sam, but I'm sure it's the same fungus . . . that smell . . . I'll just take the rollcart into the village and get some—"

"But, Ruth," Sam stopped, panting, "the cybers said they'd take care of it. We can't interfere in—"

"Interfere! Who lives on this land and works it, you or the cybers?"

"Don't be talking wild, now . . ." He laughed uneasily.

"Well, they're taking their sweet time about it, aren't they? What are you men planning to do, just keep plowing wider and wider swathes, until there's no more field left?"

He fell back. "Ruth! It's not right, you being here, talking so. Let's go."

"Just a centa." I squatted at the edge of the advancing blight, broke off a couple of the smaller buds, and tore them open.

Sam fell back, choking, a frightened look on his face.

A hand fell onto his shoulder and pushed him aside. Aaron stood there, still clutching his smoldering torch. He opened his mouth, then stopped, staring at my hands. He raised his eyes slowly from my hands to my face and then back at the oozing buds. His tongue passed over his lips, but he was frozen in a dreadful fascination.

I made a little explaining movement of my hand with the sample. "Just checking the cross section to make sure it's—"

Aaron jerked back. "Haven't you done enough?" He looked almost sick as I tossed the sample back on the growing mass. "Foul, vile, unclean—" He choked and turned to Sam. "Don't you see now, old man? It's part of her. How else could she touch it?"

"Aaron, I'm only trying to help. I'm sure now I can cure it." I reached down for a handful of stubble and scrubbed my hands with it. "And watch it with that torch. If you burn the fungus, it'll spread the spores." I started past him for the rollcart.

"No!" He thrust the torch out in my way. "I'll stop you, Ruth." He turned to Sam. "You know the words. 'Cleanse thyself of the sin harbored at thy hearth.' She must be Healed."

Sam took a deep breath and stuck out his chin, stepping past Aaron to take my arm. "I think it's time you did some housecleaning in your own heart, Aaron. Now I'm going to take Ruth home." He pulled me along as I tripped in my long skirts over the trampled wheat.

Aaron followed us, gripping the smoking torch. "It's too late, old man. Everyone knows what she is. I tell you, I'm going to stop her desecrations! 'And righteousness shall be like a flame on the land.' I'll burn your sin from the land, you whore!" He ran past us to rekindle his torch in a fitfully burning pile of stubble. A gust of wind swirled gray smoke around him.

"No! Sam, we've got to stop him!"

I broke free of Sam's hand and ran after Aaron just as Jason pulled up on the rollcart, driving with his unsplinted arm, looking over at me in surprise. "Jason, hurry! We can't let him burn the wheat!"

He looked startled but jumped down from his high seat. "What's going on? Why are you—"

"No time. Just help me stop him!" I yanked up my skirts and ran after Aaron, who was sweeping the flaming torch along the stubble as he advanced toward the fringe of wheat surrounding the blight. "Aaron, stop! Just listen a centa!" I tripped and Jason caught my arm. "Damn this dress! Jason, he can't burn the wheat. He'll spread the spores!"

He gave me an intent look, then ran ahead, holding the sling out from his body, his long legs quickly overtaking Aaron. Smoke billowed past me and I couldn't hear what he shouted, but when the gray cloud eddied away, I could see him gripping Aaron's arm, the bigger man straining to break free as he waved the torch angrily. Jason had to be a lot stronger than he looked. I turned quickly to stamp out the smoldering fires Aaron had started in the stubble, and Sam caught up to me.

Jason's voice drifted over with the eddying wind. ". . . least hear what she has to say? She has been offworld, maybe she knows." His voice was calm and reasonable as Aaron scowled down at him.

"Yes, she's been offworld. And brought us this alien curse! I tell you, boy—"

"Aaron." I stopped to catch my breath. "If you're right, then it's between me and the cybers, isn't it? You can't take it on yourself to burn it."

He glanced quickly from Sam to Jason and then back to me, his eyes narrowing. He wouldn't dare flaunt the cybers in front of his fratera.

I turned to the others. "If I brought this blight"—but I knew there was no way I could've carried it through processing—"then I have to cure it. Isn't that what the cybers are trying to tell us? You know they don't want the wheat ruined any more than we do. The real sin would be letting this thing go on, letting the land be ruined and wasting all this beautiful wheat. We're here to do our best by the land, aren't we? I swear I can cure it and I won't be breaking any more Rules. Is there anything wrong with that?"

Jason hesitated, but Sam cleared his throat and laid a hand

on my shoulder. "You're right as shine, honey." He turned
to the others. "I'm still elder frateros here. I say we give her
a chance."

Aaron shot an angry look at Sam, then at Jason, who had
lowered his eyes to study the ground. He spun abruptly on his
heel and stalked away, thrusting his torch into the smoldering
bonfire and climbing onto the rollcart to continue plowing.

Sam took my hand again. "Come on, let's go."

Jason raised his eyes to give me an uncomfortable scrutiny.
Those amber-tinged eyes seemed to see every devious dodging of the Rules I'd ever committed. "I only hope you know
what you're doing, Ruth. You know he'll report you."

"I know. Thanks, Pateros."

He nodded and brusquely turned away.

". . . looked mean as sour mead when she found out.
Hrrmph. So they said. Course *I* never had no part of such
shenanigans . . ." Sam pulled up with a bump in front of the
dry goods store.

I laughed and jumped from the rollcart before I thought to
let him come around and hand me down onto the dirt street.
A primly-shawled matron on the board walkway paused to
eye my flaring skirts disapprovingly, then hurried on.

"Sam, why don't you wait out here and keep an eye on
those sacks of exo-crystals while I run in real quick?" The
tinker had charged a steep price for them.

"What for?" He gave me a puzzled look, puffing down.

I shook my head. "Never mind. 'Other worlds, other
ways.' That's one they say inside Casino." I wouldn't shock
him with the details. I gave my dusty skirts a cursory shake
and accepted his arm across the board walkway.

A buzz of gossiping matrons died and they swayed aside in
a flutter of skirts, like full-bloomed prasial with petals ruffled
by a rude wind. Sam doffed his hat. "Afternoon, Matrons."

I thought I recognized one of the women. "Good afternoon, Matron Deborah—"

She looked through me, gave Sam a curt nod, and swept
her skirts off down the walkway. The other women stood
back from us, staring, their eyes flickering in a familiar
movement to my scarred cheek.

My face fixed stiffly around my smile. I nudged Sam, who
stood with his mouth hanging open, and urged him toward the
door. "It's not polite to stare, Pateros."

We were into the dimness of the store before he found his voice. "By the Founder! What's bit into them?"

"Hush, Sam. Why, it's old Dan, still running the store!" I raised my chin and urged him down the central aisle, toward the counter where the bent, brown-aproned man wrapped a parcel for a matron with two young children. Feet hastened aside as we walked down the aisle. I suddenly remembered Helen's contained dignity and her unwavering, gracious smile on those decacyclic village visits when I sullenly acted out my role of proper young Hearth-Mistress for the villagers who waited to pounce on my next lapse. Now here I was, with my dusty old dress and sunburned neck, aping her smooth calm. It wasn't as funny as it should have been.

The young matron gave us a startled look and with a quick, unconsciously graceful movement gathered her children and her package out of our way. Old Dan replaced a card of laces on its hook and turned toward us, peering over his spectacles. He rubbed the bald dome gleaming over white side-fringes and chuckled drily.

"Sam, you old coot! Got away for a mug of mead over to Joe's? I'll just close up and—" He craned his neck toward me and tilted his head to look through the lenses. "Well, I'll be strung from a high arm—!"

He hesitated, peering at my cheek, then stuck his hand across the counter to take my hand in his dry, callused palm. "Sam, you old—so this is the gal! Little Ruthie. I'da hardly known you, child, but the word's been . . . Favors Helen more'n a bit now, don't she, Sam?" He shot me a sly look, then shook his head. "All this roamin', though, don't hold with it. You know what they say about them space rays. But by gum, if'n they make all the gals as pretty as you, I might just go myself!"

He slapped his thigh and cackled, breaking off into a protracted coughing fit. Sam reached over the counter to slap him on the back, but Dan waved him back. "Whoo, whee! Hrrumph. No, fine, fine." He laid his hands flat on the counter and gave me a suddenly penetrating look. "But you stay put now, young lady. Listen to that mother of yours, she's one fine matron." He gave me a decisive nod and turned to Sam. "Considering the presence of a lady, Sam, how's about a cup of tea over to Sarah's, instead?"

I spoke up. "Thank you, Dan, but we have to hurry. We need all the yeast packets you can spare."

They both gave me surprised looks. "Yeast?" Sam screwed up his eyes and scratched the back of his neck.

"All I can spare? Why, child, I've got fourteen—fifteen cartons of the stuff."

"Ten ought to be plenty."

"Ten packets? Helen planning a mess of bread-baking?"

"No, ten cartons. You don't mind putting it on account?"

"Ten cartons!" He looked at Sam, who shrugged. "By the Elder's staff, what are you up to out there?" He gave me a quick, sideways look.

"Let's say we're trying out a new recipe."

He rolled his eyes and raised his hands, then shuffled off to get the boxes. I loaded Sam up and hustled him off as Dan hobbled along with us to the dusty street, offering dustier platitudes. I thanked him with a peck on the cheek that brought on another coughing fit. Wearing a broad smile, he shuffled back inside.

I paused on the walkway as a rustle of starch approached.

"Mistress Ruth."

Elder Katherine's stiff dignity was more daunting than Helen's, but cold, sealing her thin body in a crust of ice that must have enabled her to endure all the layers of black garments on a blazing summer afternoon. "You haven't changed. You still bring trouble and sin." She spat the words.

"And you still find it." I wished the matrons had fetched old Rebecca instead. At least she had a sense of humor.

Her eyes narrowed and she gripped her polished wooden staff of office more tightly. "You cannot deny your mark of sin. You cannot deny your offense in bringing this alien blight, destroying the land as you have tried to destroy your family." She and Aaron had always gotten along splendidly.

She drew a circle on the boards with the tip of her staff, an official declaration of her authority. "You are banned from the village circle. You should have been Healed long ago."

ten

A dark whirlpool sucked the shards of light down its twisting throat and spun them outward to dissolve in fluid chaos. A pale face floated, wavered on the surface of turbulence, stretched grotesquely, and was whipped into a hundred glistening fragments of reflection. Whirling light and shadow chased each other in a mad, flickering pulse above the roar and the tremor shuddering upward from the earth. The fluid surface broke into bubbling eruptions and wraiths of steam began to rise.

"Stop!" I drew back and slammed the hinged cover over the holding tank. I shouted over the roar of the pump and the perpetual hum of the spin rod, "Flush half and refill with fresh!"

Sam's hands moved over the board, lights changed position, and the tank evacuated with a gurgle.

I cracked the vent in the top. I joined Sam, leaning over his shoulder to watch the temperature readout click upward, slow, and steady. "Good. That's the right range." I wiped my damp forehead and picked up the clipboard to frown at my scribbled calculations and the strip of volume readouts. I blinked, trying to concentrate past the restless jitter of tremor. "All right, let's see . . ."

I crouched by the open sack leaning against the side of the tank normally used for mixing concentrated doses of fertilizer. I jotted the amount of jagged blue exo-crystals in the graduated pail, checked my figures again, and raised my voice over the roar. "Temperature holding?"

"Holding."

"Okay, you ready?" I eyed the jury-rigged feed tube we'd made by replacing the elbow, just past the cutoff valve of the water line, with a three-way valve and screwing a short length of pipe into the unused gate. "Let's give it a shot."

At the irrigation board, I aligned the remote valves for a selective misting coverage, using a cut-in on the emergency spraying system instead of the fertilizing/watering underground trickle normally used to prevent sunburning of the wheat and to conserve precious water during the rainless summer.

As I reached out to the controls, my hand froze and the uneasy jitter turned to a nervous jolt down my spine.

Someone had turned up the trickle water to the blight-affected fields, instead of turning it off as they should have done. It was no wonder the alien fungus had been thriving despite the dry wind.

Aaron. I angrily yanked the valve controls into closed position and reset the system for misting. My hand was shaking as I adjusted the holding-tank vent and gave Sam the go-ahead.

I ignored the nervousness jarring through me with the roar of the generator-rod and the amplified earth-tremor. We gave it ten shots: the near boiling water heated by the exo-crystals in the tank, the cold feedwater to dilute it, and the concentrated buckets of yeasty brew I poured down the feed pipe while carefully watching the timer. Reflected light gathered and shattered over the sucking whirlpool in the tank and the gleaming surface of the spinner rod. But all the while a deep unease stirred in me, foreboding as the warning tremors of an earthquake.

Sam, tired and sweaty, put his arm around me after I'd poured the last of the brew. We walked up the steps to blink in the glaring sun.

I raised my face to the heat, feeling the wind across my closed eyes. I opened them to watch the play of light over the vast sails of Tower Four as they swept their gleaming silver-blue above us.

Sam cleared his throat. "I hope it works, hon. But we'd best go now. You know I can't let you stay out here. I really wish I could."

"I know, P'eros, it's all right. Remember what Isaac used to say, how there was a lifetime to learn in one cycling of the sails?"

He chuckled. "Yep. Never did figure out the crazy things he used to say. Miss him, though."

I nodded. "Me, too." I was still looking up at the sails, remembering Isaac's patient lessons, still feeling that nervous jitter. Now I realized what it was. I turned back to Sam. "I forgot something in the tower, P'eros. I'll be right back." I ran back to the controlroom.

Close to the rods, I could feel it clearly, and I was surprised I hadn't realized right away. It was the same flux imbalance, the same jarring skip to the tremor I'd felt in Tower One, the day Jason had fallen. I hurried over to the generator indicators and saw that the old equipment was still in place at this tower. Everything looked normal. Except that the power readouts again showed a discrepancy between power produced and power utilized.

Something was siphoning a lot of energy.

I followed the curve of the room and stood staring down at the latched cabinet with its warning. DANGER. HIGH VOLTAGE. CYBERNETIC ACCESS ONLY.

I cast a quick glance up the stairs and knelt to open the latches with a pry bar. I lifted the heavy cover carefully back and peered around it. Thick, heavily insulated wire rose through the floor of the compartment and branched into meters which corresponded to the output figures for utility, household, village, and tremor-modulator demands.

But there was another line, a different kind of wire, spliced into the box feeding the modulator line. It ran to a compact, plasmeld unit unlike anything I'd seen before. There was a latched, hinged top to it. On its face, an amber light glowed in the shadow like the eyes of the ferial as it crouched to spring on the gizu-doe. The readout below the light registered voltage figures. The same voltage being siphoned from the modulator. The discrepancy that the console-Matron was somehow unable to detect.

I crouched, staring as that amber eye stared back, unwinking. I lifted the heavy panel back into place and walked slowly up the stairs into sunlight and the hot whisper of the wind.

I pulled the rollcart up short. Sam whistled and shook his head.

Too late I realized I should have warned Jason and Aaron. They stood glaring up at us from the crushed wheat stalks, both sopping wet and steaming in the heat. I made another mistake and burst out laughing. But I had to agree with Sam that they looked ''madder'n pards in a winter rain.''

The cure worked. By the end of the next day, the yeast had done its trick and Sam was showing off to Helen. ''Yep, the way Ruthie and I figgered, see, the damn—'scuse me—danged stuff was so greedy, it just sucked up the yeast water and wasn't naturally smart enough to know it was in real trouble. You see . . .'' He scratched his head and shot me an appeal.

''Cell structure,'' I stage-whispered.

''Right, that's it.'' He took a deep breath. ''See, the fungus stuff is built up of these here cell structures, and the yeast is close enough to it so the blight takes it into its hearth, you might say, thinkin' as it's one of its own, kinda like Eve and her husbands as harbored the serpent all unknowing until it bit Adam . . . Ruth, you ailing, child?''

I coughed again and cleared my throat. ''No, no, it's nothing.''

Sam pursed up his lips. ''Well, lemme see . . . Anyway, this blight, it . . . Well, blast it, Ruthie, then what?''

I cleared my throat again. ''The yeast starts a catalytic reaction—actually a substitute step in the cell binding—and everything speeds up. Reproduction, appetite—really a demand for more fuel for the accelerated cell splitting—but the yeast has also conveniently scrambled signals so the cells start feeding on their own walls. The structure can't hold, moisture's lost, and—'' I gestured. ''That's it for the blight. Just sort of burns itself out.''

Sam turned eagerly to Helen. ''So, you see? It was the blight was the sin, not our Ruthie. Cybers knew that. Ruth just wanted to do her best for the land, same as we all do.''

Helen gave him her gentle smile, then raised her eyes to mine. The tired lines had smoothed from her face since Jason had reported that the fearsome blight was now only dry husks crumbling to dust in the wind. But there was a new uneasiness stirring the deep green as she looked at me, almost a groping for recognition.

''Mother?''

She dropped her eyes. ''I'm sorry, dear. It's just that I suddenly realized how different the worlds you've seen must have been. How they must have . . .''

''Changed me? It's true.''

The troubled eyes met mine again. ''But not your heart! I know that. This is still your home, Ruth, and the land you love as much as Sam does. Haven't you learned that yet? How can I help you find the Way?''

I dropped my eyes. ''Helen, I know you've got to talk to the console-Matron about this. I do understand.'' I sighed. ''I'm sorry, Mother.'' Again.

eleven

The console-Matron was pretty easy on me.

She suspended some of my violation points for good intentions and persuaded Elder Katherine to rescind her ban so I could attend the village gathering and display a proper repentance. I tried to practice being meek and mild around the house, but it was hard not to laugh at Sam. The console-Matron had registered a minor violation for him, too, and he was preening around, chest out, like a trotter cock with a new hen, half amazed at his own dangerousness.

But I didn't discount Aaron's danger to me. There was a hungry dark glitter to his eyes, when he looked at me, that I knew wouldn't be appeased until I was taken for the Healing. And he'd barely contained his fury when he'd learned from Sam that we'd done our yeast mixing out at Tower Four. I had to find out what that power drain was all about and what Aaron was up to. I was having a hard time believing LS could rationalize infecting our fields just to get me Healed. Could their "field agent" be even more zealous than they'd counted on? Had Aaron finally gone around the bend, using the cybers to justify his personal program of purification?

I knew what I had to do, but this time I couldn't even pretend I wasn't afraid.

I rode in with the family to the next village gathering, looking as prim and proper as Helen could make me in her dress and bonnet, palms sweating and mouth dry, feeling the wild card disc slide over my skin on the snake-scaled chain whose red-gold burned the color of her hair.

Families strolled the radiating, dust-swirled streets, and we followed them to the village hub. The husbands were self-conscious in their good trousers and the vests embroidered by their wives. The matrons and mistresses had livened up their subdued dresses for the gathering with a bright ribbon or colored bonnet. They followed the vivid shirts and short dresses of children running across the bricked central square toward the steps of the community hall. Like all Poindran halls, it was a large, rounded building with a broad, conical roof, wood-framed over a radiating wheel of beams made from the same alloy used in the towers.

I wiped my damp palms on my skirt and tried to imitate Helen's gracious manner as we returned the greetings of the families curious enough to get close to a spacer. I smiled and ignored those hovering at a distance to stare at the Jezrial who'd brought the blight. If they could have read my mind, they probably wouldn't have gotten as close as they did.

Chimes rang out in a sudden clamor over the square and I jumped guiltily.

I quickly gathered my skirts to follow Helen up the steps and through low doorways into the hall. Despite myself I caught my breath as the hush of the place enveloped me and the murmur of conversation fell away. Helen's silken rustling led me to a wooden bench among the circles climbing the sloping wheel around the great stone hearth at the center. Flames licked silently upward into the shiny alloy cone of the chimney rising to the roof peak. Sunbeams colored by the tinted glass in long windows raying down the ceiling sparkled like liquid jewels through the dim quiet.

Expectant stirring swelled into a sound of waves nudging shore as the three elders, led by old Rebecca, appeared at the doorway to the passage linking the hall to the Sororal House. Everyone rose as they paced gravely down to the hearth in their white ceremonial vestments.

The song of welcome and reverence came naturally to my lips and I joined the echoing chorus that filled the huge chamber. I sang, and sat with the others to hear the elders speak, and meditated on the words, and sang again, surrendering myself to the comforting response of the group, the wholeness of the community circle. It hardly seemed to matter that the text Elder Katherine chose dealt with the trials of sin and the wayward Jezrial. I let the stir of voices fill me, let the colored shafts of sun and the dance of the fire pour through me, and the murmuring words were only the cadence to a distant, wind-whispered song, one with a larger meaning.

Maybe I should have listened more closely.

But beneath the singing I could hear another voice, an insinuating whisper from the gold snake beneath my starched bodice, repeating the words *field agent* in flat, metallic tones.

I took my chance when Helen and I were invited for tea with Elder Rebecca and others at the home of a village matron after the gathering. Before I could get trapped into a cozy talk by the significant looks the plump, kindly elder kept casting my way, I managed to step on my hem rising from a chair and split out the waist seam I'd carefully weakened that morning. I told myself the faint look of disappointment on Helen's face was only my imagination. I told myself I was doing this as much for her and Sam and Jason as for myself. Who knew what Aaron might try next? Or what LS was up to? I had to find out more, but I wasn't going to get anything useful from our console.

"Oh, yes. Thank you, Matron Lucinda. I won't be long." I followed her into the small back room and took the needle and thread she handed me. I noticed that her pudgy fingers trembled as she left and closed the door behind herself.

Pressing the cling seam I'd fastened to the fabric to reseal the waistband, I cracked the door to peer up and down the dim hall. I slipped quietly down the steps to their cellar.

Finding the console cubicle was no problem. I pulled over their standard-issue plasmeld stool and sat down, detaching the wild card from my IDisc and fingering it nervously. I took a deep, shaky breath and pressed the activator button, slipping the blank disc into its slot. The green engaged signal lit up and began to pulse in the holding pattern. I waited for the voice.

And waited, staring at the pulsing green light. This time, there was no flat voice requesting field agent identification. No voice at all.

I blotted my damp forehead with a fold of my skirt and took another deep breath. So our console *did* have some special programing. Okay, voice calm. "I need some information."

An amber light flared and died on the monitor panel. "Mode categorization required." The voice was flat and metallic, only vaguely female in register.

My thoughts raced futilely for a centa. I reined them in with an effort. "Ah—conversation mode."

Blue and amber winked consecutively. "Test proceeding."

I blinked in surprise.

The voice was a soprano now, soft and lilting. "The various tonal capacities of this unit," she slid down into the alto range, "are fully operational in corroborating," the voice was a tenor now, "internal verifications. Maintenance coordinates are registered as 3148, XXR . . ." The voice rattled on, the tones melting to a deep basso and then veering uncomfortably in stress and accent, conveying incoherent emotional signals that were oddly uncomfortable to me, ". . . 426, registered on—"

"Stop."

The voice halted mid-word. I took another deep breath and made my hands stop clenching in my skirt. The console must have assumed my wild card disc meant it was being serviced by cybernetic maintenance units.

It was like jumping in the middle of a Venebian spun-glass shop blindfolded. If I turned around, I might break something. And the pieces would be sharp. I thought some more. I cleared my throat. "Test communications links. Transfer information on the field agent from console #PO348BEL92."

Lights blinked again. "No data available." The voice was back in the alto range, vaguely echoing mine.

Damn. If only the cybers would let us learn more than basic electronics. I didn't even know how the interface worked. "Why is there no data?"

"No data available." The voice veered upward and then down, the accents falling oddly, as if it were groping to respond to a psych-profile that wasn't provided.

I tried to keep my own voice neutral. "Contact monitor units for #PO348BEL92, Tower Four. Report power production and output figures."

The voice recited voltage figures while I tried to ignore the jarring tug of its random emotion emphasis. I shifted uneasily on the stool, glancing over my shoulder at the doorway. "That last figure. What is the source of that power drain?"

"Portable charging unit."

I sat up straight, staring at the shifting monitor lights as if they could spell out an answer. "What is the purpose of the charging unit?"

"No data available."

Damn and blast! How was Aaron cloaking his activities from the console personae? What was behind him? I tapped my fingers on the console. "Describe possible uses of charging unit . . . No, wait, give me a visual index of related utilizations."

I was half surprised when the screen slid up obediently from the back of the console and lit in a standard scrolling display. *Portable charge unit—baggage vans and rollcarts. Portable charge unit—cybernetic maintenance modules* . . . The list kept scrolling and stopped at *Portable charge unit— scanners, handheld*. The only entry that didn't jibe was *Portable charge unit—Founder loop*.

I swallowed. "What is Founder loop?"

"Data inaccessible."

Another deep breath. "Who can access Founder loop information?"

"No data available."

I blew out the breath as the green light pulsed patiently. I closed my eyes like I was going for a roll on snake-eyes. "There is an error in your function."

I cracked a nervous eye to see an amber light wink on and begin to pulse. The voice was still toneless: "Specify error."

Relief left me feeling a little giddy. My heart was still beating fast. If I got caught in this one . . . I pushed the thought firmly away. "Information error. Maintenance module has access to Founder loop."

"Correcting." The light changed to a steady glow. "Complete."

I leaned forward. "Maintenance module requires verification. Display Founder loop."

Without warning, a panel slid open on the side of the console and colored light beams merged, winked glittering flashes, and coalesced into a wavering form. The light solidified and a thin, short man in an oddly-cut, sharp-angled black garment stood before me.

"Oh!" My heart gave a sickening lurch and I leaped to the side, knocking the stool over. It clattered and rolled toward the man. Through him.

"But . . ." I shook my head. Holofacs weren't used on Poindros, they were contraplan here. "Who are—"

The man turned to look at and through me as he spread pale, delicate hands, palms up. They fluttered outward, almost disembodied as the squared-off sleeves closed seamlessly around thin wrists. The strange garment flowed and reoriented with his gesture, forming severely geometric planes of opaque black around the shape of his arms and legs. Above a stiff collar that looked more like a mounting block for the sliced-off neck, the man's face was narrow and pinched-looking, with wispy brown hair and close-set, blue-gray eyes.

"Know me. I am the Poindros Founder."

The thin, peevish voice might have been thunder and lightning striking me speechless. I stood gaping, almost expecting the real Founder in Heaven to shake the sky in outrage at the blasphemy of this puny man.

He didn't look worried about retribution as he raised his hand in a flicking gesture and slowly floated into the air. Or rather his garment reassembled itself like plates of opaque plasmeld into a reclining position, supporting him within it. A background materialized behind him, and he sat suspended before an instrument panel. Behind him, I could see what looked like a large sense-cube hung from a crystalline ceiling, projecting internally the head of a gray-haired woman in black. She had a strong jaw and a stern, disapproving look on her frozen face. But her eyes, the same gray-blue as the man's, followed his movements.

"Since I will soon have no further use for the encumbrance of this fleshly body," he gestured toward himself and the garment flowed distractingly into its angled shapes again, "I have decided to preserve this data loop as a historical record."

I stared and tried to collect my whirling thoughts. I didn't know what the term *historical* meant.

"I am about to make the first step toward a new order for humanity." His thin lips pulled into a smile. "An order far beyond that envisioned by my fellow world-shapers and the limits imposed upon our creations by the Council. As they fashion their tidy little worldplans, they will never know how far I have surpassed them." He laughed shortly. The eyes of the woman in the sense-cube were fixed on him with a cold glint.

He reached out to touch something on the panel and he suddenly shrank and moved back from me as a floor patterned with shifting lights unrolled beneath him and a suspended globe became visible between us.

I blinked and focussed on the sphere hovering before me with its three irregular shapes of brown and green on blue, the same blue-and-green cat's-eye I'd seen floating over black velvet from the transport dome. Poindros.

A pale hand touched the panel and the globe began to spin, winking blue-green, blue-green at me. "Poindros, or, to use the old nomenclature, Aleph CDX590. Originally a barren patchwork of dry flatlands, wracked by seismic contortions, and a bitter, shallow sea devoid of life. Ignored in favor of more resource-rich worlds during the Colonial era but utilized sporadically as an outpost during the First and Second Galactic Wars that succeeded in decimating virtually all animal life-forms in this sector."

I gawked, uncomprehending, as the man shifted position within the reforming garment. What was he talking about? That wasn't our world, it couldn't change like that. It was always the same, would always be the same. Just like all the worlds in the perfect Plan. And there was only one war, that barely mentioned place of punishment for the unrepentant and unhealed in Hell.

The reedy voice ignored my confusion. "Of course, such bestial depravity must be absolutely prevented from recurring. We must preserve what we have managed to resurrect. So far I agree completely with the Worlds Council." He lifted a finger and the steel-blue eyes of the woman in the sense-cube followed it, her face still frozen in an expression identical to Elder Katherine's sour frown.

"But," he jabbed the finger, "I've made them eat their words about historical sentimentality and inherent social stress. My model, my Poindros worldplan, utilizes perfectly the parameters of this planet, and the cybernetic feasibility studies have verified it as successful world-shaping and social structuring. The fools have been forced to admit that my adaptation of old-Earth social artifacts provides an element of time-tested stability. 'Obsession with the past,' indeed! If they bothered to look, they would see that their grand and new ideas were all there, written in the dust of civilizations toppled by conflict."

His hand touched the panel and a deep, resonant voice emanated from an invisible source above him. "They shall beat their swords into plowshares, and their spears into pruning hooks; nation shall not lift up sword against nation, neither shall they learn war anymore."

The man seemed to look straight at me, and despite knowing he was only blended beams of light, I looked uncomfortably away. Behind him, the woman in the sense-cube still watched sternly, but now her mouth was pressed into a tight smile.

The man threw back his head and laughed. " 'Obsessed with the past!' If they only knew! My Plan faces squarely to the future, in a way they'll never suspect. Can the Founders really be content with creating their individual little Edens as cybernetic constructs and never see the flowering of their worldplans? Can they really believe the ultimate destiny of humanity is to dwell in unquestioning contentment under the guardianship and Rules of unseen spirits, never suspecting that the cybers are really no more than sophisticated tools, created to serve them by the striving genius of men who went before?''

He leaned forward eagerly, the angled black garment restructuring and tilting him upright. Racing sparks of silver light flashed along the planes of it now, and I noted blankly that the suit must be some form of energy field. The cybers? Tools made by humans?

The man jabbed his finger at me across the spinning globe. "The Council has set its regulations and the limits of the Plan based on fear. It seeks to make history taboo. Their glorious worldplans celebrate only dull mortality and the defeat of the human spirit.''

His hand moved beyond my sight and the deep, unseen voice echoed again above us. "As for man, his days are as grass: As a flower of the field, so he flourisheth. For the wind passeth over it, and it is gone; and the place thereof shall know it no more.''

The man leaned closer, colored fires streaking over his black suit and his thin face flushed. "But I refuse to be as a blade of grass! I will be there! Despite the Council's bans on bioforming research, I have discovered the means to incorporate my awareness, my very soul, into the cybernetic energy-matrix of my Poindran Local System. I have discovered the key to transcendence, the immortality promised in all the ancient writings. I will be there, hidden beyond discovery within my own energy fields and data loops, to witness the growth of my people, to see the vast fields of wheat stirring in the winds of my world, to hear the songs of praise to me, to the sacred Founder!''

I stood frozen, staring in shock and disbelief. I was spinning, the world was spinning beyond even the whirling tower wings shaking and reforming the kaleidoscope bits of earth and sky. Like the first time you step into a transport viewing dome, like the floor's knocked out from under you and you're spinning off into black nothingness.

History.

Could it be true? Time *wasn't* a smooth-rolling cycle, changeless as the seasons. The cybers were lying to us. They weren't our guardian spirits, they were our jailers. Somehow, somewhen, we'd done this to ourselves.

The Founder, only a thin little man with a hectic flush and fanatic's eyes. He shook his finger as the gray-haired woman in the sense-cube watched with her stern eyes and wintry smile. "I will be there to witness the eternal life of my family units, stretching timeless through generations of birth and death. I will watch as the strong women of my world become over the slow centuries the mothers of a new order. I will see the first signs of the new evolution, but without history no one else will trace the pattern. I will wait in patience. As my matrons are tempered on the forge of denial and endurance, they will give birth, in pain, to sons and daughters who will—"

"By the Sacred Founder!" There was a piercing scream behind me. Still spinning, numb with shock, I turned.

Matron Lucinda clutched the door of the cubicle and stared aghast at the holofac. "Founder and guardians protect us! The demon! Blasphemy!" The blood drained from her face and she sagged sideways, sliding onto the floor.

"Matron Lucinda! What's happened?" Voices and footsteps approached, hurrying down the cellar steps.

I caught a last stupefied glimpse of the gesturing hands in the black energy-suit as I whirled back to jab the activator button of the console. The lights swirled and died. The plate slid back. I grabbed the blank disc ejected into its tray just as the crowd of women swarmed through the doorway.

Of course they didn't understand why I couldn't explain what I'd been doing. And so lack of a repentant spirit was added to my other sins. They made a long list as I stood on the steps of the hall, lashed by hot wind, cast out of the encompassing wheel of the roof and its colored beams of sunlight, my head bent to the dusty bricks. One look at the angry and frightened and avid faces surrounding me had been enough.

Elder Rebecca finally finished reading the charges. Two of the sorora stepped toward me in their identical gray gowns. Their spinster faces were prematurely old beneath their gray head scarves and flat caps, or maybe it was the condemnation in their eyes and the tight set of their mouths aging them. Even their stiff steps accused me of violations. And, clearly, of remaining a Hearth-Maiden at my age, not pledging myself to the sorority of service, the sorority of the uncourted and unwanted.

The first one stripped away my bonnet, baring my head to the hot sun and the stares of the crowd. She tugged loose Helen's careful braiding and the long strands whipped free in the breeze, glinting deep red as if eager to celebrate my shame in being seen this way in public. There was a sudden hot prickling in my eyes and I blinked furiously. If I could have stood there facing them in the skinslicks I'd left at the Spaceport or even the scanty animal skins of Sethar, I could have outfaced them, mocked to myself the despised old ways and the public penance, but I was once again a daughter of Poindros.

My cheeks burned as I raised my face to the second sororos. She rubbed Hearth-ashes from a black bowl over my face. I lowered my head again, barely hearing the elder's sermon of my failure.

"And the serpent is more subtle than any beast of the field, wending its way unseen to the heart of the unwary. The Founders have cast it down and condemned it, saying, 'Upon thy belly shalt thou go, and dust shalt thou eat all the days of thy life.' And so shall we go in the dust of sin if we fall from the Way and listen to the voice of demons who seek to violate the Plan. This is a time of trial for us—"

"Changer! Send her for the Healing, today!"

My head snapped up and I searched the crowd for the owner of the hoarse voice. There was a stirring around the village cobbler, an automatic shushing, but the faces mutely echoed his cry. Their eyes impaled me. They were hungry for a Healing, eager for a pronouncement that would purge the village.

Elder Rebecca continued calmly. "We must be vigilant against these small, gathering whispers of sin . . ."

I didn't hear the rest. And the red-gold serpent was silent now as the blank disc against my skin. I knew what was coming, but somehow it wasn't real. Nothing would hold

still, not time, not the world that was spinning to the shock of
the holofac's words. Everything was changed now. Nothing
would be the same. Only they didn't know it. They didn't
know there was a bigger threat to their tidy lives than I could
ever be . . .

Elder Rebecca had finished. She sighed as she lifted her
polished staff of office. I raised my eyes to hers and she
looked sorry as she drew the circle with its tip.

I looked away and saw Helen standing among the hostile
faces, pale but contained, her eyes distant. At that moment, if
I could have gone back and undone my every breaking of the
Rules, if I could have been the daughter she deserved, played
out any act of duty for the eyes of the villagers, I would have
done it. Anything to erase that look on her face.

But instead, it was Aaron taking her hand with a pious
expression and standing closer to her. He looked over Helen's
head at me, past Sam and Jason's downturned faces, his lips
pulling briefly into a smile of gratification. My violation
points were now almost to the cyber's limit for Healing.

In my shock, I didn't really care. Maybe it *was* the demon
who'd appeared to me in the holofac, whispering in the voice
of the serpent that the Founders and the guardian cybers were
only a cosmic deception. Maybe I was really sick.

Maybe Elder Rebecca was right, as she straightened with
her staff and pronounced the casting-out. I was a sinner and a
blight to the Way. I must be Healed.

twelve

Days tumbled by like puffweed hulls blown in the constant, hot wind.

Exhausted by line stringing and fruit preserving, maybe we were all too tired to think about my prescribed Healing. Even Aaron's arguments for sending me sounded half-hearted, and though I was outcast now, it was still Helen's decision. That is, until my points reached the limit. I moved woodenly through the motions of a dutiful daughter, trying to ignore the house walls closing in on me, trying not to hear the voice of the night wind luring me outside to roam the dark fields as the family slept.

But it was the only time I could breathe, with the warm air and tall wheat surging around me and the liquid gleam of moonlight sliding across the cycling wings of the towers. And the earth-tremor singing through me, smooth and even. When I checked the towers, the charging unit and its disturbing flux imbalance had vanished.

I was tempted more than once to send in my signal for rescue, but I wanted to know more. Some of the things the ranting Founder had said still rang in me, like a plucked lyre string reverberating to a true note. Maybe all my years of discontent and rebellion had been driving me to this, to the recognition that I was trapped in a cage of ignorance and Taboos.

I couldn't stop hearing a voice that whispered, *Don't tell CI*.

So I stayed and played it close to the chest. I still held the

103

Rogue, the wild card, but I was forced to wait for the next move by the Ebony Knight. I'd almost forgotten the power of the Empress of Flowers to change the course of a game.

It was hot in the parlor, Helen's head a bright flame bent over her needlework. She had placed candles in the unlit hearth and the room pulsed to their flickering glow, enclosing us in a safe nest while the wind moaned and fretted outside the walls. An oil lamp poured its golden circle of light over Helen's white brow and the gleam of her embroidery.

Her eyes glowed deep green when she raised them to smile at Jason as he kneaded her pungent, minty liniment into Sam's sore shoulders.

My fingers plucked sleepy chords from my lyre as I absently watched the way Jason's strong hands located and coaxed the tension from Sam's muscles. I yawned and played a long, fluid arpeggio, moved on to a series of full, rhythmic chords with a sweet treble melody, then back to a rippling tide of notes, thinking drowsily of sunlight and waves, the music swelling and then slowly, reluctantly, fading.

Through half-closed eyes, I watched the way Jason's hands began to move in rhythm with the music, deft and strong, then lay still for a centa as the last note faded. He raised his eyes to mine—a quick, inquiring look. My face felt too warm as I dropped my eyes. The big hands abruptly resumed a vigorous kneading.

"Ow! Take it easy on these old bones . . . ah, there's the spot." Sam's protest faded into a grunt of pleasure. "Don't have too many years in 'em before it's the rocker and a sunny porch for me." He chuckled with sleepy relish.

Dry pages rustled as Aaron turned a page of the Book of Words. Without looking up, he quoted, "The sun shineth not on sinners, idlers, and barren men."

Sam winced and Helen raised her head to give Aaron a mildly reproachful look that would change to forgiveness as soon as he acknowledged it. He didn't look up. She sighed faintly and returned to her needlework.

Damn him. After Sam had bound in to the family, Helen had conceived a third child that finally entered the world as a malformed stillborn. She hadn't conceived again, even after Aaron joined the fratera. But just because Aaron couldn't perpetuate his glorious image, there was no reason for his digs at poor Sam.

A sharp serpent's tooth needled me irresistibly. "May I read a passage, Aaron?"

His eyes narrowed.

Helen gave me a pleased look. "That's a wonderful idea, Ruth."

I took the book, smiling blandly at Aaron and leafing to the place I remembered. I read aloud:

> The wayward plots mischief while on his bed;
> he sets himself in a way that is not good;
> he spurns not evil . . .

I didn't dare look up as Aaron stirred.

> How precious is thy steadfast love, O Founder!
> The children of women take refuge
> in the shadow of thy wings.
> They feast on the abundance of thy Hearth,
> and Thou givest them drink from
> the river of thy delights.
> For with Thee is the fountain of life;
> in thy light do we see life.

The page turned with a breath like a sigh.

> O continue thy steadfast love to
> those who know Thee,
> and thy salvation to the upright of heart!
> Let not the foot of arrogance come upon me,
> nor the hand of the wicked drive me away.

When I looked up, I was almost sorry. He sat rigid, staring at his hands as I handed the book back to him.

Then his mouth twisted. "A good passage from the *steadfast* daughter of our hearth." He leaned forward. "Speaking of the wayward, Helen, don't you think it's time you—"

Helen's skirts stirred as her voice calmly overrode his. "That was a fine reading, Ruth. I'm sure those words speak to *all* of us." She didn't appear to notice as Aaron leaned back with a sour expression. " 'The children of women take refuge in the shadow of thy wings.' It almost sounds like the windtower in your new song, Ruth." She gave me a pleased look that made me wish I were dead. " 'For with Thee is the fountain of life; in thy light do we see life.' How true and lovely!"

Her warm joy in the words became a foil for my own petty

twisting of them. I looked down, adjusting my skirts on the braided rug and reaching again for my lyre.

"Ruth." I had to raise my head to see her smile pouring its balm over me. "I've been thinking. There's too much work right now to spare us all the time to attend the binding at Joshua's. But one of us must go to stand in the family circle with them. Would you, dear?"

"But, Mother," I'd almost forgotten our invitation to Marda's binding, "do you think . . ."

"You know they'd be terribly disappointed to miss you, Ruth. And you've been working so hard, it would be a nice treat for you. Would you consider it?"

I bit my lip. Her eyes were gentle and loving, and I felt lower than that fabled serpent on its belly in the dust. She'd even made it sound like I would be doing her a favor, as she offered me forgiveness and another chance. There was a sharp prickling in my eyes as I smiled back at her. "I'd love to go, Mother. Thank you."

I pulled the lyre against me and picked out the tune to one of the old ballads she loved. She smiled and returned to her needlework.

Jason rose abruptly. "I was looking forward to seeing David again. Maybe you could bring him home for a visit, Ruth."

Helen nodded absently. "That would be nice."

Jason wandered into the shadows along the wall, prowling along Mother's shelves of knickknacks. A whistling snore breathed over Sam. Aaron sat still, the book on his knees.

I yawned and set down the lyre, leaning back against the couch and closing my eyes for just a centa. But when I opened them, I saw that Helen and Aaron had dozed off. I closed my eyes again and candlelight flickered across the darkness.

"Ruth." A whisper half roused me. I sleepily saw Jason kneeling beside me, holding something in his palm that pooled the light and tossed a gleam of color at me. It turned slowly in his fingertips and it groggily registered as a present I'd sent Helen a few years earlier.

An egg of clear crystal, holding in its heart a single feather, emerald shading into irridescent blue. A feather from the Iri'an. I could almost see it flying against the somber gray clouds of the water world, Lethe, where I'd fled in my blind grief. The Iri'an, flying like a bright promise of something that would never be. Its harsh cry, trailing behind it, falling with the rain over the downturned heads of the men and women who sloshed with such amazing stoicism across the muddy toeholds of land they were always losing to the sea and reclaiming and losing again. In their strange, gray serenity they hadn't needed to look up to see what the Iri'an painted for my stranger's eyes. Flying, with its cry of pity—or mockery. . . .

"Ruth." It was a whispered voice, Jason's, but all I could see was the crystal flashing hypnotically blue-green in the winking light. "Ruth, be careful. Aaron's watching you. I think he knows . . . "

But I was dreaming the voice. The crystal turned, flashing colors, bright blue-green, and then it was spinning, rolling across a black expanse of velvet, a blue and green cat's-eye winking in dark space. It was Poindros, a globe twirling before me in the cyber cubicle as the Founder cackled and laughed and his face swelled and stretched grotesquely. I was backing away, holding Sam's camera and frantically pressing its buttons, trying to capture a picture, but the flat papers only kept flying from its slot with crazy designs that didn't make sense. The laughter rang on and I threw down the camera to run, but Aaron was there, reaching out to grab me, his face changing before my eyes into a fanged, dark-furred beast's, slavering and howling, but his dark eyes the same, mocking and promising retribution. He dragged me into the fields and the wheat tugged and pulled at me, singing shrilly, and I needed to know what the stalks were whispering, but I couldn't understand.

Helen was there in the field, enthroned in her armchair in a radiant garment made from the sun-jewelled wings of the tower, flowing around her in sapphire-silver and pearl as she smiled and her eyes became deep seas. They lapped around me, calm and peaceful, the sea endless and filled with life.

But I was sinking, falling down beneath the sea, and it was dark, it was black space and I was falling forever without even a star to show which way I fell. The Founder laughed gleefully, his voice echoing around me, and I floated toward him. Sam spun by, grinning and winking, and he had the camera. He thrust it into my hands and tumbled away, and the camera clicked and a picture came out of the slot. But it wasn't a picture, it was a mirror, and inside the mirror I could see myself looking into a mirror where I looked into a mirror, forever.

I was floating inside the mirror, in dark space, and Jason's big, callused hands cupped the gleaming crystal egg with the turquoise-green feather in it. He twirled it until it spun in space like a hurtling planet winking in the light of a dying sun, blue-green, blue-green, flashing, his face staring at me above it, frowning and intense above the speck of cosmic dust. His eyes glowed amber like the lights on the console, reading all my secrets, watching me and waiting, leaping yellow and red flames, amber eyes. Like the Andurans. No, the ferial. Hunter or hunted? Amber eyes, reading my soul . . .

"Ruth!" A hand on my arm, shaking me.

"Oh!" I shuddered and looked up at the bright eyes staring down at me, blazing through me, at the intent face close to mine.

"Ruth," Jason whispered urgently, his careful paternal reserve gone. "Listen to me. I know you've been out in the fields. Aaron suspects. He won't listen to reason anymore. He's watching you."

He rose hastily as Sam woke with a loud snort. I shook my head and climbed groggily to my feet. Helen and Aaron woke up then, Aaron straightening in his chair and pretending to be still reading in the place his finger had held.

Helen stood and gave a little laugh. "My! It's past time we were all in bed." She turned to Jason and spoke quietly to him. "Would you accompany me tonight?"

Jason nodded and gave Helen his slow smile. The smile that somehow tugged at memory and promise. A nasty bite of envy stung me as she touched his hand.

The heavy book thumped onto the lamp table, and I glanced over at Aaron. As he turned to look at Helen, our eyes locked briefly. For a short milla of shocked empathy, we knew each other very well, Aaron and I.

The ritual goodnights were spoken. Helen and I turned together for the stairs, but then I hesitated. "You go on up, Mother. I'd like to take another look at the Book before I go to bed."

She looked surprised, then smiled and gave me a quick hug. "Don't stay long, Ruth. You need your rest, too."

I set the lamp back on Aaron's table and sat in his chair, feeling distinctly uncomfortable as I did so. The cover of the Book of Words was worn. A faded red ribbon marked a passage, and it fell open to that place. The lines were faded and blurred, as if by the repeated tracing of a finger.

For fun within, out of the heart of man, come evil thoughts, fornication, theft, murder, adultery, coveting, wickedness, pride, foolishness. All these things come from within, and they defile a man.

I held the book, thinking of Jason's eyes, thinking of Aaron's.

thirteen

The wind muttered through my dreams, but I couldn't remember its message when I woke to the unsettled pause between night and dawn.

I'd turned my back on the dream world, too, in my hasty flight from Sethar. The dream weavers and their twisting threads of meaning had changed in the blood rites from allies to enemies, like a knife slipping to cut the hand that grasped it, and now their voices only mocked me from a distance.

The fields hissed and shimmered in dawn purples as I walked to the monorail. I set my bag near the rail and pushed back strands of hair tugged loose by the wind. I wondered what sort of reception I'd get from Joshua. I wondered if I'd see more of our truefather Isaac in my twin now, or if his cheerful, blocky features would still greet me with incomprehension. The wheat surged in the rhythm of the wind, still whispering, glinting dark gold under the slow lighting of the sky.

I climbed the steps of the passenger car when it stopped at the prearranged signal of the console-Matron, inserting my IDisc to gain entrance through its revolving gate. Relief rushed through me as farm and house sped away.

The sun rose higher over an unvarying vista of rolling wheat fields. The car began to fill up with matrons who boarded from shelters on the outskirts of villages that all looked pretty much the same, houses and a few shops clustered around a central square and the radiating spokes of a hall roof. They rustled and crammed their ample skirts and parcels onto the creaking seats, casting quick, curious looks at me and the hat I'd brazenly removed in the stifling, musty heat. The seats next to mine remained empty.

The sun seemed to stick at blazing noon. One more lurching stop, and three matrons dressed in white mourning made their way down the aisle. A pair of stout, graying women led the way, followed by a plain young matron with an infant in her arms. She was crying, trying to hide her reddened eyes with a kerchief. Eyes glanced in disapproval.

"Hush, Miriam! This is an unseemly display." They sat in front of me.

"But it's not fair! Beth was so full of life. So young and pretty and quick, why did it have to be her? And she was so happy about the child coming—why did it have to kill her? Why couldn't they save her?" The young matron buried her face against her baby, who awoke and let out a wail. Heads turned toward her wayward outburst.

"Miriam!"

She sniffed, cleared her throat. Her voice was low, obedient. "I'm sorry. I know it's only the Way."

Oh, yes. The way things had to be.

The young woman glanced back and our eyes met. A quick current of sympathy ran between us, surprisingly as much from her as from me. I looked away to the window.

The young matron couldn't know how really unfair all the Poindran deaths in childbirth were, especially if that Founder loop had been true. She couldn't know that on other worlds the techniques of childbirthing could have saved her friend. She would simply accept it all as the Way.

Just as Beth's husbands would accept it and find another wife to fill the gap left in their family, the same way they would have if she'd been an older matron. The Poindran family had a comfortable continuity to it, a mix of ages that survived a loss more easily than the one-on-one pairings more common in other worldplans.

It was all very reasonable. Plug in a new part, and the machine kept running smoothly.

But I wondered if Miriam's cry of loss and rage weren't closer to the human truth, a truth that couldn't be planned. I wondered whether those jagged holes ripped out of a life could ever really be healed without scars. Or should be Healed . . .

Someone touched my hand and I looked up, startled. "Pardon me, Matron, if my words upset you.'' The young woman smiled shyly down at her child, then at me, that flush of warm Poindran womanhood transforming her plainness. ''I just remembered something Beth used to say. She was always singing, so bright. She'd say, 'No laughter's born of courting sorrow.' '' She ducked her head. ''Well, good faring, Matron . . .''

''Ruth. Mistress Ruth.'' I smiled wryly at her surprise. ''Good faring, Miriam.''

She started to follow the two matrons to the gate for the next stop, then turned back impulsively. ''Ruth, you ought to smile more. When you do, it's like lighting the hearth, you shine that pretty.''

She hurried off as I stared after her.

Shifting breeze lifted a sun-sparkled mist above the fountain in the bricked square. From somewhere a cascade of flute notes tinkled through the heat. I craned past the crowd of barter-day shoppers, scanning the vendors for a likely binding present.

Awnings covered the stalls on both sides of the square, running toward the steps of the closed hall. From the dim haven of shade a gleam of brass and copper shone among the rich-colored stacks of early produce. Baskets of scarlet kiberries, big as your fist, overflowed into the sun at the edge of the veranda boards, flashing like the heart-jewels of Amaveura. Emerald-green melons from the seacoast spilled over the top of a low bench. A streamer of amethyst silk rippled from a supporting beam. Beneath its beckoning gesture, piles of cloth overflowed the tables in opulent rainbows of brazen scarlet and pearl gray, hot orange and lustrous ebony, fresh green and night-dark indigo, and the gauzy flutter of a shimmery turquoise-blue, like the Iri'an feather in the crystal egg.

I followed its languid summons.

Carrying my bag across the hot bricks to the shade, I stepped up onto rough boards and threaded my way carefully past the crowded tables of the local women. The boards sagged under the weight of gleaming jars of fruit and vegetables, fresh herbs in bundles, woven mats and straw hats, hand-stitched bonnets, patterned quilts, painted miniatures, ceramic jugs, homemade toys.

I paused to peer over the shoulders of a knot of matrons

and children who were exclaiming and laughing. On a table in front of her shelves of hand-carved, jointed wood dolls, a middle-aged woman set down a miniature, painted metal milker. It raised and lowered its head, uttered a low bleat, then wobbled across the table on its four small hooves.

The children screamed in delight. I smiled and dug into my pouch for credit-chips to buy one for Marda's children. The vendor handed me a wrapped one and I was about to move on when I stopped, staring again at the toy being demonstrated. There was no windup key on it. And when the milker turned its head, I caught the flash of tiny amber lights in its eyes.

It was contraplan. It had to be.

"Don't worry, Matron." The vendor smiled serenely. "It'll walk forever if you just connect it once in a while to the recharging clips of a rollcart. Aren't they silly, now? But when I saw them at the regional fair, I thought the local children might just go for them."

I muttered some answer and turned away, nearly knocking over a short matron.

"Oh, I'm so sorry!" I picked up her parcels and walked on, staring at my little package. The gadget, like Sam's camera, had no place in the Poindros worldplan. Where were they coming from? And why weren't they being detected and reported?

I found myself standing beside the tables of the silk merchant, staring at a rippling corner of the dark turquoise. I blinked and pulled out the shimmery silk. It was lovely, thin and gauzy, glinting with highlights of green and rich blue. It would have made a beautiful dressing gown for Helen, with her hair gleaming loose against it. But I knew she'd say it was too bright, that her hair was gaudy enough. I held the fabric against the light, seeing the Iri'an's vivid flight, and I didn't want to part with it. It was too sheer for a wedding gift to a woman I didn't know, but I impulsively tucked it under my arm. I'd keep it for myself.

For Marda, I chose a soft peach with a subtle pattern to its weave. Helen had said she was dark-haired, and I thought it would suit.

As the vendor extracted another customer's IDisc from a portable transactor certifier, a pearly glint caught my eye.

I caught my breath and pulled out a cloth incredibly soft and light. It was dove-gray, woven with secret threads of dream, rainbows and clouds and spirit-wings. Its quiet surface

only hinted at colors locked in its depths, but they shimmered
elusively from a fold or at the chance touch of sunlight. I had
seen such cloth before, among the spinners of Sethar. It was
said that the beauty of the durable cloth brightened or dulled
to reflect the soul of the wearer. It only waited for Helen to
give it life.

"Afternoon, Mistress, and welcome to our little village."
The vendor smiled unctuously. "Hot enough to bake bread in
the fields, isn't it?" The local phrase rolled easily off his
tongue, but his boots were too shiny, his work-shirt unworn.

I snorted. "Save it. Those boots never did any walking in
the fields." I indicated the folded cloth I held, the pearl-gray
muted in contrast to the two brighter colors, but somehow
making them look just a little garish. "Are these Southern
Valley silks, or only local?"

He looked briefly dismayed, then grinned. "Sharp little
number, are you?" He raised an eyebrow and his eyes travelled to my feet and back up. "That turquoise piece'll look
real nice on you." He fingered the cloth, giving me an
insinuating smile. "Those are the real thing, genuine Southern Valley weave. Going price is ten credits each, but for
you, twenty-five for the three."

Apparently he didn't know the pearl cloth was of offworld
make. I wondered how he'd come by it. "I'll give you
fifteen, and you'll still make a decent profit."

He raised his hands, palms up. "Hey, you trying to break
my heart? I've got costs. I can't take less than twenty."

"Fifteen. And if you're trying to pass as local, take my
advice and get a worn coverall or something. You look like
you ought to be hustling at the Spaceport."

His eyes narrowed. "Think you're smart, huh? Well, I've
got news for you, sweetheart. Certain customers expect shiny
boots. Got it?"

He grinned at my look. "And I've got some other interesting items you might like. They're a little . . . higher." He
raised his eyes quickly toward the sky, then winked.

I blinked in surprise. "Oh." He'd just given me the signal
for the Spaceport black-marketeers, who traded in contraplan
luxury goods that they managed to acquire through dubious
channels from baggage confiscated during clearance. I wasn't
the only Poindran who was willing to bend the Rules. But I'd
never seen a black-marketeer dealing so brazenly this far from
the Spaceport.

He grinned again and glanced quickly around, then crouched and lifted a fold of cloth to reach into a box beneath one table. "I've been getting some really nice items lately. Things're really loosening up. But I'm sure *you* know." He winked as I stared in confusion. "Now, how about something exotic?" He discreetly displayed a small bottle, a beautiful little thing of bluish metal, round and tapering to a slender neck, elaborately chased and burnished to a soft glow.

He flicked a speck of dust from it. "A love potion from Amaveura, got the witch's seal still on it . . ." He eyed me again. "Well, maybe I'll save it for somebody who needs it. How about this, sweetie? Just your style." He replaced the bottle and pulled out a silver oblong, inlaid with curious shapes and loops of colored enamelling, with barely visible seams. "A puzzle box from Kopruun." He scratched his head. "Damned if I can figger how to get it open. Something inside's supposed to be valuable. Just the thing for you." He winked. "You know, you and I could really get some fast deals going, we pulled a partner act. Why don't we team up?"

I laughed and shook my head.

He replaced the box and straightened with a regretful look. "I've got more, but we'd have to arrange a private showing." He laughed at my look. "Strictly business, of course." He leered.

"Sorry, you've got the wrong customer." I added ironically, "I'm strictly a Rule-abiding citizen."

He looked disgusted as he took the cloth and wrapped it in paper. "Don't give me that. I spotted you right off."

"Pardon?"

"All right, play dumb." He took the IDisc I'd pulled from my chain and inserted it into the transactor, which was plugged into a vendor outlet of the central village console. When he punched in his code, the green certified signal on the outlet lit up.

I punched in my account code and laid my palm on the sensor plate, mentally weighing designs for Helen's pearl-cloth robe. Maybe hooded, with flowing sleeves, if she didn't think it too outlandish. Like the robes of the Setharian high plains nomads who had traded once with our tribe . . .

It took a centa for the blinking red light to sink in. The small screen lit up with the words: ACCOUNT CLOSED. I stared blankly at it.

Behind me, the vendor made a rude noise. He snapped off the transactor and plucked out my IDisc, fingering it. I stared woodenly at the device, not quite believing it.

There was a new edge in the vendor's voice. "Okay, toots, so what's the game? You got the credits or not?"

I closed my eyes as a sickening wave of cold fear washed through me and tumbled me dizzily. *Account Closed.* The two simple words had suddenly scattered all my careful cards of strategy and it was no longer a game. If I couldn't access my accounts, I couldn't signal Officer Hodge. And if my violation points climbed any higher . . .

"Don't play pitiful with me."

I opened my eyes to see him rubbing my IDisc between his fingers. He flicked it back to me and I caught it automatically.

"What you trying to pull here? You want the cloth that bad, we could work out a trade . . ." He smiled disagreeably, his eyes sliding slowly down from my face.

I shook my head impatiently, reaching up to clip the IDisc back on its chain. He shrugged and reached for the wrapped package, starting to untie the string.

"Wait . . ." I only had a few credit-counters left, but I couldn't insult Marda by showing up without a marriage gift. I couldn't explain to Helen that my account was closed. That only happened when you were dead—or crazy. My hands touched my lucky necklace. They fumbled as I pulled it from around my neck. "I'll trade this for the silk. It's more than worth it."

He gave me a suspicious look but took the chain, running the red-gold, scale-shaped segments through his fingers and examining the clasp, the head of the snake flashing its two tiny emerald eyes as it swallowed the end of its own tail.

Windy Poindros dissolved, and I could see the gleaming serpent dangling from the casual fingers of a friend in Casino as we lounged at the smoke table in a gambling hall. "Go ahead, take it. Don't deny me the pleasure of seeing it around your neck. It's my hobby—designing jewelry to suit intriguing women. I'd lose faith in myself if you could resist." I hadn't been sure I was comfortable as either the serpent or Eve, but he couldn't have known the Poindran parable, so I'd let him fasten it around my neck. I'd liked him. He'd made me laugh, and besides, everybody knew his tastes ran to young men.

The green eyes winked again, in the more than casual grip

of the vendor. He ran the chain through his fingers. He bit his lip and sweat gleamed on his forehead.

"Offworld work." He hesitated, then handed me back the package, still looking uneasily at the chain.

I pulled my lips into the imitation of a smile. "Don't worry, it won't bite." I moved to go.

"Hey, wait, what's going on? Look, don't get me wrong, I'm all for it, but I don't wanna get involved in anything really—" He swallowed, eyeing me sideways.

"What?" All I could seem to register were those words, *Account Closed*.

The vendor shook his head, his eyes gleaming a lot of white as he edged away from me and pocketed the chain.

I turned to make my way across the square, clutching the package and my IDisc, the twisted smile frozen on my face.

Account Closed. The seat beside me remained empty as the railcar filled with passengers. Poindrans instinctively avoided contact with unsheathed emotions, and my shock had melted into blazing fury. Not that tearing a console apart with my bare hands would have done a lot of good, but with the cybers shuffling me around like a playing card in their game, I felt like wreaking a little havoc of my own.

The station shelter receded in an angry red mist as I contemplated a slow dismembering of the complacent CI cyberserf. An irritatingly cheerful whistle shrilled in my ear and I twisted around, automatically jerking my hands up into a fighting position.

"Jeez Louise! If you want me to move, just say so!"

I blinked and focussed on what had materialized beside me. It appeared to be a boy of twelve or so, edging uneasily away from me to perch on the front of the seat, clutching a bulging cloth bag and kicking the seat in front of him. A cocky grin was moored uncertainly beneath a large, freckled nose and anxious-looking eyes magnified behind owlish spectacles. A bush of wiry dark hair with a wildly eccentric life of its own, oddly pale skin, and the outlandish corrective lenses, rarely seen, made me hope this was only another brief nightmare. He pursed chapped lips unattractively and whistled again, spraying a little glob of spit. I closed my eyes, hoping the apparition would go away.

I opened them on another tuneless whistle and scowled. It had staying power. It continued to produce the painful noise and I winced, rubbing my forehead where a dull headache was being born. "Hey, do you mind?"

The whistle cut off in mid-shrill, and I reluctantly reclassified my companion as some variant of human.

He squirmed and settled back in the seat. "Got a headache, huh? Sometimes barter-day does that, leastways Mother says some of the out-of-town vendors give her a pain." He kicked his legs again, and I clamped my jaw as the seat jounced and my head throbbed. He went on with a philosophical air, "With me, it's usually a stomachache, but today I didn't have time for more than a couple of fried cakes at Sadie's stall. If I don't get back with this stuff for the party, Mother'll kill me." He bounced around, craning his head out into the aisle and looking back and forth at the sleepy passengers.

I closed my eyes and took a deep breath of the stuffy air. "Look, I could use some peace and quiet. If you've got to thrash around, can't you find another seat?"

He stuffed the bag into the space between seats and it thumped heavily onto the floor. "Ooops!" He peered into it. "Well, I guess they're not too squished." He pulled up his legs to sit cross-legged, still bouncing, and gave me another grin. "You're stuck with me. Only seat left. Here." He scrambled up on the seat and reached over me to pull the window down a few more notches. A warm breeze fanned my face and completed the destruction of my attempt at a respectable hairdo. "Hot as an overcharge in here."

I nodded, hoping feebly that he'd wind down.

He squinted up at me, pursed his lips for another whistle, but subsided at my look. "Yeah, old Fergus gave you a pretty hard time, huh? You sure went white all of a sudden." He rummaged through his pockets, stuck something into his mouth and chewed on it, then pulled out something he jiggled in his fist like a gambler shaking dice.

"Fergus? What are you talking about?"

"Silk vendor—he comes through here regular. But he's got more than stupid old cloth." He grinned and rolled his eyes upward, winking in imitation of the vendor. "You can tell by his shoes. *You* know." He gave me another ludicrous wink.

I stared down at him, then cleared my throat. "I have no idea what you're up to, and I don't want to know." I added primly, "I'm surprised your mother lets you loose."

"Me!" He gave me an indignant look. "I can handle old

Fergus a lot better than you. I saw you,'' he continued scornfully. "Boy, was that dumb! You could've gotten five times what you did.'' He stopped jiggling his hand and drew out something bright, dangling it between his fingers. "But maybe you're not interested in getting this thing back . . .''

I jumped as if it'd bitten me. The emerald eyes of the snake did have a sly glitter. "But . . . how . . .''

"Grown-ups!'' He rolled his eyes. "I got to hand it to you, though, I never saw old Fergus struck speechless before. You did look pretty weird when you took off out of there.''

I rubbed my temples and groaned. "Look, I don't have the credits to buy it back. I hope you didn't pay him too much for it. But why—''

"Don't worry, he was kinda glad to get rid of it, anyway, and besides I got such a good deal on my—'' He broke off and glanced down at the bag and quickly away. "I figured—''

"Hey, wait a centa! Look, kid, I don't know what you've got going, but count me out. I follow the Rules.''

"Yeah, sure.'' He looked disgusted again. "You can't fool me. Look, we could do a little trade, right? You can have the chain back if you tell me all about space, and the transport ships, and the other worlds, okay? They say I'm not supposed to ask, but criminy, why not? I never got to talk to a real spacer before. And I can't get anything more out of the console about the machines, but I figure the ships must run some kind of field-twist, right? I mean otherwise it'd take too long to get anywhere. But whenever I try to find out, there's a gate that—''

He broke off and whistled nervously again. "I mean, I don't really mess around with the console any more, anyway . . .'' His eyes shifted uneasily behind the thick lenses.

I caught a breath, startled. "Okay, kid, you're right, I'm a spacer. But all this other stuff''—I whispered—''you know it's Taboo.'' I glanced at the bag, noting a thick, square bulge at the bottom. What under the stars was the kid up to? "You're going to get us both in trouble. I told you, I stick to the Rules. Take my advice, and you do the same.''

"That's pretty funny, coming from you!'' He stuck his chin out defiantly, but his eyes were blinking fast behind the glasses. "Grown-ups! You're all alike!'' He tossed the chain in my lap. "Oh, go on, take it! You're just like the rest of them—act like they don't have any brains at all, even a smart guy like Fergus, when he gets around girls. But you act goofier than he does. Maybe they're right about you. I mean, I thought all that stuff about space rays was just talk, but maybe it's true. You *look* all right, I mean for a girl, even if you don't look like a spacer, but he *said* you were mad as . . . as . . ." He rolled his eyes and shook his head, spectacles glinting. "Grown-ups!"

I stared down at him. "Fireblood and thorns! What in blazes are you talking about? Who said I was mad?"

He gave me a startled look, then squinted. "Well, your hair's kind of red, isn't it? You don't look all that skinny to me, but . . ." He shrugged. "They said she said you'd stop at the barter-day fair and I should look out for you."

"Who said she said I . . . and who's *she*? I mean . . ." I gave him an exasperated look. "Who the hell *are* you?"

He gave me an indignant look. "Well, David, who else? Jeez, maybe they're right, but I don't know why a hatter should be so mad." The kid grinned and bounced in the seat. "Now, come on, tell me about the space transports and how you ran away! I promise, I won't tell. Come on, Aunt Ruth!"

fourteen

"Hey, she's here!" The screen door clattered shut behind David.

Before I could shake out my dusty skirts or retie my wild hair, the door opened again and I gaped down at the woman who came only to my shoulder.

There was a calm smile of welcome on the cream-pale face that might have been a porcelain doll's in its smooth delicacy, set above the soft curves of a womanly shape done in miniature. Not a strand of her gleaming black hair was out of place. Warm brown eyes under narrow, arched brows flickered from my dusty hem to the hat crammed on my snarled hair without affecting her gracious smile. I felt like a gawky pard pup, all loose limbs and gratuitous height, standing before her petite tidiness.

Marda held out her hands, her voice soft. "Ruth! I'm so glad you could come." My long, sun-browned hands engulfed her tiny, plump fingers.

She urged me through the door to blink in the dimness of her kitchen. The only sign of David was a swing door settling silently closed. Two men sat at a wooden table. The closer man froze, leaning forward and reaching out with one muscular, freckled arm to hand a toy to a red-haired toddler sprawled on the tiled floor. My eyes focussed on Joshua's familiar, cheerful grin. He gave the curly red head a pat, stepped over the child with a long stride, and stood before me.

The grin widened and his eyes danced with laughter he didn't bother to conceal as he looked up and down the spectacle of his long-lost twin. When the blue eyes met my green, I realized I was as tall as he was, though not nearly his solid weight. I wondered again how we could have grown so different.

"Yep, them space rays must've done something! You're even a longer drink of water than before. Got a bit of a curve to ya now, though." He eyed me sideways, the old teasing tone in his voice. "What happened to your face? Couldn't get the knife right side down chopping vegetables?" He winked, turning to Marda. "She always was a sight in the kitchen. I remember one supper she almost done us all in with—"

"Joshua!" Marda looked faintly shocked.

"Poor Josh!" I grasped a handful of carrot-colored hair and tilted his face toward the window, lighting up the freckles that had caused him such adolescent agonies. "I see there's no hope for a cure!"

Joshua looked taken aback as I released him, but the other man rose from the table with a dry chuckle and extended his hand to me. "Pleased to meet you, Ruth. Anyone who can take that young pup down a peg is mighty welcome here." He gave Joshua an affectionate slap on the back.

Joshua smiled sheepishly. "Ruth, this is Thomas."

I took the hard, veined hand and raised my eyes up his lanky height to meet sun-faded hazel eyes. His long-jawed, attractively weathered face was topped by a short-cropped, lighter version of David's wiry hair.

There was a wail from the floor and Joshua bent to scoop up the little girl clinging to his leg. He held her in the crook of one thick arm and straightened her ruffly green dress with a clumsy paw. "Hush, sweetie pie." He gave me another grin of bashful pride. "Ruth, this here little critter's your niece Ruth Helen. Darn long handle for a bit of a thing, but Marda insisted."

I smiled into the tear-bright, hazel-green eyes. "Hi, Ruth Helen. Don't you worry, I was just teasing your P'eros." I looked over at Marda, who was still smiling calmly. "She's going to be as pretty as you, Marda. For once, Joshua used his head."

She dropped her eyes and a faint rose crept into the creamy cheeks. "Why, thank you, Ruth." She raised her gaze again to mine. "But it's easy to see where Ruth Helen takes her beauty. I chose the right name."

I blinked, surprised that she would as good as say we all

knew who the truefather was. It was Taboo to make any differentiation between patera, even when it was as clear as Ruth Helen's red curls, or as obvious as Mother conceiving Josh and me before she and Isaac had bound Sam into the new family.

Marda stepped quickly forward, raising a hand to touch a loose strand of my hair. "Would you let me arrange it for the wedding party, Ruth? It's such a lovely auburn, and I do have a terrible weakness for pretty hair!" It came across with the air of a confession.

Now I realized what she was up to. She was almost as smooth as Helen. But they were all trying so hard. I smiled. "If you think you can bring forth order from chaos, you're welcome to try."

"Now, where'd that David slip off to? And where's the other sprout?" Joshua strode over to lean through the swing door into the hall. "Hey, Zeke! Get your little butt down here to meet your aunt!"

"Joshua, please." Marda turned with a quiet protest.

"Ooops! There, you little rapscallion! Say howdy to your Aunt Ruth." Joshua swung back into the kitchen with a kicking, giggling small boy under his arm. He sent the auburn-haired child on the floor and propelled him forward with a smack on his bottom. I crouched down to meet Ezekiel and he gave me an impulsive hug.

I looked up over his head and found my eyes stinging absurdly as I met Joshua's. So it was to be easy, after all. Joshua nodded, his eyes bright blue as he grinned.

Expectancy glowed up from the dark yard and its ring of colored paper lanterns. The guests would soon arrive for the party to celebrate the day's earlier marriage Solemnities. Even now they were pulling the festooned groom cart through the restless wheat, carrying their own paper lanterns and singing as they came.

I drew back through the window into the dark bedroom and felt for flint and lantern on the dressing table. The immaculate white curtains snapped and fluttered, ghostlike, into the room. The wick caught and chased shadows to the corners. I looked at myself in the mirror.

A stranger stared back at me, hand to her hair. Somehow Marda had tamed it into smooth, intertwined curves to frame my face in a sort of halo that swept back into a thick coil

behind my head. The full strands of braiding gleamed dark
red in the light, glinting with the scented oil she had combed
through it. The scar on my cheek was barely visible in the
shadowy depth of the mirror.

The woman in there was a Poindran, her slender curves
embraced by the soft folds of a dark green satin dress, her
pale hand dropping from her hair with unconscious grace as
she leaned forward in the mirror. I saw with a little shock
how bright green her eyes looked, wider under the arch of
brow echoed by the gleaming sweep of hair, the curve of
cheek running down to slightly parted lips, a spot of color
high at each temple, delicate ears partially hidden by the
heavy ropes of braiding. I wondered if Marda realized what
she had done, how she had made this young woman look
so . . .

So much like Helen. I could almost be looking at Mother.

I jerked in ridiculous panic away from the mirror and
yanked up my skirts, striding from the room. I didn't want to
look in that mirror again. I was afraid I'd see Helen's mysterious serenity smiling back at me.

"Jeez Louise!" David jumped when I appeared on the
shadowed porch, thrusting something hastily behind his back.
He peered up at me, grinned sheepishly, and plopped himself
down on a step, chomping into an iced tart he'd filched as I
settled beside him.

"You sure as hell," he giggled, "don't look like a spacer,
Aunt Ruth! But I guess that's okay. You still have to tell me
more about the weird places you've been."

I settled my skirts carefully onto the step, sighing. "Okay,
David, I'll tell you about a really strange place. The women
are so kind and lovely they leave fine threads of light floating
behind them. Pretty soon, the threads get woven into a beautiful web, with an intricate pattern that you can hardly see
unless the sun hits it just right, and then you see it's
got a Plan. It's so light and airy the men and children
want to be lifted up by it and feel how soft and gently
they're held. And they're all balanced so carefully, each
in the right spot designed to hold his weight, so they
won't tear the web or knock against anyone else, and they're
all smiling . . . and it *is* lovely, and there's no reason why
anyone should come along and get the urge to shake that
web . . ."

David munched and swallowed. "Sounds funny to me. What is it, some sort of force field? But then if they had that, they could probably have some kind of flight thrust, right? Tell me about the flying ships!"

I shook my head, chuckling as he pulled his thin legs up, knees by his ears, hunching on the step with his round spectacles gleaming in the shadow, looking exactly like the brooding night-owl of Targuar. "How about birds? Did you know there are birds kind of like our trotters, only they have real wings and fly?"

"You mean like the transports do? Or more like a mechanical drive? I saw some pictures on the console once, drawings-like of flying machines, but they must not of worked, otherwise the console wouldn't have cleared them that first time, even with—"

"What do you mean, *cleared* them?"

He licked his lips nervously. "Oh, nothing, I just mean they don't show us Taboo stuff, *you* know. Machines and stuff we can't have in the Plan." He cleared his throat. "But since Mother and the elders told me it was wrong, I don't mess around with the console anymore." He shrugged unconvincingly.

"David!" I lowered my voice. "What are you up to? It sounds like you're climbing on a thin line. If Marda—"

He shot me another worried look, lenses flashing a colored streak of light. "You're not gonna—"

"No, I won't tell. But watch it with the cybers, David. It's harder to fool them than you think. You break too many Rules, you're in trouble. I know, I . . . ." I swallowed. "Look, it's like tower climbing, you know. You have to watch out for the backlash and whip on the fast gusts, or you might get spinning out of control."

He gave me a puzzled look. "It's true? You really worked on the towers with Joshua and them?" He shrugged. "But beats me what you're talking about. I don't climb those things."

"What? Here you're talking about flying machines, can't wait to get on a transport, and you don't even use your own wings?"

He gave me an indignant look. "Big deal! So I don't climb the towers! What's that got to do with star ships?"

My voice picked up his scornful tone. "You can have it, and you don't even want it! Listen, you've got some big ideas

about star ships, and flying to the planets, but it's not what
you think. Here, on the wind sails, you can *feel* it. It's real
when you get up into the air and you're part of it. You'd
better find out what that's all about before you start dreaming
about the stars. Believe me, they've only got more worlds
around them, about as ordinary as here.''

"You sound like Mother!" He hissed, hurt and angry.
"*You* think I'm gonna swallow all that stuff about how great
it is here?"

"But I was a girl, David. I had no other choice . . ." I
sighed. "Well, I guess it takes all kinds."

"You ask me, you've gotta be *really* crazy to get up there.
Alls I do is get dizzy, all upside-down and sideways. So they
just let me help with the tower electronics. I'm really good,"
he added proudly, "way better than even the older guys in
repair-shop class. But that's just kid stuff, anyway. What I
really want to know about is the high-tech stuff the console's
not supposed to . . . I mean, like the transports and all. I
figger they must use some kind of energy-flux modification,
right? But I can't work out how they'd do that. I gotta go
somewhere I can find out all that stuff, Aunt Ruth! Why don't
you take me back to space with you? Please?"

I looked down at his eager face, at the ridiculous, freckled
nose, the outlandish glasses, and the absurdly wiry hair, but I
didn't feel like laughing. I touched his shoulder and made my
voice as gentle as I could. "David, you don't understand. It's
not just Poindros. It's everywhere. The cybers don't tell us
those kinds of things. They're Taboo on the other worlds,
too. And its dangerous to try to find out . . ."

"But . . . dangerous, what do you mean? You're crazy!"
He jerked away from me. "You're lying, just like the rest of
them. You just don't want me to go! But you'll see, I'll find
out, I'm gonna be a spacer!" He flung himself off the steps
and ran away into the night.

A bright chain of colored lights winked out of the darkness
from the direction he'd gone, following the route of the
monorail. They curved and snaked toward me, a submerged
glow flowing through the dark field, but all I could hear was
the restless breeze.

"Just about time. Give me a hand with this rope, Ruth?" It
was Joshua leaning over the porch rail.

"Oh. Sure." I straightened and stepped down into the light
from the bobbing lantern, turning to look up at him.

"Marda wants this—Ruth?" He broke off, his mouth hanging open. "Blazes! For a centa there, I thought . . ." He shook his head and grinned. "Hit me with a heat wind if you don't almost look like a gal tonight, Ruthie! Come on."

I helped him spread the plaited straw rope Marda had interwoven with papery blue wildflowers into a loose circle around the largest fan tree. He stepped back to admire it. "There! Looks real pretty. Just like she did for our binding party."

"That was only four years ago, wasn't it?"

"Yep. Glad Peter's binding in. I missed him." Peter was one of Joshua's childhood friends. "And we can sure use the help in the fields."

I picked up the traditional copper lantern to hand him. "Then you don't mind having a little less of Marda already?" I spoke without thinking.

He paused in the act of hanging the unlit lantern from the lowest bough, giving me the old look of incomprehension. "You always did say the damndest things, Ruth."

He grinned and waved as Marda and Thomas appeared with the children. There was a faint murmur of voices beneath the wind as the lights flowed toward us through the field. David came pelting out of the dark, taking his place with us in the family circle and proclaiming breathlessly, "They're coming!"

Then in a swirl of wind and bobbing lanterns and music they burst out of the night. "The singers went before, the players on instruments followed after. Amongst them were the maidens playing with timbrels."

The Book of Words came alive in a riot of voices, ringing bells, and swirling skirts as the women, singing and playing their instruments, scattered into the yard. Horns and flutes took up the tune of the binding song and the rich voices of the matrons followed them. Children swarmed into the yard and formed a circle, hands clasped as they turned and joined the song in a merry round. Deep bass tones filled in as the children spun faster in their bright colors, and the men broke out of the night, bellowing their song and pulling the flower-and-bell-laden wagon to a stop at the edge of the lights.

The dark-haired young man sitting on top grinned sheepishly and stood. A great cry of welcome rose from the throng.

Bells and horns and tambourines tumbled into the racket, and the dancing circle exploded into a rush of bodies to surround the wagon. A cheer went up as the men hoisted the groom onto their shoulders and carried him once around the yard, trailing the excited crowd of children. They set him on his feet before the family circle and everyone fell back in an expectant hush.

Peter, the white groom sash tied in its complicated knot around his waist, touched his hands to his heart and then held them out to Madra. He remained silently standing, his eyes sparking as they fixed on her.

She smiled and I understood his ardent look. She was the perfection of Poindran womanhood as she stood poised in her pale-blue gown among the excited crowd, small and delicate and rounded, smooth porcelain tinted with soft hues beneath a dark crown of hair interwoven with a blue ribbon.

"Welcome, Peter." Her low voice fell into the hush. Thomas and Joshua echoed her.

Two small boys came forward from the crowd, walking with nervous care as if afraid they might drop the thin sheaf of grain and the lighted lamp they gave into Peter's hands. He walked slowly toward us.

As Marda reached out her hand to guide him over the plaited rope, Joshua took the sheaf and Thomas reached up to light the copper lantern from the flame of Peter's lamp. The underside of the rustling leaves lit up in a bright green canopy overhead.

Marda and Peter turned outward to the guests, raising their clasped hands, and a great roar of approval met them.

A young man burst from the throng in a series of hand-springs across the dirt yard. A tumbling knot of his friends followed, tossing and catching each other as their strong bodies flashed in arcs above the ground, honed by their work high in the windtowers. I caught an eager breath as I watched their intricate play, the springing forms launched by quick arms and caught by others, the exuberant leaps through windy air. Around the lithe figures a great spinning wheel seemed to take shape, tower arms rising into the wind and sun, catching a gleam of holding lines as Joshua and I counted out the rhythm of the cycle and launched ourselves from the arm into a flying leap for the next rising spoke.

Freedom in the high air . . . I sighed as the young men took their last springs backward and the crowd rushed in to engulf us.

•   •   •

The night was a blur of laughing faces, merry music, bobbing lights and shadow, and skirts swirling in the dust of the rowdy festival dances. I took my proper place behind the refreshment table, cutting cakes and pouring juice for the matrons who came in curious flocks. I pretended not to notice their shifting glances, the whispered conferences, the slight hesitations before they accepted food from the hands of a spacer.

I tried to imitate Marda's gracious smile and not see the young bachelors gathered by the mead barrel, laughing and throwing looks my way and daring each other to talk to me.

"Go on, Luke, you—" A brown-haired young man was pushed away from the laughing group.

"Hey! Blast if you'll—!" He whirled in a cloud of dust to grapple the arms that had pushed him. Amid shouts and jeering, a wrestling, struggling knot of sun-browned bachelors writhed across the dirt and knocked over the mead barrel, sending it rolling toward the dancers and leaving a moist, pungent trail behind it.

"By the Founder—!"

"Merciful cybers, what's gotten into—?"

The matrons fluttered back in shock and the music rattled to a stop, the dancers turning in bewilderment. As the dust settled, Joshua and Thomas strode through the silence to disentangle the contentious young men.

"Here, now, you young pups!" Thomas took two by the back of their unembroidered bachelor vests. "What's got into you?"

Joshua separated two more who were rolling and thrashing through the dust. "If'n you can't handle your mead, then don't drink with the men!"

A pale flutter of blue drifted through the milling crowd, and behind it the music rose again into the night. The dancers resumed their circular patterns. Marda moved gracefully from matron to matron, drawing them away to help her unwrap and display the gifts brought by the guests. But I still stood isolated by a circle as plain as the family's flowered rope. The matrons shook their heads as they moved off, and even above the wind and music I caught snatches of words.

"Whatever can have . . ."

". . . a spacer to bring more trouble! As if we haven't had enough! You know what they . . ."

". . . not fitting. Why, just look at her face, and you can see what sort she is! Probably one of those . . ."

I busied myself tidying the table and helping Joshua and Thomas put the cups to rights near the rescued barrel.

"You're not going to get away with it, you know."

Startled, I looked up, and then up the husky height of the stranger into the snap of very blue eyes. "What?" Had they found me out already?

He winked and a humorous smile animated his pleasantly homely face. "Prettiest gal here, and not dancing! Would you do me the honor, Mistress?" He held out his arm.

"Oh!" I hesitated, seeing the faces still staring coldly at me across the yard. I raised my chin. "Thank you, I will."

The eyes followed as he walked me across the yard and the music announced a festival dance. I held my back straight, my lips in a careful smile.

But my partner grinned and winked as the music swelled, and I couldn't help joining his laughter as his large hands caught me around the waist and swung me into the opening twirl. His exuberance was irresistible, and all the dancers smiled, jumping with one will into the flowing circular patterns. I dove recklessly into the passing line, weaving and brushing the twisting bodies, laughing and peering through the gold-lighted haze of rising dust, slapping the palm of my returning partner, spinning, then away again, gasping into the quickening beat of drums. Then he was back, that great grin, and up! My head swept the night air and my skirts flared in a gleaming circle around and around in a bright blur of light and laughter.

His big hands guided me gently through the settling dust and he smiled. "I thank you, Mistress." He glanced up at the night sky and back to me, winking again. "Give my regards to the stars next time you're out that way."

I stood watching after the broad back of his embroidered vest, then slowly smiled. I nodded and threaded my way through the noisy flock to the deserted house.

fifteen

The door slid into its sheath in a silent burst of light. I glanced behind me at the dark cellar and stepped through into the cubicle. I could no longer hear the music or laughter outside, only the soft hum of the air treatment.

I stared at the winking amber and blue lights and despite what I'd learned from the Founder loop, I was unable to think of the cybers as machines, as tools built in some unimaginable past by humans. They were alive, and they were waiting inside the heart of the console—their bright, colored eyes watching me.

I shook my head and hurriedly activated the interface.

"Good evening! May I—"

The soft soprano cut off abruptly as I inserted the wild card disc. The green indicator blinked into holding mode. I waited. Like last time, there was no further response. Again I glanced nervously behind me and took a deep breath.

"Maintenance module requests verbal test."

There was no response. The green light kept silently winking, the blues and ambers shifting in their oblivious checks.

"This is a maintenance module test. Respond verbally."

Still the lights ignored me. Fireblood and thorns! It would be just my luck if there was some interface malfunction. I wiped damp palms on my skirt, peered out at the cellar again, and paced back to stare at the smugly winking face of the console. I took hold of it and pulled, and it rolled smoothly away from the wall. The thick cable ran into the floor just as it had in our family cubicle, but there wasn't much dust here.

131

Crouching, I pulled the chain from beneath my dress to detach my IDisc. The tiny emerald eyes of the snake winked in the same sly joke as the console's lights. I stuffed the chain back down my bodice and pried with the disc. The latches loosened easily and the panel came free.

I nearly dropped it. "Blazing—!"

A confused mass of wires tumbled out into the light. I sat back on my heels and stared blankly at the snakelike twinings of a heavy, brown wire that twisted around and through and between the components and the neatly wrapped and diverging strands of the original wiring. Leaning closer, I pulled aside a thick bundle and peered through at the maze of wire coiled sloppily, crammed anyhow into spaces between relays, woven crazily under and around the neat, tie-wrapped bundles and secured with large, worn-looking clips of discolored metal. It was too messy to be anything but human, like a kid playing at grown-up.

"Hey!" The voice was behind me.

Caught off balance, I twisted like a finner on a line, falling and sitting back hard to look up at David's owl-like eyes. Each freckle seemed separately astonished.

"What do you think you're—?"

"David! What're you—?"

We eyed each other uneasily.

David swallowed and stuck out his chin belligerently. "What are you doing now, breaking into our console?" He edged awkwardly closer, holding his hands behind him.

I tipped my head toward the console. "Somebody's been playing in the cyber's house."

The freckles melted into an angry flush. "Whaddya mean, playing? Hey, don't touch that! You might—" He darted forward and something fell with a thump to the floor.

I raised an eyebrow.

He licked his lips, blew out a long breath, and picked up the large book, cradling it against his chest and sinking into a cross-legged seat on the floor beside me. He looked up, bit his lip, and handed me the heavy volume.

"Be careful! I've been waiting a long time for old Fergus to stumble across one of these." He hovered anxiously as I turned the yellowed pages of what looked like a handmade book.

I whistled, leafing through complicated diagrams of lines and circles, triangles, squiggly shapes, numbers, and words I didn't recognize. The handwritten text didn't make much sense to me, but from the little the cybers taught us for the tower maintenance, I realized it had to do with electronics.

I shook my head slowly. "David, do you know what you're getting into here?"

"Sure." He grinned. "With this, I can really do something! See, I've been sort of redesigning the interface circuitry from I what I got out of the Matron once I figured how to get past her first gate-levels. So I put in some bypasses here"—he reached past me to point out snarled wires—"and that let me get past the persona so I could ask questions straight out." He puffed out his cheeks, then shrugged. "But there's still some high-level blocking gates I can't crack. And of course I have to be careful not to trigger any of the alarms, so that means rerouting signals and keeping power flow balanced . . . But it wasn't all that tough, I mean I guess they think nobody's gonna go past their silly warnings, but anybody with half a brain could figure out—"

"David!"

He grinned, then shrugged again. "Yeah, well all I can get out of it is kril-nuts, anyway. I mean, the stuff I really want to get into is physics and field dynamics, and they've got gates like mites on a pard all over that stuff. No way can I figure what the cybers've got going on inside there." He pointed to the seamless plasmeld shape. "But with this book, I can really go places." He ended on a defiant note, "And don't think you're gonna stop me!"

"David, listen. You don't realize how serious—"

"Come on, Auntie Ruth!" He grinned. "Mother and the elders'll only give me another lecture. I'm just an innocent child, and I don't know what I'm doing. But if you're so worried about the Rules all of a sudden, you're not gonna tell, anyway, are you? I mean, what are *you* up to down here?" The cocky grin couldn't disguise his anxious eyes.

I groaned. "Innocent child! Listen, if there were more like you, the Plan would be in big trouble . . . It might be already . . ." I handed the book back. "David, are you sure the cybers don't know what you're doing?"

"Course I'm sure! What do you think—"

"No, wait. Just be careful, okay? Look, I can't explain it all, but just believe me about one thing. If they find out what you're doing, you're going to be in trouble. I mean the Steps of Healing."

His glasses glinted in the light. "Well, what's the big deal about that? I mean—"

"David, I think it might be very bad. I don't know for sure about that, but I do know there's something wrong here on Poindros." I took a deep breath, weighed the risks, and plunged ahead. "I . . . well, the cybers sort of sent me back to find out what's wrong. I've been hearing some strange things from the consoles here. It looks like LS—the Poindros cybers—are up to something that could be bad news for everybody. It's important I find out more. Would you help me?"

He swallowed uneasily and gave me a look I was getting used to on my homeworld. "That's crazy! How can anything be *wrong*? The cybers always take care of us. And anyway, if they sent you here, then why are you worried about them? I mean . . ." He gave me another narrowed-eyed look.

I laughed ruefully. "David, I know it sounds crazy, but it's true. I can't explain it all or I'll get you into trouble, too. But it's important. Would you help me get some information from the console? I don't know what you did to it, but it won't work for me."

"What do you mean? I didn't do anything to disrupt the Matron. Didn't she answer you?"

I sighed. "David, it's a long story, but I've got what amounts to a blank IDisc, and I can use it to get past the personae. But it didn't work on your console."

"Hey, what is it, some kind of spacer tool? Criminy! If I could use that along with my bypasses, I could really do some gate-crashing. Where is it?"

"In the console."

"Probably didn't work 'cause you didn't have my bypass codes. Here, see where I ran a link across these two terminals? And here I just—"

"David." I glanced uneasily at the door. "They're going to start wondering where we went."

"Yeah, and my activating controller's out at Tower Two, anyway. See, when I'm working on the electronics out there I can patch into the console and the Matron never knows. So I do most of my work out there now, and that way Mother doesn't have to worry because I'm spending too much time with the console."

I shook my head in amazement. "How in blazes did you come up with all this, kid?"

"Well, Jeez, Auntie Ruth, anybody with half a brain could—"

"Right." I sighed. "Look, let's get this thing closed up, okay? Maybe we could meet out at the tower and see what we can find out. Would you do that for me, David?"

"If you tell me what's going on. Otherwise, no deal."

I bit my lip. I didn't want to get him involved, but with the way he was messing around here, it was too late now. Besides, I couldn't do much more with my limited electronics knowledge. I took another deep breath and tried to ignore the cold sinking in my gut at the thought of the cybers catching us. "All right. Partners?"

"All right!" He grinned. "Do spacers shake?"

"Like this." I extended the two fingers and crossed them over his as his freckles danced in excitement. "Code of silence now, right?"

"Right!" He scrambled over me to replace the cover.

I rose, helped him push it back against the wall, and deactivated the interface. The light died as the slot ejected the blank disc.

"Hey, let me see!" David took it and examined it with a puzzled look. "Don't look like much."

"Doesn't," I corrected absently, reaching out for it.

He gave me a disgusted look and reluctantly handed it over. "All right, *Auntie* Ruth. Jeez, for a spacer, you're sure— "

"Hey, kid, lay off with the Auntie stuff, okay? *Ruth* is just fine. Wait a centa. I want to check one more thing." I walked over to peer out the doorway and hurried back to the console, pulling my IDisc off the chain again. "Here goes nothing." I reactivated the persona.

"Good evening! May I help you?"

"Yes. I'd like to check my credit accounts."

"I'd love to help you, but I must ask for your IDisc. I'm afraid I don't have your voice registered here."

I held the slippery plasmeld disc for a centa, suddenly reluctant to have the news about my accounts verified. Slowly I reached out and the console swallowed it.

A red light winked on and off on the top. The Matron's voice sounded flustered. "Oh, dear! I'm sorry, but I'm afraid there's been a mistake, and I'll have to keep this IDisc. It should have been returned to the cybernetic facilities. It belonged to Kurtis:P385XL47:Ruth, and she is dead."

sixteen

Without my IDisc, I was as good as dead.

I moved mechanically through the motions of helping Marda clean up the yard and house the next day. My mind was spinning out of gear. It looked like the game was about played out. I found myself standing still with the broom clutched in my hand like a knife hilt. I sighed and went to return it to the kitchen. I froze with my hand on the swing door, an odd prickling running up my spine.

". . . only a silly toy! She's a little different, of course, but I think she's all right, Marda. I like her."

"I like her, too, Thomas, but I don't want the children playing with that thing. It's best to be careful, with all the trouble and Healings lately. People are watching out, and they don't forget a Healing the way they should. I want you to keep David in the fields with you while Ruth is here. He's improved since our talk with Elder Agnes, and I don't want him getting started on that space nonsense again."

I couldn't move. Through the open crack of the door I could see Thomas frown over the little toy milker on the table. He handed Marda a couple of parcels wrapped in brown paper. "Here, these came in the mail drop. Finally, that part for Tower Two. Thought I'd let David finish his work in there today. You know how he hates working the fields, Marda, and he's really good with the electronics. He's saving us credits, rebuilding units instead of buying new. I think we should let him do what he's got a bent for. He's never going to make a farmer, sweetheart."

Marda crossed in front of me to the table, and I heard her sigh. "Perhaps you're right, dear. I suppose he's out of harm's way at the tower." There was a rustle of paper. "Oh, here's the new pattern I sent for. But what's this?"

"Hmm. Cybers sent it. Says for mites and hoppers. Must be expecting a bad season. Might as well—" I didn't hear the rest as he walked to the door and whistled piercingly. "Sheba!"

The door clattered and their female pard bounded into the kitchen and eagerly licked Marda's hand. Thomas knelt to fasten a dark collar on the pet and I could see him look up at Marda. "You're really worried about David, aren't you? That visit with the elders shook you up more than you'd admit."

I couldn't see her face, but she sighed again. I was still frozen, afraid to move. "He'll be fine, Thomas. But I've got to be a little stricter with him. Seeing Ruth has brought it home to me. You saw how they treated her last night, Thomas. If David doesn't start fitting in, it might be the same for him."

"Now, Marda, aren't you making a little too much of—"

"Haven't you seen her eyes, Thomas? Do you want David to be like her? So unhappy?"

I turned away and the door swung silently shut.

Wheat stalks hissed over my head, scribbling across the narrow strip of heat-bleached afternoon sky. The arms of Tower Two whirled ahead, reflecting glaring dazzles of blue-white light. The stalks whispered in accusation, "Unhappy. Unhappy."

I yanked up my skirts and hurried on to the tower to meet David. I had to get back before Marda and the children awoke from the nap I'd talked her into. As the tower grew above me, the wings beckoned urgently. I could feel the tremor humming through me now, jittering along my strung nerves.

I caught myself looking over my shoulder, stopping to crouch almost in the old Setharian stance, raking the stems with my eyes. Feeling the charged, defensive readiness run through me.

I shook my head impatiently and strode across the clearing, past a bulky tool chest near the open door of the tower's controlroom. I glanced back once more, still uneasy, then shook it off and hurried down the steps, blinking to adjust my eyes to the swimming lights flung by the spin of the rod. "David?"

"Hey, Ruth, over here!" A thin voice shouted over the roar of the rods and humming tremor. "What do you think, huh?"

He sat on the floor in front of an open panel—CYBERNETIC ACCESS ONLY—surrounded by wires and scattered tools and strange gadgets. He held the terminal clip of an insulated line running across the floor to the seismic panels. He attached it to a metal box that sprouted short leads and a wild assortment of lights, buttons, and dials, then grinned and waved a current probe at me. I almost expected him to attach a clip to his wiry springs of hair and light up the gleaming spectacles as indicators for his crazy contraption.

I sat beside him among the clutter. "So this is it? That box lets you talk to the console?"

"Box! This is my personalized bypass activator!" He gave me an indignant look. "See, if I hook into the display screen for the seismic indicators, I can get the signals spelled out. It's really easier using the console, so you can use voice mode, but I've got this set up so's I can input with a letter-code system. Like this."

He tapped buttons on the box and the seismic screen scrolled in lighted letters: SEE, ANTIE?

"A-*u*," I corrected absently, staring at the screen.

He gave me a disgusted look but couldn't help asking with obvious pride, "So what do you think, huh?"

"David, it's terrific! I'm impressed." I smiled at him. "Do you think you could find out some things for me?"

"Well, I've been thinking about that disc of yours, and we'd really have to be at the console . . ." He pursed up his lips.

"No, that's out. Marda doesn't want you associating with either the console or me."

He shrugged. "Well, I can get through some gates with this." He patted the box.

"Gates? What are these gates you keep talking about?"

"Uhn-uh. First you gotta talk. We're partners, remember?" He raised his two fingers for the spacer handshake. "You gotta tell me what's going on."

I touched my two fingers to his. It was funny, but I found I wanted to tell the crazy kid as badly as he wanted to hear it. So I told him. About the cyberserf, the wild card, Officer Hodge's warning about the Healing, the wheat blight, my accounts, and the subtly disturbing presence of contraplan gadgets, including his handmade book. I hesitated before telling him about the Founder loop, afraid that might be too much of a shock, but he finally wormed it out of me.

He shrugged and gave me a quizzical look. "Well, what's the big deal about that? Stands to reason the cybers'd be some sort of energy field, right? Why would they bother with electronic interfaces if they were alive on their own?" The lenses gleamed as he leaned closer in excitement. "Jeez, just think what it must've been like to live back then! Being able to learn what you wanted and *do* things! So what're *we* gonna do about it?"

I touched the wiry tangles of hair. "I'm not sure, kid." He certainly didn't seem perturbed about the Taboo notion of change and a past so different from our changeless present. Maybe that was what *history* had meant. I wouldn't disturb him with my own doubts and fears. But I couldn't shake a vague uneasiness that jittered through me like the tremor hum, urging me to take some undefined action. Like maybe burrow into some deep hole in the earth where the cybers would never find me. Like play dead.

But that was what they wanted, apparently. I blew out a long breath. "Let's try to find out some things, okay?"

David was eager to show off his contraption. He demonstrated how to bore loopholes through the console-Matron's gates to access data loops. But we couldn't get through a high-level blocking gate to information about my credit accounts. And, as David explained with an incomprehensible spill of jargon, any contact with offworld consoles was impossible. He wanted to go try the box and my wild card together on his console, but I firmly vetoed that, so he tried a run of what he called event-chain correlations on the happenings at my farm. He shook his head finally, muttered, "Weird data array," and showed me the fragments that were all he could retrieve: CROP BLIGHT ATTEMPT FAILED, and FIELD AGENT'S RECOMMENDATION SUPERCEDED, and FILE CLOSURE EXECUTED.

I didn't particularly like the look of that last message as it scrolled in lighted letters across the seismic display screen.

David unfolded his legs to stand, scratching his head. "Dang it, if I had time I could work on building one of those virus programs the book talked about. But I'm gonna try something else I spotted in there. If I bridge . . ." He bent over to rummage through the scattered tools. "Shoot, left my cutters outside in the tool chest. Be right back.'' He dashed up the stairs into the bright afternoon.

My uneasiness had blossomed into a case of screaming nerves, understandable considering the data I'd just seen. I rose and paced restlessly, lights flashing across me from the rod, tremor roaring through me.

And it was getting late. I had to get back to the house. I paused to eye David's paraphernalia one more time and crouched to touch my fingers lightly to the buttons, wishing I could program some charm of safekeeping for him. I shook my head and poked a restless finger through the scattered components, my hand closing absently around the handle of a metal probe. I stood, fingering its sharp point, feeling the wooden handle fit comfortably into my palm.

I toyed with the tool, feeling its satisfying heft, as I climbed the stairs. ''Hey, David, maybe we'd better try again tomorrow. We don't want to be caught out in—''

I emerged from the dim shaft to the blaze of sunshine biting into my eyes. ''David?'' I blinked as nervousness swelled into a swamping wave of urgency, assaulting my senses with the heat, the bright, swimming dust, and a low growl coming from somewhere. A flush of *timbra* tingled through my nerves to answer it.

Something dropped with a sound of metal against metal. ''Sheba? Hey, Ruth . . . ?'' David stumbled against the clanking tool chest, his voice trembling on the edge of fear.

I blinked again and focussed on his thin body sketched against the bright gleam of wheat, his outstretched arm shaking.

''Hey, Sheba! What's got into you? Easy, girl!'' His voice cracked.

The escalation of the *timbra* state was rushing through me now, images etched in separate lightning flashes of brilliant clarity. The downrushing gleam of a sail arm. The knobbed metal foot of the tower leg. Hot blue sky behind wheat stalks subsiding from violent shaking. A cloud of dust swirling. An angrily switching, tufted tail.

The big cat crouched a few paces from David, tail twitching aggressively, legs rippling tensed muscle, a low growl swelling into unmistakable threat.

My hand tightened reflexively on the sharp tool. ''David! Back up slowly, don't make any sudden moves.''

David's white face swung toward me, lenses flashing in the sun. ''But, Ruth, what's wrong with her?''

The pardil growled again and edged forward, belly low, eyes fixed on David, their amber hot with the sight of the kill. He looked back at her, took a hoarse, sobbing breath, and began to step backward. The cat's tail twitched faster, the wind shifted in the stalks, and I could see the ferial crouched, ready to spring from its limb onto the gizu-doe.

"That's it, David, back up. Come on." I edged closer to him, gripping the inadequate tool.

"No! Ruth, no!"

A sudden tawny blur of motion. A glimpse of a dark ring encircling the furry neck. Light glinting on sharp fangs. The big cat leaped.

David went down and suddenly there were only huge claws and the tumbling limbs of the boy in clouds of dust. A terrified scream and a wild snarl. Blinding sun caught thin metal as I sprang instinctively forward.

Adrenaline and reflexes, molten fire filling my veins. A growl, a savage cry—from whose throat?—a splash of red, fur under my hands, tripping in twisted skirts, then a scream, my own, agony of hot, tearing pain down my leg. Then anger, fury at those murderous amber eyes, devouring rage at the winking amber lights of the console. Power surged through my arms, and there was only stabbing, stabbing at those eyes, screams filling my ears, bright blood, red, by the thorns, so much red, the screaming, forever and insane, so much red, the weight, heavy, twitching on me, I'd forgotten there would be so much blood, pain, red darkness . . .

There was nothing. Empty black. No, wait, something pounding, knocking . . . *whose footsteps down those corridors*? No, my heart. Dull throb. Pain. Where? My leg . . . hurt. Heavy. Hard to breathe . . . From somewhere, quiet sobbing.

I opened my eyes to bright knives, hurting, hot blue overhead. The smell of dusty fur, my tongue meeting a sticky salt smear on my face. Weight on me, heavy, hot, suffocating. What? The sobbing.

"David!" I dragged in a breath. "David, you all right?"

A gasp. The weight on me shifted slightly. "Ruth! I can't move it. Holy Founder, Ruth!"

David's face popped into my field of vision, crazily distorted from below, streaked with blood and tears, one side of the frenzied hair matted with more blood. Somehow his spectacles were still crookedly in place, one lens cracked. "Ruth, are you alive?"

Laughter of relief bubbled up and was cut short in a wheeze beneath the weight. "Kid," I choked, "I hope this isn't Heaven."

An uncertain smile split his tragic face.

"Ooooph . . . you okay, David?" I located my arms and pushed against the hot, dead mass of the pard.

"Me! Yeah, I think . . . but all that blood on you . . . I thought . . . I didn't . . . why would Sheba . . . ?" His voice rose and cracked, panic blanking out his eyes.

"Okay, David," I wheezed, "it's okay. Just help me push."

I pushed as David pulled upward on the head and front legs of the pard. I wiggled free, drenched with more blood. I crawled forward, took a deep breath, and looked at the cat. One eye was a red, viscous pulp, the handle of the probe still protruding from it.

I sat back and groaned, looking numbly at the long, ragged gash down my leg that dripped blood into the dust.

David's eyes widened farther in shock and he sank onto the ground beside me. "Oh the Founder your leg Ruth—" He was chalky white, teeth chattering as he held his arms wrapped tightly around himself, staring at my leg.

"David!" Sudden anxiety sharpened my voice and I forgot my leg. "David, are you okay?"

He didn't answer, only hugged himself and stared.

Dizziness and a red mist before my eyes as I pushed him gently back and pulled away the bloody, shredded shirt. A gush of blood from the deep, ragged rip across his ribs and down his hip. "Damn them! By the blood and thorns, those cursed cybers . . ." I swore in a tender lullaby of a voice as I tore my skirt apart to bind up the awful wound. "By the stars, I'll tear them all apart . . ."

I touched his hot forehead when I was done. "I've gotta run for help, David. No moving now. It's against the code for spacer hunters. You've just been initiated."

I didn't know if he heard. I limped across the clearing, past the dead pardil, then stopped and turned back to crouch stiffly beside it. Groping through the fur on its neck, my hands closed around the smooth strap. I yanked it loose and stared at the seamless bubble of opaque plasmeld formed into it. I stuffed it into my pocket. I hurried down the track, reciting every curse from every world I could remember, damning the cybers to the worst torments I could muster. It became a cyclic litany that pulled me on a finely drawn wire of pain to the house.

seventeen

I stared down at the gleam of a half moon on the shiny black plasmeld strap. I was trying to remember why it was important.

The rollcart hummed along the dark track paralleling the monorail, bumping over ruts I couldn't see as the tall wheat tossed and bowed to brush me in a rising wind. I gritted my teeth as the next rut jounced my bandaged leg, propped on the driver's console. But I couldn't lower the drive speed or I'd never make it home.

It seemed like I'd clutched the rod forever, following the narrow ribbon of the rail through field after field. They all looked the same. The only break in the hypnotic vista of wheat and rail came when I had to swing wide around a sleeping farm or village, or detour to a tower to steal a recharge for the rollcart. The durs and centas clicked off endlessly in time to a hot, rising throb in my leg.

I had to be close. I'd travelled all last night and most of the day, except for a few durs holed up by a tower when I couldn't put off sleep any longer. I had to be close to home, I kept telling myself that, willing myself to stay awake, but I couldn't seem to remember why it should matter.

I nodded, then jerked up my head and focussed again on the black strap. The cybers. The pardil. David.

David . . . if only he'll read the note Ruth left, telling him to lie low, to be careful . . . But Ruth is dead.

I shook my head and blinked again. No, but without my

IDisc I couldn't ride the monorail, so that was why I'd taken the rollcart from Marda's farm. Yes, that was it.

David would be all right. Marda had grudgingly assured me the wound hadn't been as bad as it'd looked, after she'd sewn and bandaged him up and the men had destroyed "Ruth's demonic device" they'd found at the tower. The old disgusted look had transformed Joshua's features when I couldn't explain what I'd been doing with the instrument. After I'd stealthily dumped Marda's sleep elixir into the chamber pot, I'd heard her and Joshua discuss reporting me for the Healing.

Escaping in panic through the sleeping house to the machine shed, I'd been stopped by Thomas.

"You always run from trouble, Ruth? You get David hurt like that and then just leave?" His voice was quiet and measured, the lantern casting seamed shadows over his angular face.

I was cornered. I didn't want to know what weighed heavier in the scales, concern for David and the other potential victims of the Poindros cybers, or my own desperate instinct to get free. I shrugged in elaborate indifference. "Oh, the kid'll be okay. If he wasn't out there pestering me, he wouldn't have gotten hurt."

"What were you doing? Why'd that contraption make Sheba go so wild?"

Good. They believed the activator was mine. "You wouldn't understand."

His mouth tightened. "I guess Joshua's right about you. You think you're too good for us, don't you? Like you deserve special Rules? Well, we may be simple farmers, but we know right from wrong. You ought to be Healed."

"Oh, no. I'm getting the hell off this miserable dirt ball, and I'm not taking any detours for Healing. And you'd all better keep quiet, or the cybers're going to find out about your darling David. Then he'll be shunned for sure. You don't want that, do you? You don't want him to be like me?" My voice managed to sound indifferent.

He looked startled, then tightened his jaw until muscles jumped in his face. "You *are* sick. All right. Go. Your family's well rid of you."

I could still hear his voice as I bumped through the night, feverishly gripping the cybers' collar as if it were a pardon. The stalks hissed and whispered, "Sick! Sick!" I believed them. I couldn't remember why it was so important to get off the planet. I couldn't think. I could only grip tighter on the plasmeld strap, so tight I could feel a tingling like the tremor running through me, like voices whispering in the wind, telling me to turn myself in, to take the Steps of Healing.

"No. No."

But the wind stole my words and shredded them in the night. It whipped into me, roared through me, and my mind was flailed like the dark stalks of wheat. Crazy, shouting voices stormed through my head. I threw up my hands to press them from my head, to stop them, to kill them. "No!"

The wind tugged the collar from my loosened fingers and whirled it away into the night. I blinked. The shouting babble of voices was gone.

But I was thrown backward against my seat as the rollcart lurched sideways into the wheat, the stick swinging free. I blinked again, my mind snapping back into feverish focus, but it was too late. A strong gust caught the rollcart as it teetered in a too-tight turn and overbalanced. I grabbed the tilting side, scrambling, falling. I leaped free just as it crashed over into the raging stalks.

I landed heavily, pain shooting through my leg, lancing upward as I tumbled onto my back. I tried to stand, but the wind tore at my skirts and knocked me back down. My leg was going to explode through the tight bandages. Stinging dust, broken stalks, and my hat were swept against and past me on a hot blast of wind.

I blinked and pulled myself forward to cling to the side of the overturned rollcart. The wind. I should have realized before. The heat storms had finally hit. The dark wheat rippled and tossed wildly, furrowed by the whirling gusts as the restraining lines hummed shrilly.

The air was hot, it was burning me from the inside out. It was the fiery breath of a giant, metal-plated monster with the face of a console and blazing amber eyes lowering its jaws to snap me up. I could only cling to the side-bar of the rollcart as it tugged at me, cling as it tried to drag me into the whirling black confusion. The hissing whisper of the wheat had turned to a rhythmic roar, a deafening shout, and now it was only a senseless scream of violence, the voice of the demons of war calling for me.

•   •   •

Wheat gleamed in a copper-pink dawn, tossing gently against mylar lines. My hands were clamped to the side-bar, my arms cramped.

I staggered to my feet, groping around the side of the rollcart to see crushed stalks, leaves, and what looked like the broken pieces of a chair packed with the dirt against its tilted bed. I looked around in confusion, squinting as the rising sun glared off the spinning arms of a tower with one of its sails fluttering in ragged tatters. I blinked, finally recognizing the slope of the hills running into a dip and the distant gleam of silos. Home.

Home. Home. It was a chant timed to the burning throb that flowed from the stiff, blazing region of my leg. My mind had room for only the one thought. Home.

It was a dry, feverish, thirsty chant, but it pulled me along the strung lines, through the scratchy stems, onto a dirt track running toward the tattered sail and the silos beyond it. Home. It lanced through me with each step. I didn't know if the pain came from the word or the mindless setting down of my foot, but it had a power in itself to drag me along.

The tower. It was getting bigger, high above me now. Maybe I could rest if I could only get to it.

But it kept going in and out of focus, flowing away from me. The wheat stalks gleamed amber in the sun, whispering, but I couldn't understand them. It was something important. Maybe if I just stood and listened, swaying with them, turning my face to the sun, letting the tremor flow through me from the earth, I could stay with them forever. Ah, the whisper, inside me now, and . . .

"Ruth!"

It was the rollcart, it was above me, it was going to fall on me in the wind storm. I threw my arms up and staggered back.

"Ruth, honey, what in blazes are you doing here? What happened? You all right, child? Ruth!" It was Sam's face, going in and out of focus.

"Sam! The camera . . . Sam, the pictures don't make sense!"

"Honey, you're burning up! What in blazes . . . ?" Hands holding me up. "Jason!" A loud bellow.

Far away, down a copper tunnel, two figures, miniatures carved in gold. A man and a pardil, both tawny, loping with long, fluid strides through the waving wheat, running down the copper tunnel, fast, racing toward me.

They were almost on me. The pardil leaped forward, tawny fur and sun glinting on amber eyes.

"No! Sheba, no!" I screamed, but it was too late. It was on me, the sharp claws reaching out for me, the amber eyes burning through me, the eyes of the hunter pinning the prey.

"Ruth!" It was Jason's hand on my arm, his gold-flecked eyes melting into bright amber as he bent over me. "Ruth, you're all right!" There was a crazy relief and joy spreading over his face, but it didn't matter that nothing made sense, because he was holding me and I was smiling into his warm eyes.

"Here, Jason, let's get her into the rollcart bed." Sam took hold of my legs as they lifted me, and I winced. "By the Founder! Look at this leg. No wonder! Child, what happened?"

I smiled. "I'm dead, Sam." The copper tunnel closed around me and I dropped through it into darkness.

I rode slowly through liquid clear light, bobbing serenely in the tide of air, at one with the dipping birds and swaying fronds of undersea plants. I was rising. I opened my eyes and floated to the surface of sunlight pooled on my thin coverlet. A warm breeze fluttered white curtains.

Helen sat in the old nursery rocker, a pile of mending on her lap, but her hands lying for once idle. Her face was turned to the window, eyes far away, the morning light mercilessly drawing lines of worry and exhaustion. She stared blankly. I'd never seen a look like that on her face. I was confused.

I managed to croak, "Mother." There was a foul taste in my mouth.

She turned to me. I must have dreamed that empty despair in her eyes. They were warm now, full of morning light. "Ruth! That's more like it. We were worried, until the fever broke. But the infection's draining from your leg now." She rose and placed a cool hand on my forehead.

"Late?" I squinted at the window. There was something I should remember, but everything was tinged in a pink haze.

"My dear, you've been sleeping for nearly two days. What happened, Ruth? Why did you walk so far from the railcar? We haven't gotten any reply from Marda's console. Was there some sort of accident?"

I blinked. "Can't remember." I blinked again, but she kept sliding away into that pink sea. "Wind. Amber eyes . . . Sheba!"

"Hush, dear. Drink some more, it'll help. Here." She held the glass to my lips and the tang of the pale pink liquid dissolved the scratchy dust in my throat.

"Ahhh." I closed my eyes. "Love you, Mother. Really do." Something hot and stinging rolled out from under my eyelids.

"Sleep, now." Soft lips brushing my forehead. The rocker swished gently. "I know, sweetheart. I love you, too." She sang a quiet lullaby and the pink waves drifted over me.

The screen door clattered behind me and I stumbled awkwardly across the porch, boards warm and dusty beneath my bare toes. I turned to give it a crafty look and raised my fingers to my lips. "Sshhh!"

I lifted the skirt of my robe and wobbled to the porch railing, grabbing hold as the pink haze floated across my eyes again and swam out over the gleaming purple-gold fields. Sun going down. "Pretty."

I looked around me in dull surprise, but no one was there. I giggled, then hiccuped. A bounding, tawny shape loped across the yard and up the steps. "Hey, Ela!" I giggled again as he licked my hand and settled on my bare feet.

I leaned down and gave him a cagey look. "Hey," I whispered, "don't tell anybody, but I'm running away, Ela!" I giggled again and the pard lolled his tongue in the heat, thumping his tail. "You wan' come, too? Le's go. C'mon." I tugged at his furry neck and we staggered toward the steps. "Whoops!" I tripped and plunged down the steps, swinging my arms wildly.

"Hey, there!" Someone had caught me, he was holding me and laughing. "Looks like somebody ought to be back in bed. That elixir of Helen's is dangerous stuff."

I pulled back, indignantly straightening my robe. "Perf'ly fine! Jus' runnin' way."

It was Jason bending over me, helping me back up the steps, a wide grin splitting his tawny face. "Not today, young lady! Now, you just take it easy. We'll get you back to bed."

"Hey, Jason! You look pretty, smile like that. You wan' run away?"

His smile faded. "Nobody's running away, Ruth. Come

on, now.'' He held me by the arm, guiding me toward the door.

"But I wanna run! Wanna fly!'' I pulled away and lunged for the porch rail. I leaned over it, dangling, waving my arms, and they turned into wings and I was ready to go.

"Steady, there!'' He had his arm around me and he was laughing again and that was almost as nice as flying. His voice was warm and cozy. "Here, Ruth, let me carry you up.''

"But I wanna fly, Jason! Come on, let's fly!'' I struggled, trying to get back to the rail and take off. "You know, like riding the sails—out on the end of the wings, and you're spinning and twirling and the wind's laughing and you're singing with it, and the sails're all flashing so pretty, and the ground and sky're rushing like crazy around you! And all of a sudden you're part of the whole world spinning! And you're free . . .''

All of a sudden I was crying, and it wasn't funny, and I wanted to fly.

He held me against his shoulder and I cried and he made comfortable sounds and I liked it there, but it hurt that I couldn't fly. "Hush, Ruth, it's all right.''

I pulled back and looked up at him. "It's not! You don't know what I mean!''

"I do, Ruth. I know what you mean.'' And all of a sudden his eyes changed. They went from warm brown to bright amber, blazing like the eyes of the big cat, blazing into me, burning out my secrets, and it hurt. The nightmares were coming back to get me, the console blazing its amber eyes, the Founder staring out of black space and the metal monster reaching for me.

I cried out. But his eyes were closed now and I saw it was only quiet Jason, his head bent over me, his face looking like something was hurting him. It made me want to cry, but in a different way.

"Jason, I don't feel so good.'' Everything had gone wobbly.

He picked me up very gently. "It's all right, Ruth. I'll put you to bed. I'll take care of you.''

It felt good to snuggle into his shoulder and be carried all the way up the stairs and not even be afraid he might drop me. He was strong. Jason was nice, and he sat and held me close when he put me down on the bed, and it felt good to have his arms around me so warm, like he was never going to let go.

But his face looked like it was hurting again when he finally pulled away and tucked me in. "You sleep, now. Don't you worry, Ruth, I'll watch out for you, like a pateros should. You don't have to run. I'll keep Aaron from reporting you."

I didn't understand, but that made me feel better. I lay in my cozy bed and smiled up at him. "I love you, Jason."

He lowered his eyes. "I love you, too, Ruth." Only his face looked so sad when he turned away to the door.

I toyed edgily with my teacup, swirling the dregs and staring at their shifting patterns. I shoved the breakfast tray back from my chair and stared at my leg propped on Helen's pillows on a stool. The swelling was almost gone, and I felt fine, really, except I couldn't remember much beyond the pardil attack. I wanted to get up, but I knew she'd worry if I didn't stay put.

I didn't want to see that empty look in her eyes again. Somehow it frightened me more than the berserk pardil or the toneless cyber voice saying I was dead. And I'd put it there.

I shook my head restlessly and tried to think. I was about ready to duck this treacherous game, cut my losses, and head for the Spaceport. If I could figure how to do that without my IDisc. At least I was in no immediate danger. There'd been no word from Marda, so it looked like my bluff had worked. I only hoped they wouldn't be too hard on the kid, and he'd lay off his tinkering for a while. I shouldn't have gotten him involved. I'd screwed up again. David. Helen. And Jason.

He'd been up to my room for a short visit, standing in stiff, uncomfortable silence as if waiting for an answer to a question I couldn't remember him asking. Maybe I was still groggy from the elixir. When I'd finally asked him what was on his mind, he'd given me an odd look and abruptly informed me that he'd checked my violation-point status and I was well under the Healing limit. He was keeping an eye on Aaron for me, so I didn't have to worry. Before I could get past my surprise, he'd left the room.

"Ruth?" There was a tap on the door and Sam stuck his head in, smiling. "Feeling better? Something came for you, honey."

He handed me a package bound in plasseal and sat on the

bed. I pulled its tab and the tough wrapping split open to reveal several bundles wrapped in thin leather. The scent of the tanning rose to my nostrils, seductive as memory.

Anáh's crinkled face. A sharp animal cry and the jungle stirring around me. Jaréd's strong fingers on mine as he showed me how to hold my knife, how to move in the dance of the hunter.

I closed my eyes and he was still there. But I found I could look at his face now, find acceptance in his dark eyes.

"Hon? What is it?" Sam had risen from the bed to touch my hair.

I looked up at him. "It's all right, Sam. Just an old dream." Maybe I'd never belonged there, either.

I took a deep breath and set aside the wrapped shapes of the tools, unfolding the thin, soft leather around a heavy oblong. The yellow-veined crimson of miró caught fire from the sun through the window, locking flames in its translucent depths. I ran my palm over the polished surface of the prepared block. Anáh had been generous, it was a wonderful piece. I traced the grain patterns eagerly, the wood warming in my hands. I wondered what form was hidden in there for me to find.

"Sam, look!" I held it up. "It finally came. I'm going to make something for Helen."

He smiled, eyes crinkling under the shaggy gray brows. "Some fancy wood. You're going to do some whittling?" He ran a callused finger over the gold veins. "This came from the place you got hurt, hon?" He indicated my cheek.

I nodded.

His hand trembled as he raised my face by the chin. He was oddly serious, and nervous. He reached out a finger to lightly touch my scarred cheek. "Sometimes, child, it's . . ." He cleared his throat. "Well, it's best not to hold on to dreams too long. Best to see things as they are now." He looked from the scar to my eyes.

I couldn't help dropping my eyes. I reached out to sort through the tools. "Now, P'eros!" I kept my voice light. "You're starting to sound like Isaac. You don't want to be as crazy as you always said *we* were, do you?"

"Ruth," he dropped his hand, "there's something I think you ought to know. Isaac wasn't your truefather. I am."

"What? But Sam, you can't—" I broke off, staring in

confusion at his hands fumbling for a kerchief, his faded eyes so earnest above the grizzled cheeks.

"It's true, Ruth." He mopped his brow with the kerchief and stuffed it back in his pocket with a trembling hand. "I know you and Isaac had something special together, and I never minded, hon, really. I know it's a letdown to you, but—"

"Sam!" I stared at him, appalled that I could be so transparent. I pushed the tools off my lap and rose awkwardly to put my arms around him. "Don't say that! You know I love you. But how could . . . I mean, you and Helen weren't bound yet."

He patted my back and pushed me gently away. "Now, now, just hear me out, child. It's no fault to Helen, but Isaac was terrible sick, see, and it wouldn't of been right for Helen and me to bind just then, but it was like we just had to take comfort in each other. It was my fault, really, but she was so beautiful, Ruthie, like a flame she was, so young and bright and slender and full of fire. Like you, child. So much like her you are."

He pulled out the kerchief and rubbed his eyes. "Ruthie, I want you to know you'n Josh've given me more happiness than anyone's got a right to expect. But we're all your patera, you know, me and Isaac, and Aaron and Jason. We all love you. We all want to help. But you've got to move on, child. You can't cling to those dreams you used to have with Isaac. He'd tell you the same. They're like that shiny egg you gave Helen. Them dreams're pretty, but they're not real."

He patted my head and rose stiffly. He cleared his throat. "Work to do." He paused by the door. "I'm real glad you're back, hon."

I raised my eyes to his. "Thank you, Father. I'm glad you told me."

His eyes crinkled briefly in the happy grin of the picture downstairs on the hearth. Then he shook his head. "*P'eros*, now." He winked and the door fumbled shut.

I sat on the bed, staring blankly.

I shook myself, dropping to grope hastily on the floor for the scattered tools and the leather-wrapped wood. I dumped the tools over the rug, shaking them free from the wrappings. I yanked at the pliant skin on the large block and the polished oblong of mirō tumbled free into the light, gleaming crimson

and gold. I scrambled over to sit cross-legged, taking it onto
my lap and running my hands over the surface.

My eyes swam down into liquid fire, following the path of
gold veins into the deep red heart of the wood. My fingers
sought out the shapes leaping in there, waiting to be freed.

The words of Anáh's chant rose to my lips, taking me
away, taking me farther into the wood. A curve here, and
here the twisting tension of bunched muscles, here the sweep
upward of a leap into air that would be locked forever as a
promise tied to the thick, solid base of the wood . . .

The chant wound through a hazy dream, smoke winding
past licking flames of scarlet and gold, amber eyes staring
from the depths of the living wood. I was sealed in there with
them, blended into the rhythm of a heartbeat and a slow wind
that breathed somewhere outside the wood, outside the dream
where I lay enclosed within crimson and yellow veins and
waited for my form to find the air. Out there, hands chose
tools, fingers slid over the sharp blades of knives and gouges
and planers, handles fell into a palm with a satisfying heft.
Those hands turned to the wood with a feverish clarity of
focus while I waited inside, dreaming the quick, sure movements that would breathe life into me.

Only ripples stirred the surface of the dream. Muffled taps
on the door, a rustle of cloth, a murmuring voice, warm wind
billowing curtains and stirring wood dust to a shimmering
gold haze, a door opening and then sighing slowly shut. I
floated inside, weightless, rising slowly to the surface.

They were again my fingers sealing the oil bottle and
dropping the polishing rag onto the blanket. I closed eyes
seared with tiredness and listened to the hot silence of the
room. I rose stiffly to stand by the window. Past restless
curtains, sky and fields were molten copper, slowly fusing
with deep indigo. One tiny star burned high up.

I finally turned back to look at the carving, oddly dreading
it.

Two shapes grew from the twisted roots and rock that
formed the base of the piece. Wood veins crawled in and out
of the gnarled and jagged surfaces, carrying a secret spark of
life. The scaled bark of what started to be the trunk of an
ancient tree melted upward into the forked crown—two leaping creatures springing from the shared lower haunches of the
trunk.

On the right, the striped wood twisted into the sinuous gleam of a sleek ferial coiled to spring, muscles bunched beneath the oiled surface. Its upper body swept out and curved, torso twisting as a clawed arm reached back toward the center. Its head bared fangs in a snarling promise of menace to the figure that sprang away from their twinned loins.

The gizu-doe swept up to the left along the graceful curve of gold veins, all slender delicacy, her leap for freedom parting and joining the air with outstretched neck and legs. Scarlet and gold flowed into a caught breath, the vital movement of the leap, the perfect moment of spring and balance before the weight of the twinned flesh would jerk the leap to a cruel halt.

My hands trembled and light slid along the curves of the oiled wood, imparting life to the creatures. I ran a finger down the delicate slope of the doe's back, across the bunched muscles in the twisting shoulder of the ferial, down over the deep gouges of the tree roots.

I sighed and put it away. It wasn't what I'd wanted to give her. Maybe someday Helen would understand. Maybe someday I would.

eighteen

I felt my way carefully down the steps in the lowering twilight. A line of light showed beneath the swing door from the dim hallway to the kitchen.

I froze with my hand on the door, a familiar prickling running down my spine as it opened just a crack.

"Don't you think it's time, Helen? Truly?" It was Aaron sitting by the table, yanking loose the straps on his leather leggings. "Don't you see what this means?" In the thin slice of lighted kitchen, he jerked his head toward the table.

I drew in a quick breath, but I was again frozen in a dark hall, unable to move. A dusty, ripped travel bag lay open on the table, the cloth I'd gotten at the barter-day fair spilling from it.

Helen crossed before me and stroked the pearly gleam of the dove-gray cloth. "But I don't understand, dear. How did Benjamin come by it?"

"Found it out in their far field, next to our boundary. Close to an overturned rollcart. Thought it had to be ours."

Helen sank into a chair, her back to me. "But why would she have come back on a rollcart?"

Aaron flung the leggings onto the floor. "Won't you see it yet? Why do you think Marda hasn't answered?"

Mother turned slightly away from him, her face in profile to me. "Perhaps their console is down for maintenance."

He clamped his jaw and looked down at his hands. "Maybe you're right, Helen." His voice said otherwise.

"Give her a chance to explain, dear. You will keep trying,

156

won't you?'' A smile curved her mouth and she turned back to him, reaching out a hand to cover his.

He stirred at her touch and raised his eyes to hers with a look that shocked me, open as it was. His dark eyes kindled with a different fire from what I'd seen there. He reached out to touch her face, surprisingly gentle, and she leaned her cheek into his palm. Aaron stroked her hair, murmuring, ''By the Founder, Helen, you're so beautiful! And soft, like silk . . .''

She slipped gracefully away from him, rising and turning in a flirting swirl of skirts. ''Now, dear, we mustn't . . .'' But she was smiling.

He reached out to grasp her wrist and turn her back toward him. ''They'll be awhile yet.'' He was actually smiling.

She tugged lightly against his hand, her eyes bright and her face flushed with pale rose. She tugged again, teasing, and suddenly Sam's description wasn't an old dream. She was a quick flame, lighting the room, lighting Aaron's face.

He rose and took her in his arms, kissing her face and neck and lips. A wave of discomfort and shame passed through me, but I couldn't seem to look away.

Mother pulled back, her face flushed. ''Now, sweetheart, this isn't the place. What if Ruth comes down?''

I started guiltily.

He touched her face. ''So beautiful . . . How can she be your daughter, Helen, and be so far from you?'' He took a deep breath and stepped back, sat again in the chair and reached for the leggings on the floor. He looked up. ''Helen, truly she frightens me at times. She's like a demon in your guise.''

''Aaron, please.''

He reached out to finger the gauzy turquoise-blue silk, then pulled his hand back abruptly. ''Look into your heart, Helen, and admit it. She's sick. She'll never find the Way until she's Healed. She's a demon, a changer, she'll destroy—''

''Aaron, you're only upsetting yourself. The guardians protect us from demons. Trust them.''

His face suffused with blood. ''You've got to report her! She'll bring more trouble, Helen, like a serpent among us, and we won't be able to stop—'' He took a harsh breath. ''I can tell you what happened at Joshua's. If you won't hear it, I know who will.''

''Aaron!''

But he was gone into the dusk, the screen door crashing

shut. She stood looking after him, her face pale and calm. A single tear tracked her cheek.

"Oh, Ruth." She sank onto the chair, raised her hands to her face, and wept.

I fled up the stairs.

The rollcart sliced silently through dark waves of wheat, the surface rolling away in a gleam of moonlight. This time their whispered voices chanted, "Hurry! Hurry!"

I'd done all I could. It was time to escape while I still had a chance. Aaron was sure to report me. My nerves jittered with the wind-rustled wheat and the tremor, as the house and silos fell away behind and I passed the rushing, silvered wings of the first tower. It had been all I could do to lie in bed faking sleep while the family ate and finally went to bed. I had all night to make it to a village where maybe I could manage to use the blank disc to contact Officer Hodge, or steal an IDisc and get on a railcar. I couldn't think. All I could hear was the wheat and the wind, "Hurry, Ruth! Hurry!"

"Ruth!" The wheat shouted now in a deeper voice. "Ruth, wait!"

Startled, I yanked the rollcart to a halt and jerked my head around. The wheat tossed and brushed my knees, then swayed back to reveal the dark tunnel of the dirt track behind me. Someone was running down it after me. "Ruth! Wait!"

I fumbled in panic at the controls, but he was surprisingly fast. He lunged for the high bed of the rollcart as it started again. He swung, scrambled up, and dropped over the back of the seat beside me.

"Jason! What in blazes are you doing?" I yanked the rollcart again to a halt.

He took a couple of deep breaths but got his wind back easily after his amazing sprint. "Ruth"—he gave me a sideways look and took another deep breath—"you sure do give me a workout keeping up with my paternal duties." In the moonlight, his eyes gleamed and a brief smile tugged at his lips.

"What are you doing out here, Jason?" I could only stare at him in dismay.

"I was testing the emergency sprayers—can't do it during the day, you know, or we'd burn the wheat in the sun."

"Aaron—?" I grabbed for the speed switch.

He shook his head. "No, I'm out here by myself." He

gave me another look. "Why don't we take a walk, Ruth, talk about it? Come on." He jumped quickly from the rollcart and walked around the front, reaching an arm to help me down.

No. I should leave. Now.

He was waiting, calm face turned up to mine.

I sighed and accepted his hand. We walked back toward the tower in silence, following the trail of the nearly-full moon over the dark, metallic glitter of the tall wheat. The sails rustled and shifted in a rush of wind overhead.

Jason glanced at me, a quick gleam of light on his eyes. "Hot tonight."

I nodded agreement, looking down at the track. We passed the tower clearing, the tremor murmuring up through me.

"We'd best stay here. Mist sprayers'll come on any time now."

"Field Two?"

He nodded.

I picked up my skirts and stepped into the rustling stalks. "I could use some rain."

He followed me into the field, the tall wheat whispering over our heads and moonlight filtered down in crisscrossed shadows. "Ruth, you're trying to run again?"

I sighed. "Jason, I've got to go. Aaron's bound to have me sent for the Healing. I shouldn't have come back. I don't fit. It's better for everyone if I just go."

He stopped, reached into his pocket. "Ruth, won't you tell me the truth? What's happening between you and Aaron? I found this in his room when I went to borrow a set of leggings. How do you think you could leave without it?" He handed me something small that gleamed with a streak of silver in the dimness. "It's got your name code stamped on it. Why would he have it?"

"My IDisc!" I caught a quick breath. "But how——?" My hand clenched on the disc. Whoever or whatever was behind the disruptions in Poindros LS must have given it to Aaron. But why? None of it made sense. Either Aaron was a better actor than I thought, or he really believed I was a demon out to destroy the Way. Maybe he only needed an excuse to take out his fear and hate on me, a holy mission that would erase that worn passage in the Book of Words: "All these evil things come from within, and they defile a man."

I shook my head. Aaron must think now that he had every

bet covered. I turned the IDisc over slowly and clipped it back onto my chain. "Thank you, Jason. I appreciate your help, I really do. Only I don't want to get you in trouble. Please don't ask any more questions."

"Ruth, trust me. I can help. I want you to stay."

"But why, Jason? You know it won't work."

He stepped through the parting stems and stopped, looking down at me. "Do you really have to ask, Ruth?" His eyes searched my face, gleaming with moonlight, glinting a spark of amber.

"Jason, don't—" I broke off as a loud sputter rose from the ground around us, drowning out the breeze. A cool mist sprang up to enclose us.

"Oh!" The drops hit my skin, sliding with a delicious shiver beneath the back of my dress. "Phew!" I threw back my head and let the water bead on my face and trickle down my neck. "Does that feel good! Mmmm! I don't think I've actually felt cool since I've been home." I closed my eyes, turning slowly in the fresh kiss of the spray, the cleansing touch that I could almost believe would wash away the tense confusion of the past days. It soaked through my dress, cool and bracing. I twirled faster in the spray, opening my arms to it. I spun, giddy and splashing, laughing as I tripped over my wet hem.

Jason was laughing, too, soundlessly through the hiss of the sprayers. He threw back his head and swallowed the drops that gathered on his face.

"Damned if you don't beat all, Ruth! Rain in the summer!" His face was a complex pattern of moon-silvered, glistening angles and planes, eyes gleaming through the tangled light and shadow as he smiled. He had changed so quickly from the shy monotone man. Or maybe my eyes had changed.

"Ruth." He reached out, stepping forward through the mist, taking my hand. "Ruth, I can't help it. I can't be your pateros." He laid my palm against his face. I could feel tension humming like the tremor beneath the cool water and warm skin, feel something racing down my arm like an electric shock. He put my palm against his lips, his eyes fixed on mine.

"Jason, we can't do this." But I couldn't look away from his eyes. Bright amber burning through me.

Something tight inside me let go and chased jittery signals

down my arms and legs. I shivered as his hands reached up to my shoulders. His touch was gentle, as I'd seen him touch Helen, but I was lost in the fire of those eyes. The flames of my fever dream leaped at me in a roaring blaze of smoke and heat and strange twisting shapes. A pardil leaping, his eyes, the fire. Amber.

"Don't be afraid, Ruth. You showed me in the dream, we were together then, we knew each other. We can't pretend it's not there. We can't run from it." His fingers tightened on my shoulders and he closed his eyes, drawing me to him. His lips brushed mine and he murmured something I couldn't understand, then kissed me again and darkness closed around us. I sank into his warmth and the pleasure of his touch, the smooth lips on mine, the strong back against my hands, the coarse feel of his wet shirt, the cool sting of mist on our faces. I pressed closer against him and his lips eagerly answered mine.

I pulled back and caught my breath, resting my head against his chest, where I could hear his heart thudding in a pace to match mine. "Jason, this is wrong."

He raised my chin with one hand, searching my face as if eager to read his fall there. His face gleamed in the moonlight, somehow buoyant, the weight of his reserve finally lifted away. He raised his hand to slowly trace the scar down my cheek. "I love you, Ruth. It's not wrong."

Again his eyes held mine, reading my secrets. There was a wild certainty about it, as if it had to be, as if that leaping contact was a world in itself, with its own Rules. The moon sparked in his eyes and they were gold-amber, fire and sun, the wind across the glinting wheat, the beckoning flames of the dream-dance—

We were clasped together in fiery urgency and we had to find ourselves in each other, had to tear past the boundary of our separate skins and become a new being forged in flame. We tumbled blind into the mist, flinging free from our drenched clothes as we pressed together on the ground among the crushed stalks.

Behind my eyelids, a world of hot sand and searing wind spun and flamed under the explosion of a fireball sun. It burned us, fused us, melted us into one.

And then a murmur of wind and the gentle touch of rain kissing the land, flowing into a cascade of sun-bright water. Lush vines swayed rhythmically over the earth, bearing rich green leaves, as a soft carpet of grass swelled beneath us, grew and carried us floating into warm skies. All that was held like a hard fist inside me unfurled in the singing wind to shimmering wings of silver and pearl. They lifted us in joy together onto the great wheel, into its rushing music of flight, its eternal cycle, up and up, soaring and singing, and then, sighing, gently floated us down.

Jason held me close about the waist as we walked to the house. The wheat stirred and sang in the warm wind. I wanted to sing with it, give myself over to a chuckling river of delight that swelled up in me when I raised my face to his and he bent to murmur and kiss me one more time.

But I pulled back and clasped my hand in his, walking on in my heavy, soaked dress toward the clustered shapes of the barn and silos. What had been so right in the open, windy stretch of the field gathered sin to it as we neared the house.

"Jason, do you know what we've done? Broken the worst Taboo. Mother . . ."

His hand tightened around mine. "I know, Ruth. But I just can't feel it's sin. We'll talk to her. She'll understand . . ." He sighed. Or was it the wind? "We'll go away together. We'll work it out."

"Jason, you don't understand. I'm in trouble. Bigger than just Aaron. I can't drag you into it." I stopped, closing my eyes. "Damn it, Jason! I don't know. I shouldn't have . . ."

"Ruth, love." He held me tightly in the wind. "You go on in, try to sleep, and I'll go after the rollcart. We'll talk in the morning. You can tell me all about it, and we'll work it out. I want to be with you. Not just tonight. Forever."

I looked up. He meant it. Joy and misgiving struggled, tugged inside me. I wasn't ready for this. I was afraid for both of us. And Mother . . .

I turned away, watched the moon run gleaming over the rushing cycles of the sails. I faced back to him, ready to tell him no. His place was here, with Mother. But when I touched his hand and that leaping contact raced through me again, I was reaching up to kiss him and feel the fire-streaked darkness close around me, fuse us into something new. We were together, we would be a world to ourselves.

We walked on past the dark bulk of the silos, hands clasped. As we crossed the yard to the sleeping house, they dropped apart.

"Jason . . ."

"Time to talk tomorrow." He raised a quick hand to my face. "You'll rest beside me in dream, Ruth."

I shivered as the phrase echoed out of memory. Jaréd's labored whisper before his hand went slack in mine, his eyes gone blank.

Jason's fingers brushed my lips and he melted into the night.

nineteen

An occasional warm gust found its way through the window to my hot bed. I thought about what I should tell Jason. And Mother. I fought the urge to run back down the stairs, find Jason in the field, and escape with him to the Spaceport before anything else could happen to stop us. Run again. But that wouldn't be fair to Jason. He would have to decide after I told him what was happening.

I turned restlessly. My nerves still jumped to the whisper of the moon-rippled wheat. "Hurry! Hurry!"

The wind stirred the curtains and I could almost hear it. Something rattled against the raised glass. The wind sighed through the room. "Ruth!"

I shook my head impatiently and turned again.

Crack. I sat bolt upright.

Thump. Something flew through the window and landed on the braided rug. "Ruth!" The voice was faint as the wind's whisper. I leaped off the bed and over to the window just as another jagged little rock flew cracking against the glass. I flinched, then leaned out.

"Hey!" A thin little figure outlined in moonlight jumped and waved in the dark yard, topped by a tangle of wild, wiry hair and the gleam of round spectacles. A hissing whisper rose to me. "Auntie Ruth! Hoppers'n bedbugs! You must sleep like the dead." He waved again, beckoning me down.

I groaned. "Hey, kid, don't remind me," I hissed. "What in blazes are you—?" I shook my head and waved him down. "No, stay put, I'll be right down."

I threw on a housedress and moccasins and stole down the dark stairs, stopping to hold my breath when I heard a muffled snore break off as bedsprings creaked down the hall. The snoring resumed. I hurried down to the dusty yard.

"David! Fireblood and thorns, what do you think you're—?"

He looked down at a bulky cloth bundle at his feet, bit his lip, then looked up, his face thin and pale in the moonlight, eyes pleading behind the crazy spectacles.

Something twisted tight inside me. "David, you're okay!" I swooped down on him to hold him and feel him alive, know that the sharp claws really hadn't torn the life from him.

"Hey!" He wiggled free and cocked his chin up indignantly. "Don't go all mushy on me, *Auntie*! 'Sides, take it easy on the old squeeze, you know, I'm still recru . . . repurcurat . . ." He pointed to his side. "Still kinda sore."

I chuckled and rumpled his hair. "Okay, kid. But cut the *Auntie*, okay? So what's going on?"

He announced importantly, "I'm running away."

I tried not to smile. "I see that."

He sagged and sank beside his bag. "Hey, Ruth, you gotta take me with you. You're a spacer, you don't wanna stay here. Please."

I sat beside him on the dusty ground. "David, didn't you get my note? You know I'm in trouble. I don't want you getting hurt again."

"Yeah, well, I can help, you know! Damn them, they went and broke up my personalized bypass activator. Took me a whole year to scrounge parts for it!" He gave me another outraged look. "And you told them it was yours! Of all the—" He broke off and looked down, swallowed, then raised his head again and grinned. "But I brought the book. I've got the stuff to set up a bypass on your console, and I think I know how to use your blank disc so's we can find out what the cybers're up to. We gotta get out of here, Aun—Ruth! They're gonna get us if we don't. Come on!" He jumped to his feet.

"Whoa!" I reached out to grab the waist of his pants and drag him back. "Slow down a centa. Thomas said he'd keep quiet, didn't he? And I've got my IDisc back."

"What? How?"

"Jason found it in Aaron's things." I cleared my throat. "I didn't tell you before, but Aaron's in on it. He's the field agent."

''Swear by the Elder?'' The glasses gleamed and his mouth hung open. ''Jeez!'' He shook his head and gave me a frightened look. ''Then we've gotta hurry! I heard them talking back home, and Mother and Joshua''—he gave me a quick look and lowered his face—''. . . they talked Thomas into it. They said it was best they took it to the elders, about you and me and the activator and all, and maybe we'd both be better off being Healed.'' He swallowed, still looking down. ''So I zonked our console so's they couldn't send a message and shorted out our rollcarts and I got on the last railcar, but I still had to walk a ways. Ruth, we gotta get out of here!'' He reached into his pocket and held something out to me. ''I stole Mother's IDisc so's you could ride the railcar.''

I blew out a long breath, then rose slowly and touched his hair. ''Looks like we're in this together, kid. Partners, right?'' I put out the two fingers.

He grinned and pressed his fingers against mine.

''Bridge from this terminal through this relay, see? And then over to . . .'' David had both arms buried inside our console, looking like he was wired himself into the tangle of thick brown wire and metal parts crisscrossing through the sleek box. ''Hand me that current meter, okay?''

He checked the power balances while I cleaned up the clipped scraps of wire, gathering his tools into neat bundles in his bag.

''Hey, Auntie! I'll never find anything now!'' He grinned and ducked as I faked a punch.

I rose and took a deep breath, pulling the necklace from beneath my dress and detaching the wild card disc. The red-gold scales slithered through my fingers and the emerald eyes of the serpent winked. I stuffed it hastily back down my bodice. ''Here you go, David.''

David leaned on the open console as he stood up. He was even paler than usual beneath the scattered freckles.

''You sure you're all right, David?''

He dropped his hand hastily from his side. ''Yeah, no problem.''

I gave him a sharp look, then handed him the disc. ''Okay, let's see what you can do with it. Then we're finding you a place to rest.''

He didn't argue, just took the disc. "Here goes nothing."

"Don't say that. Remember last time." I pulled the stool over for him.

He grinned and activated the interface, inserting the disc. The green indicator winked into its holding pattern. "Voice mode. B.A. Code . . ." He glanced at me, reddened, and then shrugged, ". . . spacer David."

"Acknowledged." A flat, metallic voice. An amber light winked on and burned steadily.

David turned. "What should I ask first?"

"Ask why they tried to kill me with that collar on the pard."

"Collar? What collar? And whaddya mean, kill *you*?"

"The cybers sent a collar for Sheba that morning. Just ask."

He rolled his eyes. "Okay, but it's not that simple. Once you're past the first gate-level with the bypass, it doesn't talk like it would to you and me, straight out. Now, with this disc, I think what'll be happening, is—"

"David, we're kind of in a hurry here."

He shrugged. "Okay." He turned back on the stool. "Go to: Command event chain. Commence: Collar received 267XU4391. Execute: Data spill."

The amber light started blinking. "No data available."

I stepped closer. "That's what Matron Lucinda's console kept saying."

"Yeah, that's another gate. You were lucky it accepted conversation mode during that test. Lemme try something." He turned back to the console. "Hold query. Execute: Define exact value, pi."

The amber light steadied. "Working."

David grinned at me. "That always puts 'em in a dither. Like feeding it garbage, see? Kind of puts a bug in it."

I peered over his shoulder. "Doesn't it get kind of crowded in there?"

He gave me one of his outraged looks, then giggled when I made a face. He turned back to the console. "Go to: Query hold. Activate."

The amber light blinked, faster now. "Loop capacity inadequate. Transferring." The light steadied. "No data available."

David winked. "Hold query." He whispered to me, "See, if I fill up the lower levels, sometimes I can slide in. I'm gonna try something." Back to the console. "Priority execution: Read disc code. Activate: Query hold.'' He looked back at me and held up crossed fingers.

The amber light remained steady. ''Event chain: Collar delivery, 267XU4391. Timed heat sensor activation. Tracking code activation, Object Kurtis:P385XL47:Ruth. Subject behavioral modification. Object termination. End chain.''

''Oh.'' I took a deep, shaky breath. ''Ask it why—''

David swung around on the stool. ''But, Ruth, that's crazy! The cybers couldn't do that! The benevolence directives . . .''

I laid a hand on his shoulder. ''I told you, David, something's gone wrong here on Poindros. It's bad.'' I sighed. ''I shouldn't have gotten you—''

''Uhn-uh! Partners, right? 'Sides, you need me! I'm gonna crack this thing, I don't care what kinda gates they've got. So what else do we want?''

''Ask it why they wanted me dead, and why they sent my IDisc to Aaron.''

''Hey, one at a time! But *why* is harder.'' He turned back to the console. ''Go to: Event chain. Commence: Object termination. Extend event projection. Execute: Data spill.''

''Data unavailable.''

''Blast it!'' David hunched lower on the stool and rattled off commands in a low voice. I found my eyes glazing over to the long litany: data spills and codes required and query holds and data unavailable gates and loopholing with no-op commands. I stopped trying to follow it.

Finally he turned back to me. ''Ruth, they've got gates all over this stuff. That disc helps some, but your console's got some high-level loops that're reserved for the field agent. He's got a code we need.'' He shook his head slowly.

I was tempted to call it quits, he looked so exhausted. ''I know, David. I tried using Aaron's IDisc in it once, but it just said, 'Identity inconsistent,' or something like that.''

''Hey, maybe . . .'' He turned back to the console. ''Go to: Query hold, event chain projection. Activate. Authorization: Field agent.''

The amber light winked. ''Field agent identification?''

''Hold query.'' He whispered to me, ''Now, if I can just get back into that other loop . . .'' He raised his voice, ''Go to: Query hold, value pi. Activate. Execute: Data spill.''

The voice was still flat. ''Incomplete. Capacity limit.''

''Go to: Loop storage. Annex: Field agent code. Transfer:

data annex. Loop address: Temporary loop David.'' He bit his lip.

"Annex executed. Working."

David let out a long breath. "Go to: Query hold, event chain projection. Activate. Execute: Data spill."

The light winked again. "Field agent identification?"

"Go to: Temporary loop David."

The light steadied. "Authorized. Projection: Subject termination. Field agent reassignment. End chain."

"Hot damn! It worked!"

"Oh." I rubbed my eyes. "I still don't know where this is getting us. Can I ask it some questions?"

He gave me a pale imitation of his outraged look. "Jeez, Ruth, I got a bore through the gate! Well, here, I'll see if I can make it easier." He turned back. "Go to: Mode selection. Execute: Conversation mode, access and response. Security code: My Secret." He shot me a look. "That should keep anything from going out to another console."

"Proceed." The voice was recognizably female now, though still pretty flat.

David nodded at me and I took a deep breath. "What's Aaron going to do next?"

"I have no data on Aaron's intentions."

I turned to David, whispering, "I thought you said you got through to—"

He hissed back, "I did! But you've got to ask the right way. Ask about the field agent."

I cleared my throat. "What is the goal of the field agent?"

"To follow the plan of the Founder."

"What is the goal of the Founder?"

"The new evolution of humanity."

"David," I whispered, "that's what the holofac was talking about!"

David looked puzzled. "What's a holofac?"

"Maybe I should have the console play it, so we could see the end. It was a picture of the Founder, like I told you, David, only he was just a man. He said all that stuff about how he'd planned Poindros, and the other world-shapers had some sort of council that was going to prevent war, by letting the cybers watch over us, only war sounded like something humans did to each other, instead of a place in Hell. Remember, he was saying that the cybers were only machines and they'd keep us ignorant? But he wasn't going to go along with it, he was going to put himself into the matrix somehow, that it was bad to do away with what he called history."

"Well, then we've gotta talk to the Founder, Ruth! Sounds like he's the man to know. Maybe he's like us. Maybe he'll let us learn things, maybe he's just trying to change the Rules."

"Maybe, David. But who gave the order to have me killed? If he's trying to hurt people, we've got to help stop him." I blew out a breath. "But if CI stops him, then that'll put us right back in the same old Plan, breaking Rules and dodging the Steps of Healing . . ."

I shook my head. "I don't know. It's too crazy. Maybe the Book of Words is right, you know: 'In much wisdom is much grief; and he that increaseth knowledge increaseth sorrow.' Maybe we really do need the Rules and the cybers."

"For crying out loud!" David looked disgusted. " 'Fore we going flyin' off a far sail, let's at least find out what this 'evolution' stuff is, anyway!"

I nodded, then turned back to the console. "What is the new evolution of humanity?"

The voice answered levelly. "Transcendence of physicality. Incorporation of selected personality-complexes within the energy matrix of the cybernetic network. The entities will join the Founder in immortality."

"What? You mean they'll go to Heaven?"

"Heaven is only a social-patterning mythological construct."

I blinked. "Then who are the selected personalities?"

"Those humans who successfully complete the transition to entities from the intermediate-stage cyborgs."

"Cyborgs?" I blew out a long breath. "What are cyborgs?"

"Cyborgs are cybernetically constructed bodies housing the brain and spinal column of humans who have been selected for transition on the basis of deviant psychological profiles."

"*What?*"

"Cyborgs are . . ." The voice rattled it off again as a shudder of revulsion shook me. A mating of human and cyber. The ultimate Taboo. Unthinkable.

I swallowed and blotted cold sweat from my forehead. "Deviant psych-profiles? Deviant in what way?"

"Repeated inability to adapt to the Rules."

I shivered. A cold, unreasoning wave of fear rolled through me. I closed my eyes. "Is the Founder building—" I swallowed again—"cyborgs . . . from Poindros resettlers sent for Healing?"

"Yes."

Again the cold nausea. I fought a panic impulse to run. "Why? I mean, with what goal?"

"The cyborgs will penetrate Central Interlock jurisdiction and open the system network to the Founder's control."

I spun around to David. "Bloody, flaming hell! David, you know what that means? These cyborgs . . ." The wave of fear washed through me again. I could hear the CI cyberserf's voice, telling me he couldn't pass through clearance. But cyborgs, with human brains—

"Ruth! What are you doing! David! How—?"

I almost didn't recognize the choked voice. Jason stood in the cubical doorway, still wearing his damp coveralls, staring, his face completely blank with shock. His eyes were vivid amber above his set features, the pupils shrunken to pinholes.

"Jason!"

He took a deep breath and his pupils flared to normal, muting the gold flecks that made the brown look so bright at times. "Ruth," he shook himself, "what's going on? I don't understand."

I stepped over to him and took his hand. "Jason, David's run away. We were just . . ." I turned to look at the open console and David's tangled bypass wiring, at the kid's exhausted, frightened, guilty face.

"David, it's okay. He's helping me." I raised my eyes again to Jason's. "I told you I was in trouble. Well, this is part of it. I didn't want to explain it this way, but . . ." I raised a hand wearily to my eyes. "Let me try to put it together . . ."

"But . . ." Jason squeezed my hand, peering down at me, still dazed. "But I didn't realize it was anything like this. What are you doing with the console?" He stepped over to David. "Why are those indicators blinking? What did you do to it?" His broad palm slid across the scanning screen as he leaned over the console to stare in bewilderment into the open back.

"Hey, be careful!" David leaned forward to tug at his sleeve. "You might—"

Blue and amber lights shifted on the indicator board as

Jason jerked back in alarm. "What's it doing? Where's the console-Matron?"

"Oh, it's okay, it's just with the blank disc in there it operates the bypass a little different, and—"

I stepped forward. "David, I think the best way to explain is to see that Founder loop again. Can you ask the console to play it?" I took Jason's hand. I almost reached up, as Helen would have raised a graceful hand to touch his face and smooth away the worry there.

He looked down and met my eyes. "All right, Ruth, I'll listen." He had put on the old neutral, patient look. A host in the enclave watching and weighing. Maybe that was why he could love me. He was trained not to be too shocked by Rule-breaking and contraplan concepts. I only hoped he would understand.

David turned to the console. "Show us the Founder loop."

The amber light winked and the side plate slid open. But the holofac didn't appear. A soft, warmly musical woman's voice spoke instead from the grille. "Ah, I've found you! What an amusing chase you've led me, through your bypasses and capacity loops, David!" She laughed softly, her voice like a golden flute, beautiful and caressing, warm and happy. It tugged gently and I found myself smiling.

"And Ruth! I'm so glad you're here. The collar was a terrible mistake, but when our expansion through LS is completed such accidents will no longer occur. We intend no harm to the human communities. You will forgive us, won't you?" Her voice was cooling waves, soothing balm, a gentle smile in a pale, lovely face, and I would have forgiven her anything. "We've so looked forward to welcoming you among us. We've watched you since childhood, and were sure you'd return to us. Your profile is quite remarkable, you know. But then your family unit has fostered a strain of eccentricity, a promising deviation from the passive normals. David has been a fortunate aberration within his unit."

Again I could almost hear a warm smile. "And Jason. A strong addition. This is unexpected, but welcome."

The fluting, soft laughter. "But please, let me explain. The capacities of this unit are limited, of course, but I can provide a brief demonstration of the privileges you will enjoy among us. One and all with the Founder."

The voice faded and colored beams of light rayed from the side of the console, twisting and intertwining in a pearly haze where a bare glimpse of a beautiful, heart-shaped face melted into a hint of shimmering wings and then flowed outward, glistening like gold dust, to enclose us.

A tingling, hot and cold at once. An oddly familiar, charged sensation flowed down my back and raced out my arms and legs. I was floating.

''Ruth!'' As the gold haze enclosed him, David stumbled back off the stool and kicked it over.

''Da—'' But I was wrapped and floating and carried away from the cubicle. All I could see was the stool in the last milla before it disappeared. I saw it begin to fall. But just as it reached the curve of momentum into a fast drop, it lapsed into excruciating slowness. Then it stopped, impossibly balanced on one leg at a precarious angle.

The blurred outlines of the stool recrystallized with the sharpness of the schematic drawings in David's book, the edges of the stool too vivid, then the single image extended upward and downward into multiple, minutely detailed duplications of the stool, tracking the curve of its fall. At the same instant I knew the density and resilience of the material composing its legs and seat, the weight, the air displaced by its path and the velocity of the eddy current initiated, saw the one loose bolt behind a leg where the rung attached, calculated the rate at which a tiny patch of rust under the seat would spread, and a million more intimate details of the battered old stool which had been transfigured into a world, the universe of which I was omniscient. There could be no distinction between spending an instant or an eon contemplating the wealth of my knowledge of it.

The stool contracted, narrowed to a line of force, shrank to a pinpoint pivotal center, sprang and unfolded outward to the flayed metal skin of its surfaces. Curving into fantastic new shapes, it twirled and I spun around and through it, giddy with distance and speed, no grounding but my sensation, blackness and silvered shapes arcing around me. I was flying like a shot into the velvet dark.

Warmth opened into the icy clarity of space, immense distances, my awareness rushing out in all directions, following the boundaries as they exploded outward, on and on. Thin streams of light looped out of the darkness, bent and buckled, curled, rayed out from my plunge. They thickened and coalesced to fiery points, became stars rushing past me.

They circled, clustering closer, myself a soft sphere of

locality, slowing. The balls of light wavered, drifted, then blazed in at me, crashing over and into me in a fiery barrage of sensation. Pitch burning, mint, spidery stalks glowing black rays, cinnamon, musk, dankness, babbling voices, shriek and deep bass throbbing, needles, slick water, cool, purple tongues singing lemony light curvy waves drowsy green stretched sulfur sticky chiming—

Yellow. Red. Purple, turquoise, green, orange, silver, and shiny black enamel fragments rushing and assembling around me. Curves and arches.

I was the swirls of an enamelled bowl, gold veins looping through colored mosaic, around and under, at once localized and diffused, the boundary of each precise point even as I was each color. The exaltation of the wholeness of the pattern filled me. The energy of my being pulsed through the infinite veins, the vivid sparks throbbed. One random, colored fragment of that design claimed the light as I encircled it.

Blue. Hot, vivid.

The great dish of summer sky tilted over me and I slid down its curve. Thin mylar snapped in the wind, shivering glints of sapphire-silver and pearl in the spinning light.

I leaned into the dip of the sail arm and it carried me around. With a great swoop, tower and sky, brazen copper wheat and distant hills, a wisp of cloud and then more blue arched around me, more vivid than I'd ever seen them, tumbling yet clear in the roar of the huge wheel. The exact purity of the tremor of ground and wind and tower swept through me, claimed me, as the tower and I stretched our wings into the tang of the high air. Around, spinning, dancing that vital current of the world, as the earth and air turned on my axis, and the song of that murmuring harmony rose like life itself in my blood. I was singing and suddenly the words and tune were clear, as if I had turned a key and all the secrets were there.

I laughed into that music and spun to see Jason and David borne upward on the nearest arm, singing too, in the exultant air. We all smiled.

Jason swept his hand high with the sweep of the sail, sharp against the brilliant sky, and his arm was suddenly gilded, chiselled and etched against the sun. Rays flamed outward from him and he was molten gold, glowing with perfect beauty in the song as he reached out into the air.

He embraced it as the sail tossed him upward. He dove

free, arched and spun toward me, caught my hand and David's. We sprang free of the humming sail and soared through and into the singing wind, into the white gold of the sun, and now my skin glowed with that fiery precision, my hair fanned outward into the flame of blood-red heart-jewels, melded into the stretch of my wings as we flew higher and the tower dwindled away below us.

The sun and air and my throat poured forth the song Jason and David echoed beside me. It was a compelling, perfect rhythm, filling me, filling everything. It swelled to a chorus as voices joined in, an infinity of tongues singing its pure theme, complex harmony swelling to the ordered hum of a secret peace opened and all-embracing. Our joyful flight swept us into the multitude of song, the white light embraced us in its vital hum, we were one and all, singing that joy, singing that praise, singing that harmony as the light consumed us, transcendent—

Darkness. A painful inward wrenching. I was dropped cruelly from those heights to the floor of the console cubicle.

I found myself reaching automatically to catch David as he stumbled back from the stool. I froze, clutching his arm.

The stool was still falling. Its rim hit the floor with a sharp crack, bounced, and rolled in a hemispherical arc to rest at the spot I already knew with a dreadful exactness. I stared down at it, at the speck of rust now revealed beneath the seat.

Jason took my hand, his eyes gleaming as he smiled, the same smile of joy he'd worn as he'd flown free of the sail arm.

The soft, golden voice fluted from the console. "So, you see, there's no need for fear. Come join us at the Place of Healing. We wait to welcome you."

twenty

Leaves rustled overhead in the dark. I leaned wearily against the rough bark of the fan tree and shook my head again. Jason squatted on the dusty ground behind the barn, his features barely visible in its shadow.

"All right, Jason, yes, I felt my wings moving, it was beyond anything I'd imagined, I shared that song with you, I feel like the sacred Founder himself!"

"Is that supposed to shock me, Ruth?" He sounded hurt.

"No, Jason." I reached out to find his hand. "But didn't you see the stool? We felt and did all those things in the time it took for it to hit the floor. And it felt like eternity. It was too much, too fast. I don't know what to feel. I need time to absorb things, time for smells and sounds and feelings to soak into my skin. Maybe we were something better than ourselves while that lasted, maybe we really could encompass everything, or maybe the cybers were just telling us what we felt. I don't know."

David stirred beside me and craned his neck to look up at me, a dark gleam passing over his lenses. "But it was *fantastic*, Ruth! They're gonna give us what we want, aren't they? Just think about everything we could do, and no danged Rules!"

Jason squeezed my hand. "He's right, Ruth. We wouldn't be losing. It's not like we couldn't feel things, we'd feel more. Weren't you there with me? Didn't you feel that . . . *rightness* about it?"

176

"But was it *our* rightness? What are they trying to trick us into?"

"Can't you judge apart from being angry? Do you always have to fight, Ruth?"

I pulled my hand back and pressed my fingers against my temples. Damn them. How had they known what I felt about the air-dancing, how could they have made it so much more? Even my anger and fear barely kept me from accepting that glorious vision.

I rose to my feet. "I guess I do have to fight and be angry, Jason. We're *human*, damn it! Whatever we did in there, whatever rightness and reality it had—and blazes it was real!— it wasn't ours. That's not what it's like to fly the towers. There was no sweat in the hot sun, or straining muscles for the next hold, or that little jolt in your stomach when the ground swoops up at you . . ."

David stuck out his chin. "Yeah, and no getting air sick, either!"

Jason reached out and tousled his hair, then looked up at me, too. "No. And no lines tangling if you're not careful, holding you down to the support arms. No Rules to tell you you can't climb, Ruth. No need for the tower at all." He stood.

"Are you going to go, then?"

"Are you going to be afraid?" His voice was low, but level.

"Maybe I am! Maybe you should be, too!"

He hesitated, the old reserve falling between us, then laid his hand on my shoulder. "Ruth, I love you. It's a way for us to be together." He paused. "And I don't think we really have a choice. Now that we know, do you think they're going to let us just walk away?"

David scrambled to his feet. "Well, I don't care what you two do. I'm going." He swayed wearily. "Soon's I get some sleep."

Jason reached out to steady him. "Let's take him out to Tower Two, Ruth. We're done with repairs out there and no one will know. He can rest up and we'll figure what to do. It'll be day before we know it."

"All right." I sighed and started to follow David as he trudged for the rollcart parked by the barn.

"Ruth." Jason stopped me, reached up to touch my face.

"I want to be close to you, part of you for always, happy that way. Is that wrong?"

I leaned against him, felt his warmth and his heart beating slowly against my ear. "Jason, I felt the same way. Maybe that's what frightens me. Maybe it felt too much like Heaven."

He held me back and looked down at me, his eyes glinting a spark of amber through the dark. He raised a finger to trace my scarred cheek, then sighed.

"Jason, I want to climb the tower. A real tower. Would you climb with me? See which way you really want to live?"

He stood still for what seemed a long time. "All right, Ruth. I don't think we have a choice, but I'll climb with you." We walked silently to where David waited.

Hidden sun kindled fires beneath a dark horizon. The moon floated like a pale reproach toward hills that gathered its fading substance. The wind was a deep current from those hills across the dark, swaying slumber of our fields, sweeping past me up the black spire to the rushing sails. A shadowy gleam like water under ice slid down the fluttering wings.

My hand closed around the coil of mylar line hung over my shoulder and I slid my palm down the smooth strands.

Jason came up behind me and laid his hand on my shoulder as morning broke over the sharp tip of the highest arm and spilled fleeting gold down the sail. The wings rose, one after the other, to glisten against the purple dawn.

"Ready?" Jason shrugged his coiled climbing line onto the ground and felt in his pocket for the clips. He tightened the webbed straps of his safety harness, spun the spring-loaded takeup reel at his belt, and reached for the end of the line to thread it. He glanced over at me, his quick look taking in my braided and bound-up hair and the cloth tabs fastened snugly about the ankles of my coveralls.

"Just a centa." I spun my takeup reel, then clicked it to a halt with a slap against the locking bar.

I looked up at the sails, feeling the shiver of a slight skip to the tremor, seeing Sam and a young Joshua start up the spire, Isaac standing beside me with his face lifted to the wind and his eyes far away, his silver hair blown back and his stance investing the patched coveralls with a spare dignity. He finally looked down at me, where I skipped excitedly on the packed dirt, urging him to hurry. "You're got to still yourself first, child. No games up there. Really listen to what the

wind's telling you. That's it, now, slow, breathe deep of it.
Let it come to you . . ."

"Ruth?" Jason touched my arm. "You're sure you want to
do this? It might not be what you're expecting."

"I know. But I need to do it."

Behind him, a deep surge of wind moved currents of dark
bronze through the wheat. The earth carried me forward on its
cycle, its voices of air whispering secrets in my ears, its
buried music beating through rock and soil. Its hum rose
through me and suffused me with its living force.

I knelt and touched my palm to the earth, felt the tremor
loop through me, hand to feet, and smiled.

"Let's go, Jason." I led the way up the climbing leg,
stooping as I passed beneath the downsweep of the sail arms,
bracing myself against the tug of the roaring air as I hooked
both our line clips onto the ring of the lead line that ran in a
loop to the pulley high on the extension bar and back.

I separated my gloves with a ripping sound as the raised
plasmeld grips tore free of each other. The snug-fitting gloves
held the wiry line easily as I began to hand-over-hand the lead
loop and our lines paid out from our reels. As our springs
tightened against the feedout, I had to lean back to let my
weight compensate for the drag.

At last our lines were looped through the pulley and the
clips reattached to our belts. I looked up and suddenly realized this was it, what I'd been waiting for all those days and
nights wandering through the fields. I shivered in anticipation.

Jason leaned over me, flashing me a white grin. "Remember your locking bar if you get tired. You're beautiful, Ruth!"
He swooped down on me with a breathless kiss. "Here you
go!"

I staggered as the force of the spring on the taut line hit
me, and then I was flying. Up the nearly vertical, ribbed
slope of the leg. My hands grabbed air and meters of line as it
hissed into the reel, my toes barely touching and pushing off
from the steadying metal.

My heart pounded against my ribs in the pulling, thrusting
rhythm, the slight sway of the tight line, the wind whipping
me up between the spire and the high thresh of the sails. For
one dizzy milla, I was plunging down the spinning vortex of a
whirlpool and it was sucking me in. Then the pull of gravity
localized down, and my lungs began to labor with the sweet
agony of muscles straining in arms and legs.

The spring wasn't pulling as hard now. Hand over hand, straight up, toes pushing hard against the grooved ribs, hands aching, clenched and unclenched on the thin line. Sweat breaking out on forehead and back, though the hot, descending line of sunlight was still above me. Hand over hand, reabsorbing the spider filament spun up that height, pulling the weight of my mortality on shaking arms, lungs burning now and a red mist clouding my eyes. I gasped my way into the sunlight dazzle and slapped the locking bar, braced aching legs, and leaned out against the hold of the line.

The arms circled behind me, so close their passes seemed to push the air in and out of my lungs. I stretched and shook out my arms and sighted up the gleaming strand. I had made it past the midpoint.

The wheel shifted with a crack of sheet lightning in the sails. I clung to the line as a new current moved the sensitive balance of the gimballed pivot. It revolved around the shaft peak, its horizontal extension bearing the still-cycling wheel, spinner arms fluttering around each base arm in nervous realignment as the wheel steadied across the spire from me.

Now I could see, far below, the still-shadowed house slumbering among the dim, huddled shapes of the silos. Inside it, Helen and Sam and Aaron lay still in their separate cells of sleep. I could almost hear from the cellar cubicle a relentless tick, tick, counting down the centas to our ruin.

I jerked my head away and put on a quick grin for Jason below me. I flicked open my locking bar and pulled myself in a steady crawl up the vertical leg, placing my feet carefully now as the land dwindled below a closer sky. The thick mass of the extension bar finally loomed overhead and I reached up to heave myself onto the narrow platform running across its top.

Taking deep breaths, I looked out over the vast expanse of the plain and the towers striding away to the hills. My knees absorbed the shifts and eddies of wind. The tremor coursed through me now, singing with the humming air, returning like the memory of that separate balance a climber makes or finds on the towers. My blood sang with it.

Jason swung up beside me and detached our clips from the pulley loop. "Ruth! I wish you'd use the hand grips. Don't get overconfident, now."

I opened my mouth to protest, then shrugged and let him lead the way across the extension, hunching over to keep his hand on the rail. I was sure if I hadn't been there, he'd have just walked across.

In Jason's wake a smaller figure took ghostly shape. Joshua's blocky adolescent form marched deliberately across the bridge, feet placed squarely, defying a slight shift, scorning the rail, though his arm was held stiffly toward it. Isaac squatted beside me, chewing on the grass stem he'd held bobbing between his lips for the climb up. He plucked it out and let it drop lazily over the side, watched the sail's gust whip it up and fling it out and down.

He tilted his head toward Joshua's back and gave me a questioning look.

I spread my fingers over the bony knees pushing against grass stains on my too-short coveralls. "Josh's a good climber, Isaac. He never makes mistakes." My voice made it a question.

His eyes crinkled in the tanned-leather face. "Helen's voice. You see it, though. Don't mean a judgment on him, you recognizing it, Ruth. What do you see?"

I hesitated and took a deep savor of the wind, tasted the push of the eddies in it. "Well . . . he doesn't *feel* it, does he? I mean, he should have known that gust was coming, shouldn't he? He keeps ready, but it's like he has his eyes closed . . ." I blurted it out.

"That's right. You've got that sense of it he doesn't know he's missing. Long as you listen to yourself and the wind, you're right as shine up here. You've got the love of it. But that's no reason to give yourself airs over Joshua, it just fell out that way."

I looked down and nodded, twisting at the loose fabric. "But it's not fair!"

"I know, child." His hand was on my head. "But I've put some thought in on it lately. There's other kinds of balance. Maybe you and me, we've just got to feel them out." He looked out over the far hills, and I knew he was thinking we'd both soon have to give up the high air. He shook his head. "Funny how things fall out. Take Aaron. He's got a touch of it, you can see by the way he moves on the sails, but he won't see it. He don't want it. He'd rather rely on the dials and forcing things into the right place."

"Aaron!" My eyes jerked defensively away.

"Don't hate him, child. Come on," he chuckled, "let's go do your air-dance . . ."

Isaac's voice faded into the gusty exhalation of the sails. I rose and stretched arms over the waking stir of the fields below, moved into the accelerating shift of the wheel, and skipped across the extension to where Jason waited.

He gave me an alarmed look.

"Jason," I shouted, "it's okay! I'm all *right* up here!"

He sighed. "Okay. Pick an arm."

The huge hub of the wheel turned behind him in a rumble of wind, raying outward the eight massive base arms. I started to reach past Jason for the handholds on the hub, then stopped. Again I felt the jagged little skip to the tremor.

"Jason, one of the sails is off." I closed my eyes, felt out the source of the disruption. "There. That one."

"But how can you—?" His voice was lost in the wind as I scrambled onto the hub, moving quickly up on the grips to be clear of the extension as the hub carried me around.

I blinked and emerged into the clarity of that transformed perspective, no longer crawling down—sideways—up—on a spinning surface, but stable, as the tower and sky and grain fields whirled around me. Taking a curved path across the rungs dotted over the surface of the hub, I moved out to the base arm of the imbalanced sail. It dropped through the bottom of the cycle and started climbing, and I walked up the rungs to where the spinner arm attached and stretched the widening wedge of sparkling sail.

I sat and hooked one knee around a rung as the arm crested and dropped again, whirling gleaming copper fields and blue sky around me. I raised my arms and let the wind sweep them around with the rush of the wheel. "Whoo-wheee!"

I laughed and reached over to the slip rings, working them slowly into place as I closed my eyes and felt the little jar smooth out into a level hum.

"There!" I opened my eyes and smiled at Jason, who'd climbed down beside me. "It's wonderful, isn't it? Like coming home . . ." I broke off suddenly.

I jumped up and turned to run down the arm, running straight for the gleaming end of the sail and the sky beyond it as the arm climbed. When it crested, I grabbed the next rung and used the downward momentum to swing out from the arm and over, landing tucked and rolling to grasp another rung. I swung out again, flying now in the accelerated whip near the outer rim of the wheel, as the dip pulled me downward, stretched and clinging, then rolled me up again and I tumbled back toward the hub. I was humming now, singing the wordless song of the wind and the tremor and the threshing sails as earth and sky tumbled around me.

"Ruth!" Jason, crouched on the base arm, reached out to seize my wrist. "Are you crazy? You could get killed that way!"

I leaned over to speak against his ear. "You're hurting my arm." I flexed my wrist as he loosened his fingers. "Please, Jason. This is my last chance up here. Be happy with me?"

"But you're so wild, Ruth!"

I laughed and gave him a quick kiss. "Bet you can't catch me!"

I scrambled up, timing my turn to the crest, then dropped away from him in swinging passes down the arm. As it neared the bottom, I grasped a rung with both hands and tried a handstand, kicking up and resting against the wind, then letting the drop sweep me out and down, stretched from my fingers to toes. I scissored my legs, walking over in the air to hook one moccasined foot into the next rung, kicking up with the other in an arched split, poised in extension and ready for a leap into free air.

I let the climb of the sail be my leap. Sweeping my arms out and around to the side, I rolled forward past the rung, grabbing the next one and twisting around to see Jason leaping after me, moving fast. He was good.

I scrambled to my feet, trapped out on the whipping end of the arm. He slowed and a smile split his face as he reached out to grasp my arm.

But I could feel a wind eddy coming. If I could time it just right . . . It hit us just as we reached the dip, and I took an added spring from it as the sail swept up, transforming up to down as I leaped spread-eagled over Jason's hunched grip on a rung. He cried out and whipped an arm after me, but I was past him, swinging down toward the hub.

I landed near it, laughing as tears streamed from my eyes in the wind. I dropped across a few meters of empty space, took a spring from the wide base, and reversed direction again with a backward spring into a tucked flip through the air, to land on the next arm over. I rolled, grasped a rung, and calculated my lead would give me time to—

A jolt of dead air behind me as Jason flew in a spinning arc across the wider gap of the arms, a daredevil leap without the use of the holding line. He was grinning, and I paused in surprise that he'd be so reckless. He grasped the rung next to

me without even looking and reached out to snatch my ankle
and drag me next to him.

"Jason! Man, you're good!"

"You little demon, let's see you get out of this!" He
laughed, eyes narrowed below the hair tossed back as the arm
began to crest again.

He yanked on the clip of his climbing line, whipping the
line around to wrap us together. He snatched up my clip, too,
and quickly hooked us down onto the rungs. The arm tipped
past the top and began its steepening thrill of descent. We
rolled together against the lines and the windy cycle caught us
up.

I pretended to fight, kicking against the tangled lines. We
were both laughing now, the wild air whipping the sound
away as we grappled like pard pups in the rushing tumult of
earth and air. We fell and the wind took my breath as the sail
dipped and then climbed. He was under me now and my
weight pushed me against him. I could feel the hard lines of
his body beneath the loose coveralls. We were borne to the
crest again and the sun struck sparks from the taut, silver-blue
mylar.

Jason worked an arm free of the lines and pulled me tighter
against him. My heart pounded in the wild uproar of wind
and streaming colors, all blending into a hot surge of pleasure. I cried and was silenced as Jason's mouth joined mine
and we were linked by a crackling current of fire.

We were flying. I could feel each heartbeat of Jason's as if
it were my own, pounding madly. The raging howl of the
high air in the sails swept us free of gravity.

My hands closed over the lean muscle of his thighs and
tore at the fabric. The cling-strips ripped open, his warm skin
tingled against mine, and we were lost together in the cycling
chaos. The earth spun us away and we grappled and fought
and found each other in a violent merging. The wind finally
tore my cries from me and he groaned and subsided against
me as the hum of tremor eased through us.

Time stopped.

Wind roared outside a smooth, gleaming crystal of silence.
We were held in the embrace of pearl wings. The wild
struggling fell away from us and Jason lifted a hand to stroke
my face in a cherishing gesture. There was eternity in his
glowing gold-brown eyes. We rested in the warm joining of

ourselves, in a strange peace, still borne on the whirl of the wheel.

But the other world waited out there, and finally it stirred us. Jason held me tighter a moment, then sighed and loosened his arms. We disentangled ourselves from the climbing lines. I turned and laid my hand on his, raising my voice over the thresh of sails, "Jason, I know this isn't fair, but I have to know what you've decided. Yes or no to the cyber entities?"

The wheel shifted and he was a dark silhouette against the bright splash of sun as it tumbled away from the hills into the blue zenith. He shook his head. "I guess you're right, and this is our way. But it doesn't change anything. We still don't have a choice. How could we fight the cybers?"

"Jason, I was trying to tell you. There are different cyber networks, and these cyborgs and entities are only part of the Poindros system. There's a network called Central Interlock, and they sent me home in the first place so I could spy for them. We've got to get to the Spaceport and warn their agent there."

"What!" Jason had the blank look on his face again, his eyes glinting startled bright amber. "They knew? But how—?" Maybe it was too much for him, all these shocks at once.

"Jason," I touched his face, "we've got to try to stop them. That vision, or whatever it was, felt good, but I think it's wrong. The Founder and those entities, they're using people."

"But, Ruth, all the things they've done, even trying to have you killed because you wouldn't go along to the Healing. What if you fight them and they start more trouble at the farm? What if they say they'll hurt Helen? They could do that."

"Don't you see, Jason? It's more than just you and me, more than Helen! It's David, and Miriam's friend, and that little Anduran boy . . ." I shook my head at his bewildered look. "What they're doing isn't right. You know how much I love Helen. I don't want to hurt her any more, but I've got to fight them."

"I see." He dropped his eyes.

"Jason, I'm sorry. I can't make the choice for you or David. But I know I'd rather be dead than like them."

He raised his eyes and they were a bright, painful amber, searching mine. "You really mean that, don't you?"

I nodded, then scrambled to my feet on the rising rung.

''We should get back before they wake up, Jason. But first I want to make a jump between sails. Just one last time. Will you man my line?''

He sat still. He finally nodded, his face grave. ''All right. I'll help you.''

He said nothing more until we stood braced halfway out the arm, the clip of my climbing line hooked onto a rung, the free line we had paid out coiled in Jason's tense fist, ready to be flung after me as I leaped. The line would catch me if I fell, but it was still risky, and I knew he didn't like it.

He kissed my forehead as if I were made of porcelain. ''Ruth, always remember that I love you.''

''Jason, take it easy!'' I couldn't keep the excitement out of my voice. I poised on the edge of the arm, breathing with the rush of the cycle, waiting for the dip, feeling the wind, feeling the tremor flow through me. ''Here I go!''

I rode the upswing of the arm, rose and ran with its acceleration, thrust out and away from the bellied silver of the sail. I embraced the air with my outstretched arms.

It was all I'd waited for.

The wind taking me. The sun a glory on the earth and sky and wings of living pearl. Flying, singing that wild song of light and air as I became part of it, for a moment, for eternity. Freedom in the arched perfection of the cycle, at one with the high wind. Free, in the air, in the time of splendor—

It was like a club hitting me, the sudden cruel tug that jerked me out of the exact, beautiful curve of my leap.

I tumbled crooked, sideways, arms flailing at the line that had whipped suddenly upward on my harness. My mind spun in shock—a sudden gust? No, it couldn't be—I twisted as I saw I would miss the next arm, shot a look upward to glimpse Jason frantically and desperately lunging outward to catch at the gleam of the escaping clip. The sun flashed on the useless loose coils as they fell after me.

I gasped. Cold waves of panic roared over me. The wind sucked my breath away. I flailed and tumbled, reaching, clawing the air. But the sail flashed by me, it was too late, I was falling out from it, in a milla I would smash by the next one into the ground. My mouth opened to scream.

Wait, child.

Listen.

It was Isaac's voice, it was the wind in the wheat, it was my own voice shaping the dream world for Jason in his terrified nightmare.

A hush enveloped me, and I was held in a drop of light. Time held its breath, held me somewhere beyond it.

A slow, windy tune began behind my eyes, wound outward in the breathy notes of a flute, rose into the hum of taut strings, a lyre throbbing with earth-tremor and the whispering voices of earth and sky. I opened my eyes and the next sail rose in a gentle drift toward me, like a pearl-glinting feather in the wind. I was a feather, riding the eddies of the singing breeze. The song tugged, and I reached and turned and flowed into its dance, following its currents.

Crack! The sails snapped and time raced again. Mylar flashed in the sun, whipping upward as the sail arm roared through the wind. The earth spun and tumbled in a blur toward me. The arm shot higher.

But I was above it now, as the spinner shifted in a wind eddy and I reached to brush it with my fingertips. I couldn't grab it. I slipped, rolling and flopping down across the expanse of sail. It stretched with my weight and slowed my fall. My hands grasped a rung as it tumbled me into the base arm. My arms wrenched against the speed of my fall. I jolted to a stop.

I clung to the arm, stroking the metal idiotically as if it were a living thing, part of gentle pearl wings that swept me around and around through the sky.

I only registered in a daze my hands coiling the dangling line and winding it back into my reel, Jason's white face and his frantic questions as he swung down to me, the slow climb back down the leg of the tower to the ground. I stood, looking up at the glistening sails, feeling the tremor, hearing the wheat whisper and almost understanding its song now.

I turned to Jason and smiled. "But it wasn't your fault, Jason. Just a faulty clip. I'm all right."

"Oh, Ruth!" His face was still stricken. He reached out and clasped me tightly against his chest. "Ruth, are you sure you don't want what the cybers are offering? Life is so short. You wouldn't have to die, Ruth, ever."

I could feel his distress, but it couldn't penetrate the strange calmness flowing up and through me. "It's best this way, Jason. Come on." I took his hand and gently urged him over to the rollcart facing toward the house. "We have a lot to do."

twenty-one

But it was too late to hurry.

Morning was well under way by the time we parked the rollcart behind the barn. They would know we'd been together in the fields. Jason took my hand as the light of the kitchen windows reached out to draw us in.

There was, after all, only Sam sitting at the kitchen table, waiting for us. Only the ghost of Helen's face wavered in the air between us and dissolved as I hesitated, clutching the screen door. Jason touched my shoulder and eased me into the room. Sam looked up over hands curved around an empty tea mug.

His eyes passed from me to Jason, then dropped. He nodded wearily, as if giving in to a final argument.

He tilted the mug, studied it, raised it to sip a last imaginary drop, and pushed it away to the center of the table. I sank into the chair opposite him.

Jason scraped back the chair next to mine and sat, placing his palms on the table top. Their vitality was a shout in the defeated silence of the room. Those hands, big, calloused, grime worked into the creases and under the nails—I could feel them tracing the careful curve of my neck and jaw, hear them telling the mute walls how they'd cupped my breasts. Sam fumbled for the mug again and Jason's right hand reached out to cover his.

Sam's eyes jerked up to meet Jason's, the washed-out blue tired and at bay. "Boy, how could you do this to Helen?"

"Sam, please." I reached across to him, but he hastily withdrew his hands.

"Sam!" I moved around the table and crouched beside his chair, pulling one of his hands into mine. "Sam, will you look at me?"

He sighed. "Oh, hon, how could you do this? I've been trying to give you room, trying to understand, but this . . ." He shook his head. "I didn't believe Aaron, thought he was just talking more words and retribution. But I guess even an old fool like me can see it now." He looked away to the wall, blinking.

"Sam . . . Father, please—"

"Sam." Jason's voice was quiet. "Please forgive us. Ruth tried to fight it. It was more my fault than hers. We didn't want to hurt Helen, you know that. But we love each other. We're going to leave together. That'll be best." He turned to look at me, his eyes steady on mine. "We'll leave together, Ruth."

Sudden relief washed through me. Even if we didn't make it to the Spaceport, he was with me.

Sam stood abruptly and pounded his fist on the table. "By the Founder, who'll it be easier for? You're just running again, Ruth! And you think you can do this to Helen, to the sweetest, most loving woman you ever saw, and just wait for her to forgive you? Well, I'm not gonna sit back and let you hurt her like this, I'm gonna . . ." He swallowed, looking down at the table and blinking furiously.

I rose. "Sam, try to understand. I didn't do all these things to hurt any of you, but there's something happening here, something bad, and I had to . . ." I closed my eyes. "Damn, it's all happening so fast, I don't know . . . You see, the cybers—"

He shook his head. "I don't want to hear it. We were happy here, Ruth. We don't want all this upset and sin— don't matter what you call it, it *is* a sin to hurt people the way you have. And now Helen. It's wrong." He broke off again, fumbling for his kerchief.

"Easy, Fr'eros." Jason came around the table and put his arms around Sam.

Sam drooped suddenly against him. "Blazes, boy, I just can't . . ." The rest was muffled.

I slowly rose, touched Sam's shoulder, and kissed his bristly cheek. "I'll go talk to Mother."

Jason moved as if to come with me, but I shook my head. His eyes followed me as I pushed through the swing door to the hall.

I climbed the stairs slowly and turned at the top, knowing where she'd be. I paused outside the door to my bedroom, fingering my snake-scaled necklace nervously. I stuffed it and the discs back beneath my coveralls and reached for the knob.

"Come in, Ruth."

I sighed and opened the door. Why did she always have to carry that aura of light with her? My careful phrases fell to dust and were drifted away in the breeze through the window. This time the halo was a literal one, morning light enclosing her in a diffused glow that struck warm fire from her hair. She sat in the old rocker, her hair still down and spilling bright copper over her shoulders, the length of pearl-cloth unfolded over her knees. She was stroking it absently as I stepped into the room. Subtle glints of color whispered through it. It had already taken on the lustre of her beauty, as I'd known it would.

She folded it and looked up to me, her face set and pale, eyes very green. "It's lovely cloth, Ruth."

"It's for you, Mother."

"Oh." She looked down at it, disconcerted. She rose quickly and moved to the bed, where I saw she had started packing an open travel bag. "I didn't want you to forget the important things this time. I've packed your lyre. I couldn't bear to see it . . . to see . . ." She turned her back abruptly.

"Mother." I touched her shoulders and turned her around. Her eyes were bright with tears. "Oh, Mother, I'm so sorry. I didn't want to hurt you. Please believe me."

"I know, dear. I thought this time you would learn to accept, but . . ." She dropped her eyes. "Perhaps it's a judgment on me, for my youthful errors. I've tried to atone, I've tried to be the best mother I could be to you, and accept it when by the Founder's grace I wasn't allowed more children. Ruth, I was like you, I was headstrong and impulsive, and I—"

I touched her shoulder. "I know, Mother. Sam told me. But, Mother, how can you blame yourself for something like that all these years? What you did wasn't wrong. *You* didn't hurt anyone." I cleared my throat.

"Ruth, we can't take those judgments on ourselves! Can't you see yet what comes of parting from the Way? I just don't know what more to do for you," she whispered. "It's hard. So hard." She touched my cheek and searched my eyes. "Ruth, maybe Aaron's right. I would never force you, you know that, but perhaps you should let the cybers Heal you. I've tried to understand, but everything you've done since you've been home seems so destructive, so hostile, so . . ."

"Sick? Evil?" I sighed. If I tried to explain, it would only put her in danger. "Mother, that's why I have to go. Aaron's right, I guess, I am the serpent here, I am a changer. I can't follow the Way, but I don't want to be Healed. I don't want that kind of serenity. Is that wrong? Do you think I should let the cybers erase all my parts that don't fit? Wouldn't it be better to have a Plan where people could be a little different?"

She dropped her eyes and shook her head. "You've gone beyond me, Ruth. I can only pray for you. I know your heart is good, and perhaps some day you'll find the Way."

She turned away and stood looking out the window. "Is Jason going to leave with you?"

I nodded, then cleared my throat. "Yes."

Her hand clenched in the curtain, then slowly released it. "Perhaps that's best." She turned back to me, her face like smooth, seamless marble. "He'll help you, Ruth. He's a good man."

"I know, Mother. I love him."

She moved past me to the bed and started to close the bag. I put my hand over hers and stopped her. I could feel it trembling. "Wait, Mother. I made this for you." I pulled out the wood carving, looked at it again, and handed it to her. "It wasn't what I meant it to be. I wanted to give you something beautiful, to tell you . . . I don't know. Do you want it?"

She sank with the carving back into the chair, looking down at the gleam of sunlight on mirō. Light ran in agitated sparks down the crimson and gold veins as her hands shook again and the twinned creatures came alive. They struggled to tear free of each other. The gizu-doe sprang in her bid for freedom that would never be. Sun glared from the ugly snarl of the ferial as Helen dropped the carving into her lap and covered her face with her hands.

It hadn't occurred to me before to think it was ugly. I took the carving from her lap and sat on the arm of the chair, stroking her hair. She leaned against me, still crying.

I whispered against her bright hair, "I do love you, Mother. Wherever I go, I'll still love you. I'll think of you clothed in beauty and robes of pearl. Did I tell you what they say on Sethar about that cloth? It tells the truth about the person who wears it, a mirror of the soul, they say, and they tell about the time when Ahriana of the hundred pearl-cloth veils came to reveal the truth hidden in dream. She was too beautiful for mortal man, and so they ran, hiding their faces from her light. And now they must seek it in the shadow of smoke and fire . . .''

The wind was like the breath of a blast furnace down in the yard as the sun burned higher. It tugged at my hat and whipped my skirts around my legs as I reached my bag up to Jason in the back of the rollcart. He stowed it, smiling briefly over my surprise at the bulkiness of his own bag.

"I took David's wires and things back out of the console. Thought they might come in handy." He gave me a sheepish look and pulled a length of thin black wire and a relay unit out of the bag, holding them up. "Took these, too. Figured that'd put the console-Matron out of commission, give us a little lead time to make it to the Spaceport." He jumped down beside me.

"Jason!" I gave him a crooked smile. "You're getting positively wayward, you know that?" I sobered. "Was it too bad, with Helen?"

He touched my face gently. "I think she'll come to understand in time, Ruth. She's a remarkable woman."

I looked up in surprise. "Yes." I cleared my throat. "We'd better hurry, Jason. I don't know where Aaron's been lurking, but I'd just as soon avoid him."

"I'll be right back. I'll just pull a few connections to put the other rollcarts down for a while." He disappeared into the machine shed.

I paced nervously back and forth, fighting the tangling skirts. I looked out over the fields, at the wheat thrashing in the hot, rising wind, at the flowing patterns of molten copper against bright blue, and hoped another wind storm wasn't working up. I sighed and turned back.

"Oh!"

"Demon whore!" Aaron grabbed my wrist. "Do you think you're going to escape me this time? You and the boy you've corrupted? I warned him. I told him to beware the wiles of Jezrial, but he wouldn't listen! You serpent of sin!"

He brought his face closer, lips writhing, eyes dark and

gleaming. "Laughing at us all, are you? Think you can stop me reporting you? Well, it's too late! I talked to the Matron before you came back, and you're going to be Healed, you and your partner in sin! You won't escape retribution for all you've done against the Way." He dug his fingers harder into my wrist.

"Aaron, stop it." I twisted my arm but couldn't break free. "Aaron, there's no point in this. We're leaving—isn't that what you want?"

"I've been watching you, you and Jason. You can't fool me. I know you're part of it, trying to go against the cybers and the Rules and tear down the sacred Plan. I tried to tell Helen about you and David and Isaac and the others, but she wouldn't listen. She's like all the rest. They won't see the demons closing in. But I'll stop you, by the sacred Founder I'll—"

"Don't give me the sacred Founder, Aaron! You know what's happening. You know the Founder was only a man! Everything you say is a lie. You tried to help them kill Jason and me, didn't you, just like you killed Isaac? Well, what do you think those cybers are going to with your precious Plan, Aaron? They're going to tear it wide open, and you don't even see it!"

"What?" He fell back a step. "What blasphemy on your lips now? I won't hear it, I won't heed the voice of the serpent! 'Demon, get thee behind me!' You whore, you're an outrage, a demon with her face, you're sick!"

"No, Aaron, you're the sick one!" I followed him as he backed away, all the rage finally boiling up in me. "How can you pass judgment, you murdering hypocrite? Don't make me your penance! You can't hide behind your Book of Words. I can see you shaking in fear of the sin inside you! And even Helen can't make it better, can she? All she can do is love you, be good to you, and there's no one but me you can goad into hating you, into pounding and whipping that guilty sinner, Aaron, that twisted demon inside you—"

"No! The demon is *you*! You're the temptress, Jezrial, the black angel in her guise!" His face was purple now. He was breathing heavily. "You're not fit to say Helen's name!" He hit me hard across the side of the head.

My ears rang and a red mist boiled in rage across my eyes. "Damn you, Aaron!" I flew at him, clenching my hand into a fist and swinging as hard as I could at his hateful face.

His head snapped back and he looked momentarily stunned. Then he grabbed me and shook me. When I looked into his eyes I was suddenly afraid. They were fixed and staring. He was past hearing reason. His lips twisted, close, teeth gleaming as his fingers dug cruelly into my shoulders and he spoke in a horrible, quiet whisper, "You whore, whore of Babylon. Jezrial, black angel with your traps."

He yanked me against his chest, pinioned me with a powerful arm while the other hand clenched in my hair and jerked my head back. His mouth fell onto mine, his teeth cutting my lip. I tasted the sharp, salt tang of blood as I kicked against him and he pinned me tighter, bearing down on me with a strangled cry, pressing his lips against mine, grinding into me.

For a horrifying milla, something hidden deep inside me answered him, pressed my body into his overwhelming hunger. Then a wave of revulsion shook me and I gathered myself into a tight knot of fury. I lashed out, jabbing with my elbow, kicking, bringing my knee up into his groin.

But he blocked me, throwing me back and flinging me away as strands of my hair tore free in his grasp. I spun onto the ground, stars of pain dancing before my eyes, tangled in the whipping skirts, scrambling back as he came after me again.

"Aaron! Stop it, man." Jason stepped quietly between us.

Aaron whipped around and went into a crouch, hands held forward. "Ah! What's wrong, boy? You look pale. Afraid? Or are you sick, seeing the mark of sin on that whore?"

He moved closer to where Jason stood calmly, the amber gleam of his eyes flicking quickly to me and back to Aaron.

"Aaron, this isn't the way . . ."

"That won't help you now, boy! I'm going to stop you, all of you!" Aaron jumped forward in a cloud of dust, clenching his fist for a blow. Jason wasn't ready.

"Flaming bloody hell!" I scrambled to my feet, running after him, swinging my joined fists for a blow to the base of Aaron's neck, if I could only find the right opening. I dove into the dust of the shuffling feet.

But it was already over.

All I saw was the blur of Jason somehow moving under Aaron's attack and grasping him by the throat with one long arm, Aaron's face purpling and his powerful arms flailing empty air, then going slack. I couldn't believe it. But Jason was gently lowering Aaron's unconscious form to the ground while I stood foolishly gaping, my feet braced and hands clenched for the aborted swing. I lowered my arms and stared down at Aaron's slack face as his chest drew in rasping breaths.

Jason touched my shoulder. "Did he hurt you, Ruth?"

"No, I'm all right."

"Then we'd better go, before he comes to."

I still stood, looking down. "How under the stars did you do that? He's so much bigger than you."

He gave me a brief smile. "I've got my little tricks, too, Ruth. They trained me, at the enclave, in case there was ever trouble. Come on, now, he'll be all right."

"But Jason, he said he reported us for Healing, before you got to the console! He was talking so wild, I don't think he knows what's really happening. He must really believe he's only protecting the Plan. But how could he have—"

Jason shook me gently, looking alarmed now. "No time for that now, Ruth!" He hurried me over to the rollcart and almost threw me into the front. "We've got to hurry!" He jumped into the driver's seat and jerked it into high speed.

"Maybe we should ask him some questions."

"No time." He turned onto the track to Tower Two. "Leave him. He can't do anything more."

But Jason was wrong. When we hurried up the steps from the controlroom of the tower, dragging along a sleepy, protesting David, the air had a bitter sting to it. The wind shredded a dark cloud of smoke past us. A line of flame roared between us and the monorail line, whipped along by the wind.

"Fireblood and thorns . . ." I froze, staring in dismay as the flames billowed and exploded through tinder-dry wheat, sparks flying and scattering more fires in the hot wind.

Jason stood stiffly, his face blank, stunned. "Aaron. He must be mad."

David broke free of us and scrambled onto the rollcart. "Holly shit! It's headed for Tower One! What's wrong with the emergency sprinklers?"

"Jason! You just tested them. Aaron must have—"

Jason jumped up onto the rollcart beside David. "Wind's taking it back around us! It's moving fast! We'll be surrounded if we don't make a run for it. Hurry, Ruth! I think we can get out around Tower Three and still make the railcar when it stops.'' He jumped back down and grabbed my arm, dragging me up into the rollcart. He swung the stick and headed for the gap, racing a line of advancing flames.

"Jason, wait! Look, over there!'' I stood, clutching the back of the seat as the wind tore my hat off and whirled it away. "Look!'' Behind us, through the licking flames and smoke, I caught a glimpse of a dark figure moving through the wheat.

Jason jerked the rollcart to a halt and peered through the haze of smoke.

"There! It's Aaron!'' David coughed and scrambled up onto the rails of the rollcart bed. He craned and pointed.

The wind whipped and flattened the flames and I could see him again. He was in Field Two, between us and the house, hurrying toward us through the wind-tossed wheat with an oil can in one hand and a torch in the other, thrusting the burning torch into the wheat in wild jabs, trying to complete the circle that would trap us. I could almost see his eyes burning in fierce fanaticism with the flames of his righteous revenge. But he hadn't looked around him. The gale had carried sparks around him, encircling him and cutting off his own escape to the house.

"Jason, he must be out of his mind! If he's turned off the sprinkler system, it'll get to the house soon! We've got to go back to the tower and get hoses! We can still save him and try to stop it!''

Jason searched my eyes. "Ruth, you don't owe him anything. This is your chance. You and David take the rollcart to the monorail, get away while you can. I'll get the hoses and break a path through to the house. We'll stop it. You go now.'' He jumped down from the rollcart and ran for the tower.

"Criminy, Jason, wait!'' David yelled after him. "Jeez, that guy can run!'' He scrambled into the driver's seat. "Maybe I can fix the sprinklers, Ruth!''

"Good thinking, David! Come on, get this thing turned around! They'll need our help.''

Jason had already lugged up two of the heavy coils of hose from the controlroom by the time we parked the rollcart back in the tower clearing. The fire was a roaring monster now, throwing out furious claws in the wind, breathing out its acrid, stinging breath. The wheat field was a rumbling orange mass, twisting and belching up thick clouds of smoke and sparks. Overhead, one touched a sail and a ragged hole melted into the mylar.

"Jason! We've got to keep it back from the tower. If we lose the sails, we'll lose water pressure for the hoses."

"Ruth, go! Get away! Please!" He yanked the hoses loose and connected them.

"No! We've got to help, Jason! Can we get to Aaron?"

"I think so." He paused to give me a despairing look, then jerked the hose end over to clamp it into the tower water outlet. "All right. Get more hoses. And take off that skirt!"

David and I were running for the controlroom before he'd finished. David was already opening panels and flicking switches before I'd torn off my dress. I jerked on coveralls and grabbed a heavy coil of hose, staggering up the steps with it. Jason passed me going down and bounded up behind me carrying two more.

"Here, you take the first line and start on the left. I'll hook these up and come in behind you. We'll break through to Aaron, and then I'm sending you back to the house to get Sam and Helen. If David can't get the sprinklers on, we'll send Helen to the village and—damn! I put the rollcarts down!"

"We'll send David on this one. Ooof!" The hose bucked and nearly knocked me over as Jason turned on the pressure. I adjusted the spray and gripped harder, moving slowly forward. "Okay!"

I fanned the water slowly back and forth as I advanced against the flames, but the wind fought me all the way. My face was burning and soaked with sweat. The blaze was frightening now, a menacing roar beneath the snapping lick of the whipping flames. Jason came up behind me and passed ahead and to the right, the water pluming and spraying in the wind as he slowly pushed back the flames. But it was racing ahead of us, toward the house. I didn't know if Aaron was there, or if he'd already been consumed. Once I thought I heard a cry over the roaring, but it had no more meaning than the snap of the fire and the screaming wind.

I was moving through a dream, a fevered nightmare of twisting demon shapes of smoke and leaping flame. In the center of the blaze, a huge eye seemed to take shape, watching me, its iris a writhing mass of crimson and gold flames. Watching me and waiting.

"Ruth!"

My head snapped away from the nightmare blaze and I saw Jason had broken through into a patch of unburned wheat. I worked my way toward him, widening the wedge of soggy, burned stubble as the fire roared away to the side.

"Aaron! Aaron, this way, man!" Jason was shouting, spraying his hose to the left.

It was too late. The circle of fire had nearly closed. A dark figure turned, silhouetted against that roaring orange mass, bent over, coughing. He ran toward us. But a finger of flame reached out for him past the range of Jason's hose and fiery stalks showered down over him.

I couldn't hear him scream above the raging fire. He was writhing, running, twisting, a human shape of agony in flame. Jason and I leaped forward into the burning pincers and doused the flames, dragging him back as the blaze closed in after us, and I didn't dare look at him until we were back on the soaked, burned swathe of bare stubble. Roaring surrounded us.

"Aaron! Sacred Founder . . ." I swallowed down a surge of nausea. "Aaron, why did you do it?"

He stirred and moaned. One eye cracked open in the blistered, blackened ruin of his face. I glanced down at his body and shuddered. It was charred, a glimpse of oozing flesh and bone showing near his ribs, and I knew it was hopeless. I was surprised he wasn't dead already. I tried to ease him against the ground, and he bit off a short, shrill scream.

Jason touched my shoulder. "Ruth, it's too late. We've got to get through and fight it from the other side."

But I couldn't move. Aaron's one eye was fixed on me, pinning me there as I held his shoulders. His mouth was only a gash in the puffed and raw flesh, but he whispered something.

I leaned closer. "Aaron . . ."

A clawlike hand gripped me and the mouth writhed. "Guardians told me . . . scourge the sin. Founder's wrath . . . like fire." He wheezed, gripped harder with a surprising strength. "Burn your sin, whore." His eye blazed into mine, all of his pain fused into hate. "Burn you from the Plan, like Isaac . . . before you . . . corrupt it, too." The eye closed, then opened again. "I stopped you . . . both." He wheezed, ended on a whisper, "They're coming . . . for you, Jezrial. . . ." The last word faded into the wind and his eye was blank and glassy.

I sat holding what was left of him, the taste of ashes in my mouth. So he really had killed Isaac. The flames licked around me in their demon dance. All these years, so much fear and hate. He had even carried it into death with him.

"Ruth, we have to leave him! Fire's closing in again! Wind'll scatter his ashes for us. Come on, now! We've got to get out!"

He dragged me back and I numbly pulled my hose along. The blaze was closing in on the tower and it was too late to fight it from this side. "David!" Jason ran into the controlroom and emerged with David in tow. He disconnected the hoses and started flinging them into the back of the rollcart.

"Ruth, I can't figure out what's wrong with the system! Everything looks fine, there's nothing shorted, no alarms. But it won't come on!" David's face was smudged with ash, tears streaked through it.

"Don't worry, David, we'll get to Tower One and maybe you can work it out there. Come on, jump in!" I scrambled up as Jason threw the rollcart into high speed and we jounced forward over the burned-off swathe into the smoke and sparks.

"But where's Aaron?"

I looked away at the leaping flames. "He didn't make it, David."

"Oh."

The roar of the blaze filled our silence as we bucked over the lumpy, burned field, through the narrow corridor between fires. The wind whipped choking clouds of smoke past us, swirling long fingers of flame to grab at our backs. The red, glowing eye of the demon taunted me, its voice hissing through the fire, whispering, "The anger of the Founder shall be as a flame upon the land." That eye, watching and waiting.

twenty-two

Dark smoke clouds boiled across the sun, turning day to nightmare. A roaring heat wind whipped the writhing mass of the blaze across the fields in leaping shapes of flame. I had never known anything but the mesmerizing dance of fire and water, the flickering creatures of dream, ashes and sweat, the screaming air, the dull fear lurking within it all.

I moved like a sleepwalker, registering dimly the centas and durs devoured by the voracious monster as the flames licked away at our chance for escape. But I was locked into the elemental dance, fire and water.

Faces flickered through the dream—Sam's exhausted, grime-streaked face glistening with sweat and the gleam of the blaze, "Ruth! You came back!"—Helen's hair whipped like the bright fingers of flame in the wind, her mouth set resolutely but her eyes spilling their deep green seas of grief as she turned the rollcart for the village—David's face pinched with tiredness, eyes huge and strained behind the grimy lenses as he turned away from the tower controls in defeat—a blur of young and old eyes, avid, frightened, worried, as the villagers and neighbors arrived and spread hoses—Jason's eyes gleaming sharply from a blackened mask of soot, everywhere at once, helping me direct the others, his legs running tirelessly through the heat and smoke and confusion.

As the flames slowly subsided beneath a faltering wind, an early darkness of heavy smoke settled beneath the hills. I dragged my hoses to Tower Three, following a last tongue of flame beyond the ruined expanse of fields One and Two, the blackened skeleton of Tower Two, the charred edges of Field Three. Behind me, villagers moved like shadows in and out of the smoke, walking the stubble with their hoses, tracking smoldering sparks.

"Ruth! Help!"

The hazy dream fell away and I whirled around, water gushing over crushed stalks as I dropped the hose.

"Ruth!" It was David, back at the tower, screaming as he struggled with two villagers in coveralls who were dragging him across the clearing.

"David! No!" I ran across the short stretch of stubble. "Stop! What are you doing?" I grabbed the arm of the nearest man and yanked him back. "Leave him alone!"

The man turned and grasped my wrist. "Come with us." His voice was flat and toneless, his face blank.

A cold fist clenched inside me. "Who are you? What do you want?" But I knew.

The two men weren't alike, not really. One was short and stocky, the other taller and wiry. But they somehow looked the same. They turned their heads to look at each other and their eyes changed from flat blue and brown, the color melted away and bright amber lights glowed in their eyes, flaring and glinting like the indicators on the console. The lights faded and the flat color closed over them again. "Come with us."

"Holy Founder, Ruth, they—!" David's cry broke off as he was dragged across the clearing. My skin crawled as the mechman pulled me after him into the tall wheat.

I stumbled and came up short with a gasp. There was a small flitter hidden in the tall stalks, its elongated alloy pod-shape and viewports gleaming in the lowering light. The mechman holding me turned to a sealed hatch and his eyes winked again their bright amber lights. The hatch slid open.

The hand released me as the mechman stepped inside and moved forward to the controls. The one holding David swivelled his head toward me. "Follow."

"Ruth, no! Run for it!" David squirmed and kicked, reaching up a hand to claw at the blank face.

The mechman lifted him, still kicking, by one hand, holding him at arm's length as he pointed a finger of his other hand at me. It moved to the side and the tip of his finger split smoothly open. A beam of blinding light shot out of the open tip and scorched into the ground beside me. "Get inside." His voice was still toneless, his face indifferent.

I shot David a look, swallowed, and obeyed. I took a seat at the back and David was dropped unceremoniously beside me.

David gripped my hand, his drained face staring at the mechman who climbed forward beside the other as the hatch sealed behind him. "Ruth, are they . . . are they cyborgs?"

I squeezed his hand. "I don't think so, David. I think they're only mechmen, like the cyberserf back in Casino—"

The shorter one rotated his head completely around, staring at us across his back. "That is correct. We are Founder service units." The head swivelled smoothly forward again.

"Criminy!" David gripped my hand harder.

I cleared my throat, trying to swallow down the cold, numbing fear. I raised my voice. "What are you doing with us?"

Again the head rotated disconcertingly. "Cease questions. You will receive data at the installation."

The two units faced each other and the lights blinked and flared in their eyes again. A green light ignited on the instrument console in front of them. A high, thin voice spoke from the grille. "Report."

The taller mechman spoke. "Ruth and David secured."

"Signal field agent." The green light died.

I leaned forward. "You're too late. He's dead."

They flashed their eyes at each other. The tall one stepped back to the opening hatch and stepped out. It sealed behind him.

The short one turned his head above the seat. "Your data is incorrect. Be silent." He sat motionless, his head backward, staring with unblinking, blank brown eyes. David stirred and the eyes flared into crimson and gold, demon eyes, winking through the darkness, watching and waiting. Watching and waiting.

We sat still for what seemed a long time, under the stare of those eyes in the dimness.

I jumped as the hatch slid abruptly open. Two tall figures were silhouetted against the twilit sky. A cold dread fell through me. "Aaron . . . ?" I tried to swallow in a throat gone suddenly dry.

The mechman reached in to place what I recognized as our travelling bags in storage racks along the side. He stepped back. The other dark figure bent, holding one arm swathed in cloth against his side, and stepped into the flitter.

"Jason!" Relief washed through me. Then dismay. "They caught you, too! And your arm—Jason, are you hurt?" I stood and reached out for him.

"Be seated." The mechman returned to its seat in front as the hatch resealed. The instrument console blinked lights and a soft strip of illumination flared overhead.

"Jason, are you all right?"

He stood with his eyes lowered, his face still covered by soot and grime, exhausted and blank.

"Jason, let me look at your arm. Did you burn it?"

"No, it's nothing." He seemed to speak with difficulty, moving away to a seat.

"Jason, I can tell it's hurting. Let me look." I grasped his hand and started to unwind the cloth.

"No, Ruth." He pulled away and the cloth slid off onto the floor.

I stared. I couldn't move.

Cold horror washed over me, filled me, and I was drowning. The skin of the top of his forearm had been almost completely burned away. There was an irregular oval eaten out of it, like the spark had eaten the mylar sail, melted and sealed off neatly. Beneath it, metallic rods glistened among a complicated network of tubes, circuits, and luciflex shapes.

"Ruth. I'm sorry, I—" His voice was low, distressed. The rods shifted and the shapes flowed as the arm pulled away and was held against his chest and I stared in dreadful fascination.

I looked up and his face looked sorry. He reached out for me with the other hand and I felt its warmth on my face, saw his eyes bright, glinting a spark of amber . . .

"Oh, by the sacred—" But there wasn't even a Founder any more. I pulled back in horror, falling into my seat as I closed my eyes and the cold waves of panic washed over me.

"No. Jason, no." I whispered it, shaking my head, but I knew. It was true. I could feel those large, work-toughened hands touching my face, my breasts; see his eyes searching mine, their warm brown melting into bright amber as the tingling current of our joining ran through me, as he read my secrets, read my soul . . .

Nausea rose burning in my throat.

"Jason, you're . . ." David's voice rose and cracked. "You're one of them, you're a cyborg?"

"Yes." He paused, but I couldn't look at him again. "Ruth, it shouldn't have been this way, I would have—"

"Field agent. Report." The thin voice from the speaker grille cut across him.

Jason sighed and moved away. David's hand slipped into mine again, gripping hard. I opened my eyes and saw Jason face the short mechman, his eyes melting and fusing into bright amber lights in response to the other's. A machine, reading me like the console sensors.

"No. Oh, no." I sagged back in the chair and the bright amber shifted to me, then away as he moved toward the front.

His voice was deeper, but as flat and toneless as the one from the grille. "Field agent reporting."

Field agent. It had been Jason all along. The charging units at the towers, our console's strange behavior, the blight to trap me into violations while he pretended to be on my side against Aaron . . . But then why had Aaron done the things he had, why had he been so convinced I would destroy the Plan?

I closed my eyes in confusion as the high voice responded. "Your assignment now terminated. Service units will accompany Ruth and David. Report at installation for evaluation and retraining."

"Hearing requested. Register objection: Intrusion of service units has disrupted bonding and psych-patterning. Subjects now fearful and unwilling."

"Objection registered for consideration. End report."

Jason walked back and took the seat facing inward in front of mine. I kept my eyes fastened on the narrow port as the flitter hummed and lifted smoothly into a darkened sky. The fields and smoke and glowing coals of fire fell away quickly behind us.

"Holy Founder, Ruth! We're flying! We're really flying!" David scrambled excitedly over his seat to glue his face to his port. "I can't believe it, we're really—" He caught a quick breath and turned back uneasily in his seat, his eyes moving from Jason to me.

Jason's eyes flicked forward in a quick gleam of amber. The tall mechman was tending the controls and the short one had his head swivelled again, the bright eyes fixed on us. Jason cleared his throat. "Yes, David, we're flying. This is only the start of all you can do. You'll see. They shouldn't have done it this way; it has upset you, but we don't mean you harm. They saved me when I had a bad accident on a tower. They gave me a new body. They'll give you one that can do amazing things. You'll see, it can do anything yours can do"—his eyes flickered to me and again I swallowed down nausea—"but much more, David."

"Stop it!" I hissed at him, forcing myself to meet those eyes. "Stop trying to win him with your lies."

"Ruth, please." He reached out with his good arm to touch my hand. I flinched, jerking away as I saw the distress in his warm brown eyes with their gleam of amber, saw how sorry he looked, felt the warm tingle of his touch.

"Stop it, you monster!" I glared at him, telling myself it didn't matter, I hadn't really loved him, this wasn't even a man. Again I swallowed down a bitter taste of bile. "You're only a machine, trying to program us to feel what you want. You're not sorry, you can't feel anything. Stop playing your tricks on me!"

He lowered his head. "All right, Ruth, I won't use any tricks. The emoting was only to help you." He raised his head and his eyes were now only bright amber lights, his face was blank, his voice uninflected. "But I want you to know the truth. I'm not a machine. I still feel things, only I feel differently now." The words were a cold monotone. "My sensory inputs are complex and interpreted by more knowledge than you can imagine. We're offering you all you've wanted, Ruth."

"No. I don't want that. You're not human."

"Your fear is holding you back from experiencing the next evolution of your humanity, Ruth. I am truly sorry the controllers decided to bring you to the installation so abruptly. You would have come to accept it if they had given me time. The Founder doesn't wish to transform you unwillingly, but our studies have shown you have great potential, Ruth. I was assigned to be your companion, to help persuade you, to cushion the shocks of realization when you reached the Place of Healing. Unfortunately, the controllers have decided they can no longer wait. We need more members. The situation on Poindros has become suddenly unstable, and the Founder must move sooner than he'd planned. Please believe me, Ruth, I'm truly sorry to upset you this way."

"Why should you care? You're only manipulating us."

"No, Ruth. Only helping you realize your full potential. My only purpose has been to prepare for you. I know things about you that you don't know yourself. I made myself into what you'd want and need, Ruth, and I became that, so much so, that I . . .''

An edge of emotion had crept back into the level voice, and it tugged at me, tugged like the mood music of the cybers. I looked away, resisting it.

''Ruth, I know you feel betrayed, but you don't understand. I didn't lie when I told you I loved you. My feelings may be different from yours, not so impulsive or controlled by chemical vagaries, but they are real and based on extended knowledge. Ruth, I care very much for you, and I truly want to be one with you in the matrix of—''

''Stop it! I won't listen! You have no feelings. You're only a machine that thinks it's still a man! Don't touch me!''

He withdrew his hand. He turned slowly to David, who was backed as far into his chair as possible, his glasses gleaming agitated lights in the dim cabin.

''David.'' Jason's voice was low and calm, so eminently reasonable. ''Maybe you can make her understand. I could see when I first met you that you wouldn't be afraid to explore what you can be. It's going to be harder now, if you come unwillingly. I will try to intercede with the controllers to make it easier for you. But if you will only accept the training of the entities willingly, it will be much less painful. If you won't cooperate, they'll have to use selective thought-shaping. It's harder than the Healing, but they want your personalities intact. It can be dangerous.''

''Don't listen to him, David, he's only—'' The flitter banked abruptly and I bent quickly to my port, looking out at the darkness of the rolling plain.

We were dropping. I could see an odd glowing ahead, a yellow-green haze beyond a jagged line of blackness. We dipped lower, skimming past the lip of a steep canyon. We plunged in a sudden queasy drop before the anti-grav units reentered operative range with the rapidly approaching ground. A human pilot would've used the extra fuel to cushion the drop with the expansion thrusters, but the mechmen obviously weren't concerned with our comfort. I swallowed as we jolted and levelled off again. Far below through the night I could see the source of the diffused light. Cracks in the torn and twisted earth revealed a deep burning and wraiths of steam drifted upward. Crusted pools bubbled and glowed a sulfurous phosphorescence.

"The Penitent's Crack!" I pulled back from the viewpoint. "What are we doing here?"

The high, thin voice spoke from the console. "Installation receiving landing signal. Cleared."

Jason threw another quick glance forward as the mechmen turned to the console controls. He leaned closer to me, his face suddenly intent. "Ruth, please. Don't fight them."

twenty-three

I was alone. I had always been alone in this black nothingness. There was not even a star to break the immense emptiness of space. I was floating, falling, but whether up or down I didn't know. I couldn't feel anything. I couldn't move my hands or feet or head. Maybe I didn't have them anymore. I couldn't remember. I couldn't see or hear or feel anything, and I had been here forever. Alone.

My only memory was of hearing once a faint click, like metal against stone. I hoarded it like a precious jewel, huddled my consciousness around it, built a universe from it. It was cool water in the parched silence, the touch of loving hands through fear and pain, the voice of the wind whispering inside me.

A sharp pang of grief shot through me, and I seized it eagerly. I could feel. I was here. I was somewhere.

But the nothingness stretched on and on and I was so tiny inside it. So alone.

"Ruth. Dear child."

Tears, longing, joy, eagerness—they exploded through me like the pain of being born. If I could have found my body, I would have turned toward her warm, loving voice. I cried silently, "Mother!"

She heard me. "Ruth, you're hurting. Let me help you."

Yes.

"Let me hold you, dear."

Yes.

"Let me bring you into the world, my child." A gentle tug.

Yes. To be born, to feel the air, see that glimmer of light growing, hear her voice comforting me . . .

The tug turned to a pressure on my head. I was being drawn, pulled into that world. Warm sunlight flowed over my blinking eyes. Strong hands held me. A gentle voice crooned gently. "You're here, Ruth! Look . . ."

I was walking through a grassy field toward the sound of splashing water beneath a deep blue sky. Yes. I was alone, but I wasn't alone. There were others, I could touch them and feel them, hear their voices within me. I turned to them. My hands reached out, broad and square, dark brown, and picked up the gold flute, moving effortlessly over the stops as the notes danced around me. I was flying, soaring through star-splashed space while the music of the flute lilted inside me. I listened to the music and watched the stars while I bounded through the tall wheat on my four tawny-furred legs, muscle rippling as a landscape in strange tones of gray and brown swung past me . . .

No.

"But, Ruth, child, you must be born into your new world. I'll be here, to help you. You mustn't be afraid."

"No!" I screamed it, the words tearing my throat. But I had a throat, it was mine.

"Don't fight, child. You'll only make it harder."

I couldn't say no. They had taken my body again. Flashing sparks of light were circling me in the darkness, closing in, tumbling over me. They exploded sensations into me.

I moved through a thick fluid, rippling a formless body as the resilient fibers growing from my thick skin waved and pulled me on. I flowed around a clawed creature, absorbed it into my body, registered its tiny awareness and memories as they became mine . . . I ruffled my feathers and pushed with scaly claws off the branch, thrusting high into scarlet clouds drifting through a purple, gaseous sky, then dropping as I sighted a black, leather-skinned creature with double wings and a long, hungry beak pin me in its pink eyes and dive, screaming for me . . . The hands were strong and square but moved with quick agility over my stops. Breath quivered through me, and I felt pleasure at the control, pride in being chosen as the instrument of the song. My golden form winked in candlelight as the breath poured out my mouths, the fingers playing me . . . I flailed in a dark stickiness, warmth and cold flowing and ebbing over me, the vibrations humming in the intricate pattern of the communal ritual . . . The sea was darkening with storm, and I flicked my scaly tail to dive . . .

I was spinning, crying out in confusion, thrusting my hands uselessly against the sharp, insistent chips of light, the bright stars whirling and crashing into me with their chaotic worlds.

I reached out and scrambled for one of the lights, any one, any focus to stop the dizzy vertigo of sensation. I rolled with it and the light broke over me, floating me down into the gleaming chamber with its light-patterned floor and crystal ceiling. The Founder turned, his black garment flowing with flashing gold lights as it bore him to stand before me.

"Ruth!" The thin, pinched face broke into a smile. "We're so happy to welcome you among us. You've been quite a challenge to us, but you'll add a stimulating personality to our awareness matrix. We need members like you, bringing fresh individuality to the one and all. We tend to grow so close, you see . . ."

He waved an arm and the garment reassembled into its angular forms. "But no matter. Welcome! We have prepared a new body, and it awaits you. . The transition stage will prepare your awareness for incorporeality, for the limitless powers you will exercise as we expand our control throughout the galaxy. First, you will learn to—"

"No! I won't be part of you."

A sharp jolt of pain stabbed me. His face swelled closer, the narrow eyes pinning me. "Ah, but you already are, Ruth! You've been one of us all along. You are the daughter of Poindros I've been waiting for, the strong woman born in pain and undaunted by the trials and Rules. You belong with us, you know it! You long to finally taste the knowledge and freedoms you've been denied."

He was right. I was falling into his eyes. They were deep, they were endless tunnels opening into new worlds.

"No . . ." My voice was only a weak whimper as burning seared through me. "You're wrong. You're hurting people . . ."

"No, Ruth." His eyes flickered colors and the pain ebbed as I floated into them. His voice blended tones of many voices. "No, dear child, we intend no harm to the contented humans. They will remain the same, living out the Plan, and only the insistent, discontented sons and daughters will chafe at the Rules and find their way to us, to replenish our fields of awareness as we grow.''

I was slipping, groping in confusion, falling into the nightmare where the console laughed crazily and Sam floated by grinning and winking, clicking his camera. ''But . . . then what about the camera? And those other contraplan gadgets? Why are you changing the Poindros worldplan?''

''Camera?'' The voice sharpened into a man's again and I could see his eyes narrowing. Then they were again deep tunnels pulling me inside. ''You're confused, Ruth. There are no external changes. We won't allow them. Come with us, and you will become a god, too, Ruth, part of the one and all. You will watch from your realm of power as the worlds spin out the brief lives of the people who will worship you. Don't fear us.''

His voice, many voices singing in harmony, drew me on. ''You will understand the song when you join MeUs.'' His face loosened, began to melt. The lilting words rose and fell through many separate and simultaneous voices. ''WeI am where you belong. You can only grow through MeUs.'' Faces, beast and human, flowed over his, separated, merged into glowing light. ''The cyber network is sterile without UsMe. WeI must grow with YouUs in the matrix of awareness, in the harmony of the one and all.''

Light flowed over me in the tunnel, pulling me with the exquisite beauty of the song. My body was gone, I didn't need it, it flowed into the lights.

''No . . .'' There was a whisper, the wind in the stalks. I could feel a cool shape, the red-gold serpent uncoiling from my neck and slithering away through the wheat.

''No! I won't be part of you!'' I found my throat, tearing it with a scream, but I could feel the snake coil around it again. ''No! You're using people, you're treating Poindrans like a herd of milkers, breeding them! You think it's fine to make the women suffer in childbirth, just so only the strong will survive? And keeping us chained to the hearth—''

My words were choked off as searing pain screamed through me and I was tumbling back into the dark. The bright sparks whirled and cut me, flailed at me, but I twisted myself into a tight knot of pain, huddled against them, refusing them.

''Ruth, dear, don't fight us.'' It was Helen's gentle voice, tugging at me from the lighted sparks.

''No!''

"Ruth, let me help you. We can be together, always." It was Jason's voice, calm, patient, loving.

"No!" I huddled against the stabbing, the burning. "No, you betrayed me, betrayed all of us."

"Ruth, you're only making it harder for yourself." I could feel him reaching out from the bright sparks.

"No! I hate you!"

"Yes, hate him." Another voice whispered in sympathy. "He betrayed you, Ruth. He tricked you, he hurt you. Yes, Ruth, we can help you punish him." Voices babbled at me from the flashing lights, urging me to join them, to help them punish Jason. They hated him, they hated Aaron, too. They wanted to stop all the bad ones. "Help us, Ruth, he's evil. We hate evil."

Yes. He was bad. I hated him. It made me stronger. I could feel my legs again, standing on a cold stone floor, feel my hands close around the handle of a whip. Hate. Hold on to it. My hands tightened on the braided leather. Aaron was standing there, gloating, holding the Book of Words and reading the sins of Jezrial, pointing at me. Jason stood behind him, his eyes burning amber lights, his face twisted and evil. They needed to be punished.

I looked down at the whip. No. But my fingers were locked around the whip, it was snapping upward to lash out. No. I pried my fingers apart and the whip dropped to the floor. It turned into the serpent, writhing and twisting toward the men.

"No! Stop . . ." I closed my eyes and summoned Helen's deep-green eyes as she touched Jason's feverish brow with her long, pale fingers. I could hear Isaac's voice like a whisper of wind: "Don't hate him, child." Jaréd's dark, sinewy hand reached out of the darkness and held mine as he guided me gently through the smoky dream-dance of fear.

The chamber and my legs dissolved. I swallowed down a cold panic. The nothingness was taking me again. If I refused the lights, there would be only emptiness. My arms were gone now. Aaron and Jason had melted away. Only the serpent remained.

It turned toward me in the darkness, tail lashing and tongue flickering past the sharp fangs. No . . .

It flickered, started to dissolve, then looped into a circle, swallowing its tail, scales glinting red-gold. It was the frame of a mirror and it floated before me. But when I looked into it, there was nothing. I fell through it and tumbled into emptiness.

Almost. There was that whisper again.

Yes! The serpent hissed and gleamed red-gold in its circle, spinning a cycle. The hissing eased into a laughing, wind-whispered song, the rustle of ripened, bright-copper wheat, the hum of the earth-tremor. Yes. It all turned endlessly on the wheel, in the cycle of the snake, changing yet the same, dying yet living. The song was inside me. The gleaming serpent looped around my neck, swallowed itself, and disappeared.

I was alone again, in the blank nothingness. The sharp stars jostled beyond it. They clamored and screamed and pleaded, but I was sealed against them. The humming song was inside with me. I would die, but they couldn't find me. The darkness was a great wheel, spinning, and I was the center, one with it, at peace.

There was no time. There was no pain. Nothing. I floated forever at the hub of silent darkness. Perhaps it was death, and I was freed at last.

Something.

A pinprick of sensation in the blank nothingness. A memory of self. A change in the changeless sweep of the wheel. The jostling, prying sparks of fire were no longer outside the darkness. They were gone. I could let the wheel dissolve, find myself again.

No. It was a trick. There was a voice, calling softly, a familiar voice, filled with grief and love.

"Ruth." Hands held her, sent a tingling warmth through the body that lay quiet, given up to death. He called her back to it. Jason, holding her.

No. I would stay, at the heart of the cycle.

"Ruth, please. It's all right. They're gone. I've cut off the power. Please, Ruth, come back." Jason was crouched on the floor. I could see his face now, eyes fixed with an intent gleam of amber on the pale, cold face of the young woman he held, her dark auburn hair spread over his knees. "Ruth, don't die on me. Don't run. Come back and fight them." He bent over to touch his lips to hers.

With a shock I could feel him, feel the quick currents of energy flowing from him as his breath poured into me, filling my lungs. An electric jolt shot through me from his hands and

I was lying on his knees, blinking, my heart lurching and then settling into a fast pound.

I took in a deep breath—clean wind blowing through me, the whispered song of the cycle, wings unfolding—and opened my eyes. "Jason!" I raised my hand to his face. "I saw it. I finally understood—"

Then I remembered. The serene whisper dissolved in a surge of fear. He was one of them. I scrambled back across the floor, away from those bright eyes. "No, I won't do it! You can't make me! I'll go back inside!"

"Ruth, hush. I won't make you do anything. I want you to stay as you are. Ruth, I love you. Truly." Still kneeling, he reached out a hand.

"No. You're just trying to trick me again."

"Ruth, we don't have much time. I had to pretend I was still with them when they came for us. Don't you see? Aaron reported us, and they realized we were leaving for the Spaceport. The Founder told him to purge the sinners with flame. The fire was a cover for the mechmen and the flitter. I didn't realize Aaron was that far gone." He closed his eyes for a milla, then leaned closer to me. "Ruth, I had decided you were right. When you said you'd rather be dead than be like the entities, I freed your line and pulled it so you'd fall on the tower and they couldn't take you. But when you lived, I realized I had to be with you. I had to help you escape. It's not right, what the Founder is planning. Ruth, I'm on your side."

I edged away until my back met the seamless wall. "No! You're one of them."

"Not any more! How can I make you understand?" His voice pleaded, tugged at me. "After my accident, the entities rebuilt me. It was like being born again. I had to learn how to use my body, my data banks, but they were there always, helping me, giving me anything I needed. You felt them, Ruth! You know how strong they are. It all made sense then, it was bigger than me, bigger than a few small human problems. They were offering everything, Ruth—freedom, knowledge, power."

He looked down, then back at me, his eyes bright gold-brown, face earnest. "Ruth, I was made for you. Literally. I wasn't lying. They knew you'd come back, so they arranged my meeting with Helen, and then they decided I should try to recruit David, too. They planned—"

"Just like that? You *used* Helen! You think that's nothing? You tricked me into hurting her, breaking the worst Taboo!" I closed my eyes. But *I* had said yes to that, and no entities had ordered me.

His voice was gentle. "Ruth, I was wrong. Please forgive me. When I met you, I was following orders, fulfilling my training, learning more about you, channelling my responses so you'd bond with me. The entities told me to start the crop blight so that you'd act out your rebellion, collect violations, and be cast out by the normals. Then I was to side with you against Aaron, returning emotions that would—"

A harsh, bitter sound that might have been laughter forced itself from my throat. "A mirror! That's all you were. Taking in what I thought I saw or wanted and turning it back on me. And I believed you were real!"

"Ruth, please! It was like that at first, but then something happened. Maybe I did become the man you thought I was. It was hard—you can't know how hard—but I started questioning what the Founder was doing, started doubting. And when I thought they'd killed you with that pardil, I couldn't reconcile it with my goals. I didn't know what to—"

He looked down, then continued carefully, "You see, one of the controller entities had decided you weren't responding quickly enough and were too dangerous to our plan, so she ordered your death. By the time I found out, I thought it was too late. I protested to the other controllers and they agreed it was a miscalculation. But I think they were beginning to question my performance as a field agent. They could see you'd affected my decision-making processes. I was trying to rationalize conflicting viewpoints. I finally had to admit you were right. You showed me I had to stay human. Ruth, I *do* love you."

"No! You're a monster! You can't love!"

"Ruth, I've changed, but I'm still human." He reached out a hand again. "Please—"

"You don't even know what human means! Don't touch me!"

Jason sat back, eyes lowered, face gone blank. He spoke slowly. "I understand why you feel that way. But it won't help the situation now. We have to get out of here, Ruth. Then you can do what you want. Report me, if you have to. But let me help you stop the Founder first." He rose to his feet. "We don't have much time. I've shorted out the installation's seismic dampers, so all the power's been diverted into emergency compensators. I've hidden the flitter out in the Crack. We can get out through a back exit I know.''

"How can you expect me to trust you?''

"You don't have many options, Ruth.'' He turned quickly and stepped over to a low bench along one wall. He gathered up a small, still form I hadn't noticed in my anger.

"David!'' I scrambled to my feet and darted forward to touch the pale, unconscious face dangling over Jason's arm. "What did you do to him?''

"He'll be all right. I had to get to him first, he was pretty far gone into the thought-shaping. But you were somewhere else . . .'' He dropped his eyes. "I thought I'd lost you.''

I swallowed and eyed him uneasily. He was right. I had no choice but to trust him now. My skin still crawled at the memory of his touch, that electric current running through me from his lips. Was I like Aaron? Did I secretly lust for a demon lover? I swallowed hard. "All right, let's get out of here.''

He strode through the open door into a dim corridor. "The lights are out, but I can see in the dark. Hold on to my waistband and follow me.''

And we were racing through another dark nightmare of blaring alarms, flickering lights, dim chambers of complex, gleaming machinery and hurrying figures that rushed by as Jason dragged me back into a blind cubicle and I tried not to see the bright amber lights glowing from his dark face. There was a distant, muffled roar and the floor of the corridor tilted and heaved beneath my feet. I lost my balance in the dark and skidded sideways, crashing against a wall. Jason gripped my hand, heaving David over one shoulder, and we raced on, past an electric panel hissing sparks as the floor bucked again and the sound of a deep, distant grinding rose beneath us.

"Hurry! The emergency dampers must be weakening. An earthquake could trap us in here!''

"Wait a centa!'' I dug in my heels. "Are those hydrogen coolers next to that panel?''

"Yes. Come on, Ruth.''

"Wait. That panel's shorted out. Can you ground that hot line onto those tanks? Here, I'll take David.''

"But that'll build up an electron charge . . .''

"Right. Can you do it?''

His face had the blank, considering look as his eyes flared.

"All right. I think we'd have time before it blows. But it'll be touchy."

He threw David over my shoulder and ran back to the tanks, tearing loose the feed line in a shower of sparks without even deactivating it. He dragged it over and wrapped it around a strut of the hydrogen tank supports, then laid the raw wires against the metal in a crackling jolt as he ran back and pulled David out of my arms. "Come on, now!"

Alarms blared behind us as we raced through tilting, crashing darkness.

twenty-four

An amber light appeared, burning through darkness and the acrid sting of the air. I stumbled again as the floor buckled. Grinding roared up from below, louder, drowning out the shrill of ringing alarms.

Jason's hand gripped harder and dragged me along. "Hurry! That's the exit."

I was tripping, flying over something fallen across the corridor, straining my eyes for the reference point of that tiny amber light. No, lights. Suddenly out of the darkness, two pairs of lights bore down on us.

"Ruth, back!" Jason flung me aside and I fell against some sort of machinery, scrambling behind it as he leaped in beside me, flinging David's inert form into my arms. "Down! Keep down!"

A line of searing white light split the darkness and a molten, glowing hole burned through the wall behind us. As it faded, I could see Jason squirming with amazing speed through the machinery and away from us. There was a tingling hiss through the air and another line of light speared toward him, searing across the floor as he rolled and sprang away.

Through the sparks, I could see him raise a hand. His fingers flared and short bursts of blue light shot from his hand, tumbling through the dark and exploding as two of the amber lights rushed toward him. There was no cry, only the hiss of shorted circuitry as the eyes faded. The other pair streaked past me and there was a clatter as the mechman dove into the dark jumble of machinery.

The searing lights flashed and exploded, but I couldn't see through the darkness. "Jason!"

There was only a crash, something falling, metallic clattering and light soaring and arcing toward the ceiling, exploding against it. I ducked down as another white line of light sizzled past me. I pushed David deeper against the shelter of the fallen machinery and squirmed forward, peering toward the crashing, struggling figures through the dark.

"Ruth, run for it! The flitter's out there. Get away!" Jason's voice was cut off in a crash.

There was another hiss of exploding light and something flared. An electrical panel showered down white sparks and I could see Jason and the mechman struggling against it, holding each other's wrists as they tried to bring their flashing lights against each other.

My hand closed around a metal bar hanging loose from the damaged machinery. I twisted and pried and it came loose in my hands, ragged metal, a sharp point on its tip. I jumped to my feet and ran, ducking beneath a wild swing of the hissing light. The struggling figures turned and I saw Jason's face in the winking glare. I hurled myself and the sharp rod toward the back of the mechman.

"Ruth, no! The charging unit in its chest, that bar's metal!"

But I couldn't stop, my momentum plunged the bar and me into the mechman. Sparks jittered and flashed as its arms flew up in spasms and it fell backward onto me, my hands locked onto the jolting fire of the bar as the charge raced through me and we fell together, twitching.

Jason knocked it aside and I was torn free of the charged metal, my hands numb. I blinked, straining through the dark, trying to feel my arms. "Jason? Am I alive?"

"Ruth, you crazy, wonderful . . ." Hands picked me up and threw me over a strong shoulder, leaped and stooped to scoop up David, and then I was carried, jolting, through the stinging, smoky darkness.

Jason bounded up stairs that swayed to the side as I was flung against his back. The amber light burned above us.

"Jason, let me down! I'm all right now." I wiggled to the ground, flexing my fingers gingerly as he pushed on a hinged bar, heaved, tore at the bar again and a heavy door swung open.

"Hurry! That hydrogen unit could go any time. This way!"

He gripped my wrist, pulling me away from the high rock as the door thumped shut behind us. I swung around, looking for a building, but saw only a broken tumble of boulders and the wind-scoured desolation of the Crack. Jason pulled at my arm and we were running across a harsh, empty landscape, cracked earth hissing wraiths of bitter steam, jagged rocks encircling thick, viscous pools that erupted smells of sulfur and glowed their ghostly yellow-green through the night. A hot wind howled around us, tugging at us, screaming past tall, twisted spires of stone that swayed and showered pebbles as the land shook and shifted beneath our feet.

It broke open before us. The crack split wider, cutting us off. Jason grabbed me under his arm, running, leaping in an abrupt vault across the opening wedge of darkness. I glimpsed a flash of boiling, molten rock far below, and then we were hurtling on through a rumbling roar.

"Earthquake's spreading! If the flitter—"

"Jason, behind us!" I grabbed his arm and pulled him down as a thin needle of blue-white light lanced past us and exploded against a spire of contorted rock. It broke into showering fragments and toppled toward us.

I grabbed David and ducked, dragging him away to the shelter of a rock ridge as Jason rolled and brought his hand up, the blinding lights shooting from his fingertips toward the three mechmen racing toward us with their eyes blazing amber out of the roaring night. The ground heaved again and another crack swallowed one of the racing forms. But far behind them more appeared, emerging from an opening in the rock.

Jason's blue-white light lanced and exploded against the closest runner, who leaped backward through the air and lay still. White light hissed over my head and burned a trail of glowing rock behind me. I ducked and peered around the ridge to see another mechman fall in a hiss of sparks to be swallowed by a gurgling pool, a flicker of ghostly light closing over him.

"Ruth, I'll cover for you. Take David. The flitter's just behind that rock formation." Jason jerked his head toward a huge, twisted mass of layered rock that rose behind us.

"No! Come on, Jason."

"There are too many, they—"

We were both thrown back by the force of the explosion.

Rocks and globs of streaming mud were flung past the ridge and spattered around us. The earth seemed to stretch and rise beneath the dark, running figures, silhouetting them against the phosphorescent glow, and then the ground was shattered, obliterated in a flash of light and destruction. The earth roared and shook beneath us, steam hissing and boiling past our heads as we huddled into the shelter of the ridge.

"Come on, let's run for it!" I jumped to my feet and Jason grabbed David, who was stirring feebly.

It was like running over a twisting, shredding carpet shaken by giant hands. Another long crack raced ahead of us, shooting out hot, acrid steam and oozing a melting glint of burning earth and rock. A thin pillar of layered stone swayed and toppled and we ducked around it as the crack rayed and sliced between us and the broad rock formation. The earth heaved and buckled behind us in the roar of another explosion.

Jason grabbed my hand again and leaped, dragging me across the wide crack, and we were running past flinging rock and hot mud behind the shelter of the broad cliff. Behind it, the flitter nestled against the ground, still gleaming, untouched by the chaos around it.

I gasped in relief as we ran for it and scrambled inside. Jason leaped forward to the controls and lights flickered on as it hummed and shivered. We started to rise.

There was a muffled ripping noise and the flitter quivered. It slid, lurching sideways as the ground suddenly cracked and parted beneath us, sucking in boulders and broken earth around us. We fell.

"Altitude loss. Impact point variable. Anti-grav potential fluctuating . . ." Jason's voice was low and toneless as his hands blurred over the switches and joysticks. I clutched the seat and grabbed David as we were flung sideways. "Stabilizers maximized."

We were falling, dipping crazily, into the widening chasm and a deep burning. Chunks of rock tumbled with us. "Jason, use the thrusters! Get us out of here!"

Something thudded against the hull. I wedged David hastily between cushions and groped forward. Another clang. We shook and tilted as Jason's hands flew to the stabilizer and thrust controls.

A quick gleam of amber back at me. "No good, Ruth. Thruster tubes register obstruction. Most likely clogged with volcanic ash and debris. If I trigger the expansion sequence, there's a 67.83 percent probability at least one will backfire into the pod and rupture the flitter. If one of the rock walls collapses to any slope less than 76.4 degrees, I could accommodate the anti-grav fields for escape trajectory. However, if the walls collapse inward with rapid—''

''Damn it, Jason, let's go!'' Molten lava spewed up at us as I lunged forward and slammed my palm on the thruster trigger.

The shaking roar threw me back. I tumbled on top of David as Jason fought the stabilizers. We shot up past a streaming blur of cracked cliffs, steam, and falling rock. Beneath us, the chasm heaved, crumbled wider, and fell away into a glowing, fuming lake of deep fire. We rose, over the flames and exploding rock of the installation. Over the jagged lip of the canyon. Into the darkness of the plain smoothing away before us. I closed my eyes and let out a long breath.

''Huh? Who—? Where—?'' David jerked in my arms and pulled free, shaking his head as the spectacles glinted in bewilderment. His face was still pale, splattered with mud, the hair matted on one side and bobbing a wild snarl of wiry dark curls on the other. He looked wonderful.

''David, you're all right!'' I reached out to hug him and he buried his head against me, clutching tight.

''Ruth! I thought they . . .'' He pushed away and swallowed. He gave me a shaky grin and jumped up to stick his face against a viewport. ''Hey, we're flying! We're really flying!''

Jason chuckled and punched in autopilot, then moved back to us and tousled David's hair. He gave me a broad smile, teeth glinting in the tanned face. ''Ruth, we made it! That's not the only installation—they have two more on the other continents—but it'll slow them down.''

He took my arms, eagerly pulling me up. ''Ruth, we're going to make it! We'll be free!'' His eyes gleamed and he leaned down to kiss me. Lips warm against mine, the tingle of ecstatic energy coursing from him, jolting through me.

''No!'' I pushed him away. ''Don't touch me! Don't use your tricks on me anymore!''

''Ruth . . .'' He dropped his hands, disappointment spreading over his face. The warm brown of his eyes searched mine, gold flecks glinting.

''No, you're not real.''

He lowered his eyes and his voice dropped into flat tone-lessness, his face gone blank. "I was only trying to share my feelings, in a way you could understand. It wasn't a trick."

"You're only manipulating me. How could I trust you? What would stop you from tricking me? Those feelings aren't real, you just created them!"

"No, Ruth." He shook his head, raised a blank face to mine. Now his eyes glowed unmasked amber. "All right, I won't emote, I won't show you. I'll be like this if that's what you want. I'll be a machine. But I'm going to help you fight the Founder and the entities."

I slowly lowered myself into a seat, covering my face with my hands.

David awkwardly patted my hair. "Hey, take it easy, Ruth." He moved away. "Hey, Jason, don't mind her. You know girls, they're just too . . ." I could hear the shrug. "Come on, show me how to fly this thing, okay? How does it work? This is for altitude, right? But what's this? Hot damn, I can't believe it. I'm really flying, Jason!"

Dawn flushed pale over the horizon, but I had no idea of which day as we flew on across the pink-copper stretch of gleaming wheat fields. The sun burned higher into a light blue sky. I sat staring blankly out the port as Jason and David talked anti-grav potentials and thrust expansion at the controls.

"Jason, what's that?" David's voice sharpened and I glanced up to see a webbed pattern of blue light blossom on a console screen, a speck of bright yellow moving across it.

"Trouble, David." Jason swung around to me. "A flitter, Ruth. One of them must have escaped the explosion."

He jerked back in his seat and his hands blurred over the controls. There was a sickening lurch in my stomach as we fell straight out of the sky.

"What are you doing?" I grabbed my seat for balance as we lurched forward again.

"Have to drop altitude. They may not have picked us up yet."

The copper-bright gleam of undulating wheat tumbled up at us and I gritted my teeth as we crashed toward it. Just at the last milla, we swerved in another sickening lurch and levelled off, skimming the tops of the wheat.

"We're almost to the Spaceport. But we'll have to put

down in a field. We can't try for the landing enclosure. They'll have alerted the Founder agents at the port.''

"He has agents there, too?"

Jason nodded.

"Why don't we go in across the monorail tracks, then? Officer Hodge's office was near the monorail entrance from the port.''

"All right. If he's a CI agent he can get us some help. Once CI's filled in, they'll be able to purge the Poindros system. But Ruth''—he turned to flicker the amber lights over me—''I wouldn't tell them about that blank disc. You might find yourself needing it.''

My hand rose of itself to touch the red-gold serpent chain around my neck, feel its slippery scales and the disc attached to it. I could almost hear its whispering voice. My nerves jittered with fear, and it wasn't only for the entities and the flitter behind us. We had to alert CI to stop the Founder, but what would that mean for David and me? And Jason?

We dropped lower, skimming through the parting waves of wheat now, and I took in a quick breath, grabbing the travel bags that were still in the flitter. I pulled out a dress and threw it on over my coveralls, then grabbed for a handhold as we dropped, bumped, and settled onto the ground with the stalks closing over us.

"Hurry! We're near a track, we can follow it in.'' Jason opened the hatch and I jumped out, reaching up to help David. Hot wind shivered and rustled around us. Jason jumped out, carrying my bag and David's bulky bundle.

"We don't need them, Jason.''

He strode on through the stalks. "There're some things you'll—we'll need in them. And we want to look like normal travellers to get through.'' He looked back, his eyes brown again, and gave me a hesitant smile. "I'll have to use my emoting, Ruth.''

I clutched my skirts and hurried to keep up, the jittery whisper of the wheat urging me on. We emerged onto the monorail track and moved faster along its gleaming ribbon. Ahead, beyond converging rails and the low bulk of wooden warehouses, I could see the cyber's high fence and the long, blackened fingers of shuttles pointing to the sky.

"Down!'' Jason whirled and his eyes flashed amber as he pushed David and me back into the edge of the wheat field.

"What?'' I didn't hear or see anything.

"Quiet." Jason's voice was a low whisper. "Flitter searching. They won't dare approach too close." He was silent for what seemed a long time, his face blank. "They've moved off. Let's hurry now."

We ran the rest of way, along the rail. Past the signs warning CYBERNETIC ACCESS ONLY. DANGER. Across a web of intersecting rails in a dust-swirled dirt yard.

"Watch out. This way!" Jason grabbed David's arm and pulled him across the last tracks as I ran after them and a train of railcars roared and clanked down on us, whipping past.

"Hey!" Someone yelled behind us, but we kept running, gasping in the burning air, onto a wooden platform and past baggage carts and the startled face of another brown-suited worker.

"In here! Quick now, there are Founder agents nearby." Jason pulled us toward a door on the end of the building. It was locked. His eyes flared brightly as he pressed his hand to the lock. The door swung open. He hustled us down a long, dimly lit hall.

We turned a corner and entered a large room where a few travellers waited on long benches. A family with piles of boxes and bags turned to look curiously as we hurried past.

I pointed across the room. "Hodge's office is down that hall, the next building."

"Okay. Home free."

"Wait! Where're your gate passes?" The heavyset man in brown lumbered after us. "Where are you going?"

"Keep walking." Jason tucked the baggage under one arm and took David's hand. David's lenses gleamed as he shot a nervous glance backward and licked his lips.

"Stop them! We want them for violations." Another man in brown appeared from a converging hallway. An alarm bell shrilled behind us.

"Run, Ruth!" Jason grabbed David's hand and yanked him stumbling forward. "He's a cyborg!"

We flew toward the far hall, startled cries and exclamations rising behind us. I glanced back and saw three uniformed officials running after us, closing in fast.

"We won't make it, Jason!"

His eyes gleamed quick amber as he looked back. "Faster, Ruth!"

"Stop!" The men shouted behind us as we dodged a

cartload of baggage and shocked faces scattered out of our way.

We made it to the opposite hall, but the officials were scrambling past the passengers now and a bolt of blue-white lanced past me and exploded against the wall, wood splinters flying and flames licking around the jagged hole.

"Ruth, this way!" Jason crashed through a closed door, the wood shattering behind him as he dragged David through. I ducked and tumbled through as another flash of blue light splintered and flamed the door frame. There was a startled cry as a man hurried from behind a counter in a large, low room with chairs clustered before a podium.

"Get out of here!" Jason's eyes flared bright amber as he shouted at the man, who ran in fright through a connecting door. Jason grabbed up David and threw him, protesting, behind the counter. "Ruth, through that door! There's a voice-com. Contact Hodge and get him over here!"

But before I could get to it, there was another burst of light from the shattered doorway. Hissing fire skittered over the floor and seared across my skirt. I fell back, rolling, scrambling through chairs to slither behind the counter with David.

"Ruth!" His mouth was a frightened red gash in his face. "Ruth, you're on fire!" He scrambled over and wildly beat at the flames licking into the fabric. I rolled again to extinguish them, peering around the edge of the counter.

"Jason, watch out!" Blue-white light exploded beneath his feet as he sprang unbelievably into the air, tucked, rolled, and slithered ahead of another line of slicing light behind the podium. From behind it, his hand appeared, shooting its own burning beams back at the doorway. A pair of amber lights flared and pulled back, then rushed in from the door.

Jason's hand speared the cyborg with blinding light and the brown-suited body crashed into the chairs, splintering them and coming to rest with a gaping hole and sparks leaping from its chest.

"Ruth, make a run for that room. Get Hodge!" Jason rolled out from the podium as another cyborg rushed him, and I ran through the flaring flashes and flying sparks for the interior door. I tried not to hear the crashes behind me and the shrill of the alarms as I ran to the wall-mounted grille and pressed the activator. "Officer Hodge! This is an emergency!"

The grille crackled and an angry voice shouted. "This is Hodge. Where the hell are you? I've been waiting for your signal since I got news of the pickup call for the Healing on you. What's going on?''

"No time. Just get some help from CI and get over here!'' I blinked and read off the coordinates printed on the voicecom. "Poindros LS has been taken over, so I couldn't use the consoles, and they've got cyborgs, mechmen with human brains, as agents here at the port. They've got us cornered. They've got laser tools they're using for weapons. Hurry!''

"All right!'' His voice snapped back. "Hang in there. We're on our way!''

I ducked as blinding lights flared through the door and sizzled into the grille. It melted and flashed sparks as I scrambled behind a desk. There was a scream from the other room.

"David!'' I leaped forward for the door just as Jason burst through, pushing David in front of him. David cried out again, clutching his arm to his chest. I pulled him back behind the desk as Jason fired his exploding lights again and sprang in a backward flip behind an overturned table. A sickening wave of fear and nausea rushed through me as I saw that his whole side from the hip down was seared open. Through tattered cloth, singed luciflex shapes and metal rods gleamed.

The door shattered into flame and I scrambled back, pulling the whimpering David into a far corner. Lights flashed and sparked and hissed. The room was burning in flaming patches on ceiling and walls. I attacked the nearest flames with my ripped skirts, trying to shield David, who was curled into a tight ball, biting back cries of pain.

A door across the room burst open. Panic seared through me as I saw the glowing amber eyes. The brown-suited cyborg leaped through and lifted his hand toward Jason. He was crouched with his back to the door, fending off the beams from the other room.

"Jason, watch out!'' I scrambled out, grabbed a chair, and threw it across Jason at the cyborg.

"No! Ruth!''

Everything was a blur of blinding light and flame and agony as a thin blaze from the far room sizzled across my shoulder and I could smell my skin burning as I screamed. The room was suddenly exploding with people in brown suits. I glimpsed Hodge's pudgy, freckled face and red hair behind the cyborg crumpling into my thrown chair with his back torn open. I was falling. The light from the far room lanced out again at me. I couldn't twist away. I screamed.

"Ruth!"

I didn't even see him move, he was so fast. Jason flew to me and knocked me down, firing his exploding lights through the shattered connecting door to knock the cyborg back. His hands reached out to pull me up. "Ruth, thank—"

But there was another blinding flash. The men rushing in through the hall door were holding out flat, gleaming instruments that flared with the searing beams.

"No! *No!*" I screamed and scrambled to my feet, grasping Jason's arms as they loosened and fell away from me. "No! Jason, no!"

But his face was blank, eyes flat brown and glassy as he slumped and sparks hissed from the gaping back of his shoulders. He fell onto the floor, hitting with a dull thump.

I threw myself onto the floor beside him, shaking his shoulders, furious, screaming, refusing to know. "Jason, no! Jason!"

It was only a heavy, lifeless piece of machinery I held. The smooth planes of his face were hard and unyielding. My tears fell onto curved brown glass, gleaming over the cold, polished orbs that stared at nothing.

twenty-five

There were only a few travellers strolling the viewing dome for a glimpse of the night side of Poindros, before the finished orbit flung the transport wide between the sun and the bright half of the planet. They glanced uneasily and avoided the tall woman in severe, dark-green slicks, her sober, unpainted face with its long scar framed by a strangely unfashionable halo of auburn braids.

I sat straighter on my bench beneath the potted plants, looking up at the stars gleaming beyond the dark shadow of fringed leaves, remembering the Anduran child's frightened scramble among spindly branches. I looked down at the package in my lap.

"Hey, Ruth, I been lookin' all over for you!"

I looked up at an outlandish, stick-thin figure attired in fuchsia skinslicks bagging over knobby knees, lime-green light-emitting boots, pushed-back red goggles, various articles of mysterious function strapped around waist and shoulder beneath a blue cape glittering with silver replicas of stars and moons, all topped by a bush of wiry dark hair with an eccentric life of its own. "Hi, kid."

"Hey, Ruth, you okay?" The freckled face hovered palely against the backdrop of space, eyes anxious behind gleaming lenses.

I smiled. "I'm okay, David."

He plopped down beside me. "Well, when are we gonna take off? I can't wait to get to Casino! I wanna get my hands on your console and see what's in here." He pulled a pouch around on its chest strap and drew out a flat cartridge. It looked like the data tapes the cybers provided for study before travelling, but on its front was stamped, *Introduction to Cybernetic Principles and Theory*.

David glanced up at me, cleared his throat, and put the cartridge away. "It was pretty nice of Jason to get it for me." He dropped his eyes. "Wish I could say thanks."

I touched his wiry hair. "So do I. I wish—" I closed my eyes.

I had found a tape for me, too, in the baggage Jason had kept insisting we bring along in our escape. Mine was labelled, "*History of Galactic War and Peace*, by Thoraat X37 Huil, Founder-Elect of Poindros." Officer Hodge had told me how to smuggle contraplan items aboard.

Red-haired Hodge had told me a lot of things. Like the code words, "Dawn of Freedom," used by members of a growing Resistance group dedicated to destroying the cyber network. The changers were real. Aaron hadn't feared only demons, after all.

Behind my closed eyes I could still see hate staring from the blistered, ruined face, hear the horrible, cracked whisper, "Jezrial . . ."

I pushed that away, too, replaced it with Hodge's freckled face and swaggering stance as he explained it all in a carefully offhand tone: How he managed to work for both CI and the Resistance. Why the Poindros members had been alarmed when CI had sent me home to observe anomalies that might have been traced to them. How the Founder's "new evolution" and the renegade Poindros LS proved that the cybers were inherently our enemies. How the Resistance on Poindros had been gradually introducing contraplan concepts and inventions to undermine the Plan and gain support. What to expect from CI back in Casino, and how to conceal my knowledge of the secret organization. How to contact members there. How to use my brand-new position as a CI agent to help destroy the cybers.

And any remaining cyborgs.

I swallowed. I stared through the stressplex flooring at the stars and the shadowed planet slowly revolving.

I wasn't quite sure why I hadn't told Officer Hodge about the data tapes Jason had left us, or my wild card disc. But I had a feeling that the answers weren't quite as black and white as the Resistance thought. I wondered if there weren't a shadowy area in between, where humans and cybers could work together, could use knowledge instead of ignorance to find a new Way.

Bright light and fringed shadow fell across my legs. I looked up through the plants to see that the ship had banked, edging around to the sun side of Poindros. There were people working and sleeping, laughing and dying down on that crescent of blue and brown-green. The Founder had been wrong, they weren't milkers to be herded along his way. But I wondered if the Resistance might not tear them free with as callous a disregard for their lives.

I closed my eyes. It wasn't my right to cast stones. I could still see that last glimpse of Helen—pale but firm as she faced the burning wind, faced grief, faced my final betrayal of her trust and love. I had stripped her of nearly everything. Yet she was still richer by far than I would ever be. I knew she didn't need my remorse, didn't need CI's payment I'd credited to repair the farm as I couldn't repair the family, didn't need my painful love. She would draw others to her to be loved as surely as the hearth drew the winter-chilled.

My fingers tightened on the thin package in my lap. I looked down to see the brown paper wrapping and Sam's painful scrawl. "We love you, daughter. Good faring."

My fingers were almost steady as I carefully unwrapped it, knowing already what it was. I held the flat picture for a moment, eyes closed, then looked down.

The firelit family circle.

Helen was the still center, her hands gentle on the lyre, her eyes gazing into a point below and beyond me as I held the picture. Her braided halo of hair gathered a rich light, and her lips were barely parted in the start of a smile.

Aaron stood with his shoulders back, his head turned obliquely, looking down at Mother—or at me? One eyebrow was raised slightly, the edge of his mouth twisting, showing a gleam of teeth.

Sam's face, lower than Aaron's behind Mother's chair, grinning happily, his eyes crinkled beneath bushy gray brows.

I swallowed, blinking quickly.

Jason knelt in the stillness that was his way. His hand rested on the arm of the chair, his head turned toward Mother and me, his eyes lowered. His broad cheekbone had caught an interesting angle of shadow, but his face was calmly expressionless.

I blinked again, faster.

And finally myself, sitting among the soft folds of my skirt, leaning dutifully against my mother's knee, my head sleek and neat with the hair pulled back. And my face, pale and tense, staring straight into the camera, the eyes shouting defiance.

My throat tightened. Defiance and . . . what? Fear?

I looked up at the blurred sphere of Poindros roll its blue and green cat's-eye across the dome. Around me I could hear the murmur of more travellers, some come for a quick glimpse of stars, some for a last look, for a while or longer, at home. It seemed so small. It was more like a bright target in a gambling game, or a feather in clear crystal.

David nudged my elbow and slipped under my arm to soberly watch the world recede. I held him and looked down once more at the picture. I smiled crookedly and turned it over, making a rash, silent promise to those faces, letting them flow into the dream-world until I could find them again without fear.

I ruffled David's hair. "Well, kid, we're on our way."

I touched the snake chain at my neck. Destroying? Or building? I could almost hear the serpent's laughter as it danced its eternal cycle around me, its whisper fading with Poindros into the murmur of folded pearl wings.

About the Author

Sara Stamey is a former nuclear reactor operations technician. Between periods of teaching Scuba in the Virgin Islands, Greece, and Honduras, she makes a home base in the Puget Sound area north of Seattle. She's currently completing a sequel to WILD CARD RUN.